THE JEWCATCHER

THE JEWCATCHER

A Novel

Ethan Mordden

iUniverse, Inc.
New York Bloomington Shanghai

THE JEWCATCHER

Copyright © 2008 by Ethan Christopher Mordden

All rights reserved. No part of this book may be used or reproduced by any means, graphic, electronic, or mechanical, including photocopying, recording, taping or by any information storage retrieval system without the written permission of the publisher except in the case of brief quotations embodied in critical articles and reviews.

iUniverse books may be ordered through booksellers or by contacting:

iUniverse
1663 Liberty Drive
Bloomington, IN 47403
www.iuniverse.com
1-800-Authors (1-800-288-4677)

Because of the dynamic nature of the Internet, any Web addresses or links contained in this book may have changed since publication and may no longer be valid.

Certain characters in this work are historical figures, and certain events portrayed did take place. However, this is a work of fiction. All of the other characters, names, and events as well as all places, incidents, organizations, and dialogue in this novel are either the products of the author's imagination or are used fictitiously.

ISBN: 978-0-595-51664-3 (pbk)
ISBN: 978-0-595-61985-6 (ebk)

Printed in the United States of America

Woe unto them that call evil good, and good evil.

Isaiah, 5:20

PROLOGUE

2

The Devil comes to Hitler in Landsberg Prison in 1924, a whiff of sulphur in a top hat. The Devil says, "Because you are one of the two most evil men on earth, I would pact with you."

Prideful Hitler quickly asks, "Who is the other?"

"That dreary Stalin—but listen to my offer. I will see you into utmost power and protect you from assassins, however ingenious."

"Ha! And I, in return?"

"What you will do to the world is gift enough. I anticipate the very destruction of civilization. Europe will be just so much Yemen."

Hitler plays the sport now, mock-patient, half-tempted. They always do that, these dupes of flattery. *The very destruction.* Gazing out of the window of his accommodating jail suite—flowers, books, baskets of hard-to-obtain fruit—Hitler asks, "What are you offering Stalin?"

"The depressing half of Europe. From the east into the middle of Germany, from Mecklenburg to Thuringia."

"*Impossible!*" Hitler screams, whirling and pointing. "Who dares to say such a thing! It is absolutely *out* of the *question!*"

Luftpause.

Then: "We must be most careful about these ... erroneous tantrums," the Devil warns his man. "Or severe measures will be taken."

Hitler feels a quick searing hiss in his testicles. A flash, no more. Over in a second. But Hitler is quite, quite still. He has learned to impress the Party faithful with his lack of deference. But he is wary now, unsure of his own arrogance.

Amiably, the Devil goes on, "I'd rather treat with you than with Stalin, anyway. *He'll* start no wars, trust me. Schall und Rauch, our Stalin." Noise and smoke. "He's so busy killing Russians, you know. And he'll never run out. It's a tremendous place, Russia."

Aroused by a favorite topic, Hitler makes a dismissive gesture, paces, announces. "A race of soulless dwarfs! Drunks! Sweet Maries! Two German divisions would cash them in in a matter of weeks!"

"You'll be surprised," the Devil murmurs.

Hitler isn't listening, but he turns, stopped by a thought. "What about the Communists? Their poisonous conspiracies, their treachery?"

"Don't worry about the Kozis. If they can't rule the world, they destroy it. It's amusing, really. They'd rather stop the Social Democrats than stop you, though the Sozis only want to debate them. You want to kill them."

"I will *eradicate* the swine! And the entire Jewish-Catholic-Masonic conspiracy!"

"Yes, yes, of course, you will," says the Devil. "Though that's not a conspiracy. That's the history of Europe."

Hitler runs a hand through his hair, sips mineral water, broods. Suddenly, he crosses his hands at his throat as his face turns up rapturously, a diva going for the high note.

"We are on the march!" he cries. "We are ruthless because we know that we are right! *And!* As for those false friends who smile with honeyed affection as they dream of betraying us—"

"Yes, but if only you didn't look like a toilet attendant," says the Devil, straightening Hitler's tie, "with the eyes of a hangman's dog. And lose the lederhosen. The Hansel and Gretel accent, too. We want a statesman, not a yodelling goatherd."

Hitler grumbles and curses, just about to blow.

"Why are the best ones always such freaks?" the Devil asks, brushing the dandruff off Hitler's shoulders.

Hitler suddenly shoves the Devil away and revs up, stamping and shrieking as his hands bang at his sides, all but exalted in his ungrateful rage. Think: if the Devil had not dropped in today, Hitler would have served his time and then disappeared into civilization's crowd of usual suspects, where carpet salesmen dream of settling scores by the millions.

"Good idea," says the Devil. "Let's get this out of the way nice and now." Looming huge and belching flame, he plays the carnival demon, reaching forth with extra hands to tear Hitler to pieces in his prisoner's luxury suite in Landsberg, the screaming head *schlopp!* off the trunk as the limbs fly and the torso bombs the floor. What a simple solution, yes, what clarity! Hitler is dumps of flesh and hair, the blood breathing in bubbles as it skates the floor.

The Devil likes to smoke after.

"Uhu, what a mess," he finally says, scooping up and plastering it all back together just before Hitler's adjutant bustles in with the post.

Amazed, Hitler stands there, feeling himself; but the Devil says, "He can't see or hear me. Only you will. Or that freaky Stalin."

"Something hurts," Hitler almost meekly observes, when they're alone again.

"Mm. I couldn't find one of your eggs in the excitement. Work around it. Now, don't expect to see me again too soon. You have to manage some of this yourself."

"But I will have my way?" Hitler asks, trying to escort the Devil to the door as if he exited spaces like an actor. "You know my plans and you assure me, ja?"

"Allwissend bin ich nicht; doch viel ist mir bewusst." I can't promise everything.

"No, wait—what's God going to do about all this?"

"Oh, I thought you knew," says the Devil, as he vanishes. "I *am* God."

PART I

IN THE WOLF'S GLEN

Berlin was a city of newspapers. There were hundreds, serving every class, every culture, every politics. To browse one of the major kiosks was to learn what everyone in Berlin was thinking. In Berlin? In the world!

Horst Pack, the least committed young Communist in all the city, was standing before the kiosk on the northeast end of the Alexanderplatz. The entire plaza was being taken apart for S-Bahn construction, so this would have been the summer of 1928. Times were good now—better, at least—and there had been few street riots. This was disappointing to Horst, who loved to watch them. Sometimes, when a bloodied enemy staggered out of the fighting or, ideally, collapsed, Horst would demonstrate martial spirit with a few kicks to his head, tscha! Once, however, he underestimated an opponent and got punched and lost a tooth. So he was wary now, volunteering for lookout and turning rare when the violence started up.

That would be soon. Horst had only to signal his comrades, waiting just a Ländler or so down the Landsberger Strasse, that the Social Democrats' parade was reaching the square. Then the Communists would fall upon the Sozis in the purely satisfying battle you can have only with those you truly hate.

It was a Berlin weekend, so quiet a town today, a city waiting to happen or a name without a place—or with too many places, competing realities. Berlin was ever under construction because it was so obsessed with itself that it was unfinishable: always more Berlin.

Horst, petending to review the offerings of the kiosk, caught the signal of a comrade standing in front of Wertheim's deapartment store. Trust a Jew, Horst thought, to build a swindle in the form of a palace. The comrade indicated that the Sozis had come into sight along Prenzlauerstrasse and were but minutes away.

Horst grinned and turned to warn a second comrade, one street off to the east. But his way was blocked by one of those pesky stiltwalkers, advertising, in a banner across his chest, Reinmar's Pastilles, "a revolution in taste."

"You should find something useful to do," Horst snarled at the man. "Maybe drowning in the Teltow Canal."

"The original is always mistaken for the grotesque," the stiltwalker replied, quite calmly. He stood ten feet tall, dressed in tailcoat, vast bowtie, and stovepipe hat. His face was chalk-white. He peered down at Horst while stamping around him, coming too close. "Ja, and the familiar is always mistaken for the admirable."

"Stick around and see how familiar it gets," Horst answered, dodging the stiltwalker and holding up three fingers of his right hand to his Kozi conspirator in the distance. Three minutes more.

"You're up to something nasty," the stiltwalker observed, coming to a stop to peer off in the direction of the others. "It shows in three fingers."

"Does it show that I knock you on your ass?"

"The terrible tide is washing over you," said the stiltwalker, now gazing at something over Horst's left shoulder.

"Hundsfott," said Horst. Dog cunt.

"Run!" whispered the stiltwalker. Turning, Horst let out a string of bad words as hundreds of brownshirts poured screaming into the plaza from Königstrasse, heading for the Commies, who had just come into view themselves, expecting to find the dear little Social Democrats.

Nazis and Reds: antagonists of the same beliefs, whacking away at each other for the right to have no rights, to take everything from all and feed it to the Tyrant. There was little in the way of heavy weapons, no commands, only noise and fighting, kicks and blows, men maddened but few, as yet, killed. Beer and biscuits after, the singing of anthems. With flags unfurled. The blood will flow. When the leader calls. Tchingerassa boom!

Horst darted behind the kiosk, but the siltwalker could not move so quickly. As the combatants closed for the reckoning, he seemed at first to float above them, then lost his footing and crashed beneath as Horst, sneaking a look, uttered a happy cry. Kill the dirty trash, he was thinking. He barred my way.

From the far end of the square, at police headquarters, came angry sirens. Horst suspected that this confrontation had been planned precisely so that the police *could* intervene immediately; the Commies preferred striking and making speeches to fighting. Chess and tantrums were their politics. It was the Nazis who loved war, as other men love women.

So the cops strode forth in their military formations, and the Social Democrats arrived at the edge of the plaza in time to bear witness with their usual bewildered looks. They might have been shepherds walking in on a border dispute among tribes on some third-century heath just as Roman legions engage them. With a shepherd's cure for problems, Sozis. Separate the parties, waste words, discover justice. They call that peace.

The stiltwalker hadn't come out badly, in the end. His hat was smashed and his wooden legs were broken off: a man like any other now. Well, who gave *him* the pass to go towering about? Horst imagined how much worse it could have been for his enemy—everyone Horst met, really, was an enemy: too smart, too solvent, too happy—as he left his comrades behind to race up the Keibelstrasse, backing into doorways to look behind. The Nazis liked to tail a fellow after the cops broke things up, finding out where he lived to get even later on. This was known as "paying the bill." Nazis and Commies alike took pleasure in closing an account many weeks after a skirmish.

So Horst took a devious route and then, impulsively, pushed open a door in the Linienstrasse. He heard music. Picking his way through darkness, he crossed, went through, and turned till he found himself in the back of a smallish theatre. Like a rat crafty by instinct, Horst hung back in the shadows. They were giving a show of some kind. In street clothes, a pianist and saxophonist accompanied a young woman in a song about someone looking into a valley from on high, addressing a distant sweetheart. The music was old-fashioned, aristocratic yet simple. The saxophone was pure Berlin sarcasm, but the rest of it was some beautiful old Germany.

Horst was no music lover—no lover of anything, really. Yet something caught him here, nourished him. He was enchanted when the singer and the saxophone took turns cutting intense little spirals into the music. He wondered what it meant when the lyrics claimed that song can "draw hearts to heaven." And he rejoiced, at the end, in the celebration of he renewal of spring; he would have clapped but for fear of giving himself away.

Now Hitler came on stage, in SA attire. *What?* thought Horst—but then President Hindenburg joined him, and the Kaiser, too, both in full parade kit. They congratulated the two musicians. "Schon am Werk?" Hitler gently asked the soprano. Already working, are you? He was feeling up her face the way some of those old characters do, pretending to be uncle when it's really about sex. Sure, and they'll do it to guys like Horst, saying, "Such a fine lad," as if sharing a secret with you, the dirty sneaks.

Hitler now shook hands with the pianist and saxophonist, and, as if stimulated by the contact, they suddenly struck up some hot stuff. The girl began dancing like a prostitute while Hitler, Hindenburg, and the Kaiser did deep-knee bends in time to the music. Then they were all singing:

> The Cannibal King, he loves to fress.
> Sozi bratwurst,
> Kozi stew.
> A la carte, they'll be serving *you*
> At the court of the Cannibal King.

So it's just acting, Horst thought. But all very convincing, even if fat old Hindenburg seemed unusually spry. Now the Kaiser put his spiked helmet on the girl and pranced around her in an unseemly manner while she took a solo:

> The Cannibal King, he lost his votes!
> Good times keep him
> Out of view.
> He's legend now, but he's coming true
> At the court of the Cannibal King!

The saxophonist laid his instrument on the piano to join in the dance, duetting with the girl in a glide from here to there as if they were joined at the hip. Some Asian dance, Horst imagined. Then Hindenburg and the Kaiser fitted themselves into this curious formation, as the pianist banged out unspeakable rhythms. Hitler danced alone, but they all sang together:

> It's history when he lectures,
> And screams and rants in fits!
> It's history when he's on the march
> And history when he shits!
> So you know he's the Cannibal King!

And just like that, so abruptly, the piano went *bang!* and it was over. All froze in position.

"And the house goes wild with admiration," said Hitler, breaking out of composition as he peeled off his moustache.

"They'll never let us get away with such language," Hindenburg predicted, starting to pull off his uniform.

The Kaiser nodded. "Why can't we stick to the old jokes about—"

"The Nazis will get you," said Horst, impulsively coming down the theatre aisle. "They won't let you mock him."

"Thanks for the tip," Hitler replied. "But police spies aren't supposed to attend rehearsals. You come to public performances—when you denigrate the players, analyze the audience by class and cultural background, and flirt with the ices Mädchen."

"He's not police," said the actress, as Horst approached the stage.

"No," Hitler agreed, feeling above his upper lip for stray bits of moustache hair. "He lacks the self-importance, doesn't he, Anni? But he has appeal, in a back alley of Wilmersdorf way." Coming to the edge of the stage, Hitler smiled at Horst, one of those old-guy-has-plans-for-young-men smiles. "Want to be an actor, do you?"

"You're ugly," Horst told him.

The man nodded. "I'm Hitler," he said, as if that explained it. "Of course, we already have Pablo, our Latin heart-boy." He indicated the saxophonist, who like the others stood watching.

"Don't the Nazis riot here?" Horst went on, feeling important at the attention he was getting. "And the Kozis, I must add. Dancing and dressing up in times of social injustice!"

"I mistook the district," said Hitler, dryly. "Not Wilmersdorf—Wedding. Right?"

"Now I leave this place," said Horst, irritated at the reference to the Communist quarter. He assumed a look of moral disapproval as he marched up the aisle.

"Do you love the gap in his teeth?" Hitler asked his cohort, as a door slammed. "It's a sign of passion, especially in Wedding. Ah! The diva is here."

"I know him," said a languidly pretty young woman, coming on stage in a tight black dress and carrying a pair of velvet pumps. "The boy who just left? He is at the bar sometimes, sniffing at me like a hound on a bitch."

Taking a stool, she sat, smoothed out her dress, and began to put on her shoes with the bland glee of the born show-off.

"That's fancy attire for a working day," Hitler noted.

"A gent took me home for good money. So I spent the night." She shrugged. "What are we up to? Am I giving my celebrated Egg Dance in the blindfold? The Garbo impersonation? A sensual tango with Pablo?"

Pablo blew out a chuckle on his sax.

"Am I the star of Mask and Shadow?" she went on. "Your heart's delight?"

"You are the love of all Berlin," Hitler assured her.

She was known simply as Jimmy, and she was more truly the love of a small pocket of Berlin's nighttime culture of bars, theatre, and sex. A Nürnberg native, she had come to Berlin for freedom and power. It was Jimmy who set the style of adopting a British name, a bisexual ambiance of man's clothing, and the Schnapsfreundin, an older woman who bought one drinks for the right to whisper honey words into one's ear. Sometimes they got somewhat more. With her slinky talk and a physique made to laugh at men, Jimmy seemed like the last hundred covers of the magazine *Lustige Blätter*—a flapper in criminally sheer blouse thrilling a shoeshine boy as she passed, a showgirl in feathers teasing the world.

Jimmy was a star, but on the small scale: the toast of the Mask and Shadow cabaret troupe and a number of bars that catered to the "special" taste. That would be the infamous Cozy Corner in Kreuzberg, the unspeakable Passage in Friedrichstrasse, the Dorian Gray, the Magic Flute Dance Palace, the Eldorado Club in Martin-Lutherstrasse, and above all The Sorcerer's Apprentice. Dance bars, lesbian bars, drag bars, pay-for-it bars, tourist bars, secret bars. The Apprentice was Jimmy's favorite, for it had no stated purpose, no favored gender, no politics, even no police raids. It was outrageous, yes: when Rupert and Heinz would show up in sailor uniforms and spend the evening trying playfully resounding slaps on each other's rears; or when Willy arrived in drag as the Countess Mariza and drove everybody crazy smoking tiny cigars; or when Ludwig threw over Marmaduke for Ferdy, to whom he swore eternal love, then got engaged to both Rikki and Dikki, all within the time it took the band to get through a single chorus of "Tea For Two." It was a tolerant place, less about sex than about a good time. A good show.

Horst was at the Apprentice on the night of the fighting in the Alexanderplatz, as was Jimmy. He made a play for her, as always.

"Off you go," she said carelessly, alone at a table, considering her makeup in her compact mirror.

"Give me a few minutes," said Horst, sitting at her table. "So I do not look a fool. Then I go."

"I saw you today."

"Where?"

"At the cabaret. You must have barged in. Did Pfuikeck offer you work? He does, to all the young men."

"That is a name, Pfuikeck? I am suspicious."

"He's our comical maestro, with many important contacts." Snapping the compact shut, she lit a cigarette. "Erich Kästner writes for us sometimes. You know this distinguished name?"

Horst said nothing, looked around.

"Kästner is known for taking advanced social positions," Jimmy went on. "We are political at Mask and Shadow."

"Yes, I see how political you are tonight in your dress that fits like lizard skin, moving your breasts to the music."

"And why are *you* here?" She laughed, a silvery riff.

"Money. Rich guys will pay."

"You sell it?"

"Smoke more, I like to see it."

But here came the Baroness, Tony, and Miss Pixie Prim. They hovered over Jimmy's table with the customary gossip. It seemed that Bijou was talking most seriously to a merchant from Thuringia not five minutes ago, when Viktor horned in with his red hair and green eyes, and suddenly they all left together!

"Bijou!" Horst sneered. "Thuringia! Who cares?"

"Who's your charming friend?" the Baroness asked Jimmy in a pensive manner.

There was in fact a genuine Baroness mixed up in all this, a wealthy eccentric who, like so many typical Berliners, came from Silesia.

"I was too interesting for Silesia," she would say, a lucky widow: impossibly well-off in her mid-thirties, rich, fit, and comely and thus freest of all nature's make on earth. She owned a handsome old house near the Tiergarten, in which she entertained and cultivated influence. Through her late husband, she was intimate with the Prominenz, the great names of the age, yet she was bohemian and enjoyed figuring in piquant rumor. What did she fear? Loss of independence. Thus, though she knew many powerful men, she preferred the company of women, especially those of modest cultural background. They could be needy but were easily pleased.

"I always knew I was born to lead a double life," the Baroness would say: the gala hostess of the public stage and the hedonist of low pleasure.

She was Jimmy's favorite Schnapsfreundin, so elegant to talk to. And what a spendthrift! Stockings from Paris—yes, the real thing! Perfume in a fairy's tiny bottle! And none of that drunken groping that so often dismayed Jimmy's table in the Apprentice. No, the Baroness seemed content to court Jimmy, merely court her, endlessly.

Well ... not exactly so. But Jimmy knew how to play her devotees: when to be pert, or cold, or smiling, all in such stingy amounts. Jimmy gave little in order to take all, but there is a trick to it, you know: never be grim.

The Baroness' motto might have been: never be sorry. She produced a bold mix at her soirees. Theatre people met the Army, writers conversed with sports heroes, politicians knew movie actors, and string players sparred with jazz bands.

The setting for the Baroness' evenings was conservative, a vast salon gazing upon the Kaiser Wilhelm Memorial Church, long, dark, high, and lined to the ceiling with old masterpieces on historical themes—"Charles V Receives the

Augsburg Confession," "The Defenestration at Prague," "The Siege of Magdeburg," and the usual homage to Frederick the Great, "Dinner With Voltaire at Sans Souci." The Baroness' staff, too, was conservative, as an almost perfectly expressionless butler directed footmen in tailcoats in the delivery of plates from the buffet. It was the kind of thing one called Very Prussian if one approved of it, and Very Prussian if one didn't.

The Herrenklub approved. Franz von Papen, the Catholic Center Party deputy, a founding member of this Club of Sirs, frequented the Baroness' evenings, often bringing with him fellow Sirs Army Colonel Kurt von Schleicher and Oskar von Hindenburg, son of the senile President of the Republic. It was whispered that they came to the Baroness' to meet actresses, but in fact they mainly talked politics and schemed while their hostess plied her trade in Zeitstars, the passing celebrities of the day.

Tonight, the star was one of those Herr Doktors of the academic world, the author of a book commingling philosophy and history with just enough gossip to attract attention. Now he went everywhere, enlarging upon his theories.

"A Redestube," von Schleicher was saying, of Germany's Parliament. A talk shop. "Too many political parties. Too many opinions. You would not have different armies in one country. Different languages, so? There should be one party, one program, and now you have heard. Ja? Now it is simple."

"Absolutely correct," said von Papen; one never knew what he meant by that. He could agree and betray simultaneously.

"Ja, it is simple," von Schleicher repeated, with a heavy sigh, as von Hindenburg, tall and gloomy, nodded.

"Just as there is one people," the Herr Doktor put in. "The Deutsche Volk. And one land, Deutschland." To this he added, with a quiet thrill, "Blut und Boden." Blood and soil, a cliché of the age. Who you are is where you're from.

Across the room, the Baroness urged champagne upon her guests, meatball pie, gravlax. Scandalized at such generosity, one guest cried, "Madam, your bank director must sleep well."

"Peasant rents, Gothic heirlooms, village bribes," said the Baroness, waving a hand. "It all happens in Silesia, so who knows?"

Ernst Josef Aufricht was telling her of the wonderful theatre he had acquired in the Schiffbauerdamm, for this former actor had turned impresario.

"It seems so much the church from the outside," he said. "Steeple and all. But the interior! A red-and-gold zoo of statuary. Poseidon, Cupid—"

"Aufricht," said the Baroness. "You are too pretty to run a theatre. Go back to acting. Make a film and be the daydream of shop girls from Sweden to Sicily."

She left Aufricht to greet Max Schmeling, the heavyweight boxing champion of Germany. Max was handsome and happy, ideal seasoning for that chowder of intrigue around the Herrenklub. When the Baroness brought Max over to meet them, Herr Doktor was advising on the importance of "national destiny." He invoked "rights of blood," "traditions of soil": and "I know what's coming next," said the Baroness, departing.

"It must be said," said von Hindenburg.

"Absolutely," von Papen agreed.

"The Jews," Herr Doktor went on, "are wanderers and parasites by nature. It is blood without soil. And so they sneak in—"

"Yes, those Jews," said Max Schmeling. "And the bakers of sweet biscuits, too."

"Why the bakers?" Herr Doktor asked.

"Why the Jews?" Max innocently replied, strolling away.

"And so we call it *Riff-Raff*," Aufricht was telling Alfred Kerr, of the *Berliner Zeitung* and the town's most distinguished theatre critic. "Or possibly *Die Luden-Oper*, but—"

"A pimps' opera?" said Kerr, accepting a platter from a footman. "You're giving an art form over to pimps?"

"Beggars, whores, thieves, arias, chorales," Aufricht went on. "It's gigantic. Entirely new."

"And that is the madness of Berlin!" Kerr replied. "Music? A chaos. Theatre? Propaganda. Literature? Mysterious experiments ... Who's your playwright?"

"Brecht."

"That pickpocket," said Kerr, affably, forking up a fantasy-thin slice of salami.

"He has genius."

"That's no excuse these days. Oh, well, *here's* quality."

For the Baroness was presenting her most special guests, permanent Zeitstars, from *Es Liegt in der Luft*, the latest hit revue, set in a department store: Marlene Dietrich, Margo Lion, and Oskar Karlweis, with the show's composer, Mischa Spoliansky. Margo was in a sassy frock and Mischa a reasonably dapper suit, but Marlene and Oskar were in black tie. The Baroness had welcomed many a beauty of the arts to her Evenings, but she was almost reverent with Marlene, and couldn't stop praising and caressing her. "The Clara Bow of the Kudamm!" the Baroness called her.

"Quite a fancy dish, this Berlin," Herr Doktor said, surveying the Baroness and her cabaret stars, the room as a whole. "They call it a capital. Of what?, one can only ask."

Von Schleicher, enjoying the presentation of the revue artists, took in the Herr Doktor with exasperation. "Why do I think I know, sir, that you are from Munich?"

Herr Doktor nodded. "A most harmonious place. A city that stands for something, a population in agreement."

"I admire the variety of Berlin," von Papen put in. "One never knows who one's friends will be, next year. Some cultivate everyone, just in case."

Max Schmeling, who was supposedly dating half the movie actresses in Berlin, was the first to meet Marlene. She mock-chided him for not having seen her show.

"I have fear of those witty revues," he said. "I never get the jokes."

"You must discover more of the town," said Oskar Karlweis. "Six-day bicycles and Paul Klee. Then you will know what we joke about."

"Movies and jazz," von Schleicher murmured to his two friends, watching the revue people tour the room. They had altered their position just enough to cut out the irritating Herr Doktor.

"She is alarmingly wonderful," said von Papen of Dietrich. "Do you know her?"

"I'm planning to," von Schleicher replied, heading over to her party. At his introduction, he declared, "Fräulein, of all Berlin's cabaret sweethearts, you are the most charming. But why do you wear a man's suit?"

"Men's clothing looks smarter on me, Colonel."

"Oh, what a smile," the Colonel muttered.

"Music!" the Baroness ordered, pampering the performers as they took place at the Bechstein. "Is the lighting adequate? Shall we adjust the stool, maestro? An announcement?"

They didn't need one, for their number, "Wenn die Beste Freundin," was a self-contained musical vignette in which two women go shopping and flirt with a mutual boy friend and each other. It was a naughty bit, the girls pushing and pulling at their man even as they saved fond gestures for each other:

> First there is a boy friend, but he fades away.
> Now, instead of him, a girl friend's making hay.

Margo put a shocked hand over her mouth as she fiddled with Marlene's bodice, and some of the onlookers cried, "Oho!" Here was the nomenclature of the arts and the estates, seated and standing, plates of lobster and glasses of Sekt in hand, attending the *pop!* of new wave. Aufricht and Schmeling loved it. Von

Schleicher was enchanted by the unique appeal of the two women in their black attire, lit by white carnations. The prudish von Papen was dubious, and the Herr Doktor couldn't wait to get back to Munich, where outrages of the day are suppressed by police action. And the Baroness complimented herself on another evening of true Berlin, the essence of European civilization, new Rome.

To Conrad Thomamüller—nineteen years old, romantic, not shy—Berlin was first of all a city of watercourses. It was woodland to be rowed past, quirky little islands to explore, villas to inspect from a distance, even strangers to wave at as one oared along. The River Spree ran through the city—right through its center, unlike that overpraised Danube that actually bypasses Vienna, or the Tiber, which most Romans never see. A second river defined Berlin's western edge, as the gullible Spree poured into the magnificent Havel on their way into the Elbe and on to Hamburg and the sea.

Here is a wonderful day in the summer of 1928, a time without penalty, of agreeable weather and no surprises at work, a summer of boating and friends and trips into town to the theatre. Conrad was fitted for his first suit. He bought his mother, for her birthday, an antique clock whose chimes brought forth heroes of ancient greatness, from Hermann of Teutoburg Forest to Wallenstein. The piece delighted her, and made her weep and love him more than ever, which embarrasses a young fellow just coming into his manly dignity.

Conrad knew this particular section of the Havel quite well, even villa by villa. For this was the Grunewald, very suburban and given to quietly spirited little houses set among carefully cultivated "wild" spots where anything might happen. There was none of the city's concentration and intensity. This was Conrad's Berlin, the one he could never be hurt in. Children dotted the shore, staring at Conrad as he rowed past. An old couple took an English tea before a house in pastel colors, as if made of schoolroom art paper. And here was "the fortress," as Conrad called it: some ancient military structure turned into living quarters. Who lived there? Warriors, surely. They must have terrible heating problems in winter, with those windowless slits in the—

"*No!*" Conrad cried, as one oar jumped off its mounting and slid into the water. Conrad lunged quickly, and got a hold on it, but at a bad angle, and it snapped in two.

Carefully steering over to the fortress' waterfront, Conrad beached his craft, and even before he turned landward he was aware of someone's approach. As he looked, a fellow a few years older than he stood before him with a stern look.

"Here it is forbidden," said the stranger. "Private."

"I need help," Conrad explained. "I've had an accident."

"That is not a concern of those living here."

"No," Conrad agreed. "But, if you will allow me to say so, even the immortal gods do not reject a helpless traveler in need. So the great Homer tells us. In the *Odyssey*."

Conrad tried a smile. The stranger came a few paces forward, saying nothing.

"I've only one oar," Conrad went on. "Could I possibly borrow a mate from you? I would certainly return it, and promptly."

The young man from the fortress was but ten yards from Conrad. His face, at first set and hard, was now open, though not quite welcoming. He said, "It is odd to lose an oar. Have you never boated before?"

Conrad blushed. "I was expert until today."

The stranger studied Conrad's boat. "No wonder you have accidents. You need painting. Caulking too, probably. And why is it called The Merry Widow? It is unwise to mock death."

"I could have called it The Swift and Shining Achilleus, I suppose. In respect of death. For didn't Achilleus give King Priam the body of his murdered son, Hector? The man whom Achilleus truly hated more than dishonor itself? And I ask only an oar."

The stranger suddenly grinned. "Give me your name."

"Conrad."

"I am Kai. I will help you."

"You are most kind."

"Yes."

They shook hands.

"Do you study Greek?" Kai asked Conrad.

"No, but I had a schoolmaster who ... I mean, I have always ..."

"Come."

He is of average height and very fair. The colors are white, pink, and dark blue. Very thin shirt open at the tie, English trousers, light cap. Brusque and athletic. He watches one with concentration, like a lieutenant on inspection day, and he says no more than a spy on a mission. He is in all most captivating, a young commander of the fortress, of whose interior I saw very little: Kai.

It was Conrad's habit thus to think up detailed descriptions of men he admired, and to work on them till they filled with air and light and character. Conrad's friend Hans Wentrepp liked his descriptions short and scrappy. "Rich and very hungry for it" was a favorite, also "Tall and rough" and "Heavy pants."

What Hans didn't get was the *romance* of a meeting, but then Hans was a Strichjunge. A prostitute. And why not, when one is penniless and uneducated, and a golden youth besides? Walther Rathenau, the Foreign Minister killed by nationalist thugs in 1922, was one of Hans' most appreciative clients.

"We never did much," Hans told Conrad, of his appointments with Rathenau. "He liked to take off my clothes very precisely, and feel my skin and say how handsome I am. 'Such a fine, fine young German lad' and all. And he would worship a bit, you know, down there." Hans shrugged. "It wasn't good sex, but it was good money."

Hans scandalized Conrad, even in that most scandalous of places, The Sorcerer's Apprentice. "Have you no ideals, Hans?" Conrad would ask.

"I suppose so. Doesn't everyone? Oh look, it's that gymnast from Stuttgart. See, in the corner, in the … yes, they say he wrestles in bed. He pins you! Do you like him, Conrad?"

Conrad had to laugh. Hans was so unfailingly cheerful and kind that one could not be cross with him. Even when he played the imp and tried to tease Conrad into renting himself out.

"That rich old thing in the stripes," Hans would whisper. "He wants you so badly he's losing his knickers."

"Hans, behave yourself."

"Or if he's a Hollywood producer?"

"I'm already in the movies." Conrad was an assistant's assistant at UFA. "And I question the purpose of rich old things in stripes. And this … this wearing of rash outfits and selling of sex. It makes us seem so different."

"We *are* different," said Hans.

"Are we made different? Or just acting that way?"

"What riddles. Wait, it's that shady Russian, Konstantin, who owes me five marks. Look at the shoulders on him! But tonight," said Hans, moving off, "he must pay up!"

Conrad hated being alone in these places. He would swear them off, then would feel lonely some night and go looking for Hans. They were best friends, Conrad supposed. From school. Conrad had other old school chums, whom he occasionally saw in a boisterous country outing that left him bored and ashamed at being bored, at least by such well-meaning comrades. But Hans and Conrad were fast friends.

Konstantin having paid up, Hans dropped in on Jimmy, who was holding court with a few of the transvestites and the Baroness. Conrad watched as Jimmy played up to Hans, ignoring the Baroness. The grand lady maintained her gravity, but surely she was grieving inside.

"Die Zeit ist da," said a voice in Conrad's ear. It's time, now. Conrad turned to find Pfuikeck at his side. "Der ist schön, der Knabe." Such a pretty boy.

"I don't know you," said Conrad, not meaning to be rude but startled by this man's presumption.

"What's his name ... Hans? You look like a Willy to me. Are you boy friends?"

"Please mind your business, sir."

Conrad concentrated on Jimmy's table, dismissing Pfuikeck, but he, after a moment, said, "I would love to see a frisky boy like you shooting his cream."

Conrad was shocked speechless.

Over at Jimmy's table, everyone but the Baroness had gone, and as she tried to take Jimmy's hand, Jimmy pulled it away with a sharp "Leave it!" Then Horst Pack came horning in with his wheedling and cursing. "Oh, I'm not good enough for you?" was his favorite line, and when he got there Jimmy replied, "You're not rich enough for me." Suddenly dreamy, she put her head close to the Baroness to whisper greedily and infuriate Horst, who stalked off.

"That Horst has such a wish for Jimmy," said Hans, back with Conrad. "Some hustler he is."

"He hustles? He doesn't seem like one of us."

"He's not."

"But he has sex with men?"

"He has sex with money. Oh ... he won't be happy now."

The Baroness and Jimmy had got up. They left the bar together as Horst fumed in the shadows.

"Here's to Jimmy," said Hans, raising his beer.

"She is my diva," said Pfuikeck, coming up again from behind the two young men.

"Are you always a sneak?" said Conrad. He gave Hans a Guten Abend and left.

Pfuikeck tried to talk to Hans, but the young man ran off when they turned up the music for a favorite number, "Frieda's Boy Friends," a comic fox trot in the American syle. Everyone paired off to dance the Texas, invented only weeks before, at The Magic Flute: couples faced each other and glided straight across the floor, performed a quarter turn, glided in *that* direction, and so on. It took an able crowd to avoid a crash, especially when singing along with the vocal, a mock-lament from Frieda:

> Ernst is quite a sugar plum,
> With eyes for only me.
> Herbert's such a generous boy,
> He lets me drink his tea!
> But they're really rather similar
> When either comes to call.
> So I guess I'll marry Hermann after all!

It was considered extra fun to yell out the name of one's light of love in place of "Hermann," and the dance floor grew riotous in no time. Nevertheless, Horst Pack stalked slowly through the chaos as if alone in the wild. He was coming for Hans.

"I see you looking at me," Horst told him. "Do you pay?"

"I pay more," Pfuikeck put in.

Horst was as startled as Conrad had been. Then, recognizing Pfuikeck from the theatre on the day of the last riot, he said, "Don't I already hate you?"

"Let me buy you a drink," Pfuikeck urged. "Let me smooth out your hair."

Horst shoved Pfuikeck so fiercely that he hit the floor with a bang; in all the tumult of "Frieda's Boy Friends," none of the bar noticed. Hans helped Pfuikeck to his feet, and the theatre manager quit the bar with "I guess I'll marry Pfuikeck after all."

Horst turned back to Hans. "You know my girl and that grand lady? They left together,"

"Jimmy's your girl?"

"So, so. She will be, when I have money instead of these others. War profiteers, burzhui, book readers. With their smiles of having too much to eat. They take my girl from me, take everything from all of us, you see this? They go to a palace and have rich sex."

Hans had been staring at the dancing and was about to go when Horst put a hand on his shoulder and whispered, "You like me, ja?"

Hans said nothing. Horst began to massage the back of Hans' neck, very slowly. He leaned in as if to whisper again but, instead, simply hovered close, with his beery breath and inveigling masculinity. If I don't get away right now, Hans thought, I'm done for.

"They threw me off the committee for not paying," said Horst. "We two make our own committee, ja? It wouldn't cost you much."

Hans looked at Horst with misgiving, but Horst got up a smile from somewhere as he ticked Hans' ear. "There must be something in it for me," Horst explained, as "Frieda's Boy Friends" gave out in laughter and cheers. "Or it would go against my nature, and you could not possibly want to do that."

Horst's grip tightened on Hans.

"I'm selling, too," Hans told Horst. "I've nothing to give you."

"Yes, you do," said Horst confidently. "You're in a fine and generous mood, and you've got it to spare. And you like me."

There was a luminous glow to be seen all over Berlin when Conrad boated up the Havel to return the borrowed oar to Kai in his donjon keep. The city is smiling at me, Conrad thought. It was cool for the summer, and Conrad had his best sweater on, the blue wool with the white stripes along the sleeves. He hoped his blown-about hair gave him a sportsman's look.

Beaching his ship, Conrad turned to see Kai coming toward him. "I am impressed that you are so punctual," said Kai, shaking Conrad's hand and reclaiming the oar. "It is well timed, so that you can stay for lunch."

"What do you eat in a stronghold?"

Momentarily bemused, Kai then replied, "Yes, it casts a shadow of myth upon these suburbs. But we were here first, and it's quite comfortable inside. My brother and I live alone, and we have no friends, so … there is the feeling of a stronghold perhaps."

"Is your brother around? Now?"

"Not today. And I am just back from a trip." Kai led Conrad up to the house. "It is my duty to inspect the running of the family business. That takes me to the west very often. Do you like to travel?"

"No, I like Berlin."

"My brother is in uniform, so I worry when he is away." Pausing, Kai turned thoughtfully toward the water. The Havel is wide at this point, the northern end of the Berliner Forst where it grows into Charlottenburg: where open land meets the town. "We have only each other and this business, which does not interest us except as a living. One must keep an eye out, or employees will embezzle everything. Do you like the water?"

"Very much."

"It is interesting to be solitary, ja? It is powerful. Come inside."

Before lunch, Kai took Conrad on a tour of the place, comfortably modern but plain. There was a music room, with a great old monster of a piano.

"My brother sings and I play for him," said Kai, slipping into the facetious accompaniment to Schubert's "The Trout." "It is most ingenious, though we have no one to perform for. Would you like to hear us some time?"

"I would love that. I don't hear real music much."

"I heard a most disturbing piece in Duisberg, on my last trip." Kai stopped playing. "By day there, it is all commercial activity. At night, one goes to the opera, normally *Fidelio* or *Carmen*. But here was a very new work. By a Polish composer. Spectacular sounds, for the end of the world. The story told how a shepherd appeared in Sicily in the eleventh century, preaching a savage new religion. All the people followed him, even the king who tried to suppress this religion. And at last, the shepherd was Dionysos."

"But that's Euripides. *The Bacchae*."

Kai nodded. "What to do when the new god comes. Resistance is hopeless and arrangements must be made."

He rose from the piano.

"In the Greek play," he went on, "it is tragic. But in this opera, it was ecstatic and dangerous. Why do you stare at me?"

Blushing, Conrad got out, "Just that you're so ... well, you speak of you and your brother being alone. Yet you're so handsome and ... popular, I would guess. You would be asked very often to the great Berlin evenings one hears of."

"When you meet my brother, you will see see what it is, 'handsome.' He is the good boy, the beloved. Come, we eat now."

It was sandwiches and beer, with salad and then cake, the best lunch Conrad had ever had.

"I so love your stronghold," he told Kai. "Might I politely inquire about the family business?"

"It is too boring to tell. What is your work?"

"I'm quite the third-lowest assistant in all of UFA."

"Cinema!"

"Well," Conrad admitted, "it's not music."

"But so sexy and famous!"

They were teasing each other, making faces and flirting.

"We might spend an evening out," Conrad suggested. "Go into town for the new Lehar, promised for October."

"Oh, waltzes and jokes. A gypsy princess meets a hussar, impasse, Dance of the Shakos, finale."

"No, this one's about Goethe."

"Singing and dancing about our national poet?" asked Kai, mystified. "It is surely outrageous."

"Well, could we not see for ourselves?"

A pause.

"I think we could," said Kai. "I feel we must!"

More sandwiches, then Conrad said, "It's called *Friederike,* after Goethe's first love, Friederike Brion, of Alsace."

"So now it is documentary operetta," said Kai, "and we are bound to go."

"Sworn to go!"

"Doomed to go!"

It was that absurd laughing over nothing that kids get into when they daren't articulate what they feel.

Cutting the dessert cake, Kai asked what sort of movie Conrad was working on now.

"A thriller," said Conrad, "shrouded in the shadows of London. A murderer is on the loose, and none can stop him except ... no. I mustn't reveal the diabolical twist ending."

"Is it sheer entertainment?" asked Kai, greatly enjoying this lunch. "Or is there a guiding intelligence in the plot?"

"Oh, to be sure," said Conrad, certain that Kai was the love of his life. "It is the theme of the Double."

Many a night, the Baroness could be found tracking through the city in search of Jimmy. It was the classic case of the excellent character with everything to lose falling for the dubious character with nothing to share. Some unknowable spring in the works of human need has been wound and must devolve.

The best one to consult with at such times was the wisest lesbian in town, Claire Waldoff. She, too, was a cabaret star, a great one. Short and plump, with a mop of red hair and an enchantingly grating voice, she sang in the local patois on a ribald political agenda. "Throw All Those Men Out of the Reichstag" was one of her standbys, and she could corrupt an innocent ditty by twirling insouciantly and carolling out, "Tutu tuta tutu" while the police spies took stern notes. Still, she outwitted almost all authority—even the perfidious god of love, for Claire and her partner, Olga von Roeder, knew unqualified happiness for forty years, to be sundered only in death.

"Kiss what you like," Claire advised the Baroness, at a table in the Apprentice, "but love only the one. That message they can paint right up on the church wall."

"You do not ever want to probe them, to overbear," said the Baroness unhappily. "But they provoke it. How they love to give the clumsy lie. No"—for Claire was about to interrupt—"I don't want to love rashly, do I? Why are all the pretty ones so false?"

"Is it only physical?"

The Baroness snorted. "Leave that to the men! You know how love can feel—the lost and lonesome heart finds home. The *needing* to be understood."

Claire nodded. "That's my Olly."

Hans joined them, sadly announcing that he had awakened in the night to see Horst going through his desk drawers.

"Scroungers," said Claire. "Burglars. And yet so lovable ..."

"Yes," said Hans and the Baroness together.

"We have been chosen, and they are the merest of mortals. We should be invulnerable to their touch, beyond the hunger. My Olly's a baroness, too, you know. She doesn't keep a salon." Rising, Claire said, "Concentrate on others who have been chosen, my dears, or you'll have to sing for your supper." Grinning, she gently gave out, "Tutu, tuta."

Some days before the premiere of Ernst Josef Aufricht's *Pimps' Opera*, Berlin's theatre and music worlds readied themselves for what promised to be the most satisfying debacle of the season. The authors, playwright Bertolt Brecht and composer Kurt Weill, were on the rise; that excites jealousy. A failure has a thousand friends, a success a thousand enemies. Then, too, the work itself was a German version of an ancient English play, reinvented in a hash of Bach and jazz band.

"It's *howling*," cried the delighted Pfuikeck to all who listened. "The *bombe-surprise* of the century!"

Pfuikeck was one of the show's many rehearsal kibitzers, thespians welcomed to criticize and enthuse. But producer Aufricht had been advised to death. Sensing a failure, the players had been dropping out without warning; the lead woman, Carola Neher, had gone off to tend to her husband, the back-alley poet Klabund, who was dying of tuberculosis.

"What, again?" was Pfuikeck's reply.

This time he did die, so Neher rejoined the production, playing prima donna with demands and remarks.

"Dump her," Pfuikeck urged Aufricht.

"I can't, not this late," said Aufricht under his breath while Neher, on stage, lured Brecht into an argument. "Besides, she's really wonderful in it. A swamp blossom under the Soho moon."

"No, *there's* your blossom," said Pfuikeck, pointing to one of the supporting women, Lotte Lenya. "Give her Neher's role."

"Lenya's Weill's wife. I can't turn this into a vanity show. Half of Berlin knows I'm producing on my father's money as it is."

Also on hand was the composer Hanns Eisler, pouring envious infections into Brecht's ear. The novelist Lion Feuchtwanger slipped in, and someone said the film director Fritz Lang was about, somewhere. Then Helene Weigel, playing a bordello madam, came down to the edge of the stage, pale and loony as a Druid. She awaited something like quiet, then announced, "You will see me play as a legless cripple on a wheeled board. Unexpectedly, I will read from a pamphlet on the insufferable hypocrisy of the middle class."

General silence. Even Eisler stops his whispering. With a conclusive expression on her face, Carola Neher storms off the stage, into the house, and out of the theatre. Weill shoots Lenya an ironic look. She merrily responds by indicating, first, Weigel; then Brecht's collaborator on the script, Elisabeth Hauptmann; and, last, with a wave and a whistle, Carola Neher's smoke: Brecht's three girl friends.

Then Weigel was struck with appendicitis; her lines were reassigned to others. The impossible Neher was successfully replaced. The leading man, Harald Paulsen, showed up blazing bright in the suit of a bon vivant, with an especially sugary blue silk bow tie.

"But you're a highwayman," Brecht told him. "Like this, you look like a wedding cake."

"My fans wish it so!"

Commotion in the aisles: Eisler whispering right and left, Aufricht looking at Lenya and wondering if Pfuikeck might be right, Pfuikeck telling everyone that the whole show is stolen from Piscator and Pfuikeck, and Feuchtwanger telling Aufricht he should call it *The Threepenny Opera*: because Paulsen's tie is as lavish as *Aida*. That sounded so right that the suggestions were coming at the gallop, and someone thought Brecht and Weill should write one of those sinister Deeds of the Murderer numbers so popular in the old days. The new piece went in during the next day's rehearsal as "The Ballad of Mackie Knife."

"Knalleneffekt!" is how Feuchtwanger saw it. Top score! But the 770-seat house was half-empty on opening night, and the audience didn't know what to make of the show after all the spiteful gossip. Then, halfway through Act One, they suddenly started cheering. "It's a hit," Aufricht cried, genuinely shocked. However, Weill was furious, because Lenya's role and name somehow got omitted from the program. Aufricht had had an erratum slip printed—"Die Rolle der

Jenny spielt Lotte Lenya"—but it tended to fall out of the booklet in the excitement. Alfred Kerr's reluctantly enthusiastic review was headed, "Who Was She?"

By the winter of 1928, the *Threepenny* music was playing all over town. Berlin was *Threepenny* mad. The Baroness wound up an imported American gramophone to play *Threepenny* dance-band medleys for Jimmy, but she hated the show, wouldn't listen. Perhaps she was jealous: other cabaret shows recorded their specialties, but never Pfuikeck's troupe. Jimmy said, "That Brecht would steal the wings off an angel, according to Pfuikeck. The cymbal crash at the end of his songs? *We* did that first!"

"Come to bed," the Baroness would plead.

"If I must" was the answer. All the same, if one but taste in just the way they love, they fly up out of themselves to shimmer in the candlelight, unearthly, something for poets.

Kai drove Conrad and himself into town in his motorcar when they went to *Friederike*, the new Lehar operetta. The auto was a hyphenated English model, with the driver's seat on the right. It had come with two different steering wheels; the rejected one still sat in the back seat.

"My brother said it was too old-fashioned," Kai explained, turning into the Charlottenburger Chaussee. "It was Bismarck's steering wheel."

Conrad reached back to fetch it. "It's a grand piece even so. What's your brother's name?"

"Gunnlaug. From old stories." After a pause, Kai added, "He is too often away, but now they transfer him to Berlin."

"From where?"

"Munich," Kai replied, in a peremptory tone marking the close of this line of conversation.

Conrad replied, "I hope you enjoy the show tonight. It's not unlike the old Greek stage, as we sit through a retelling of a familiar story. Goethe's first love and how it failed. Lehar will explain it to us as Aeschylus explained the House of Atreus."

"Yes, with waltzes."

"It's a fine evening for a ride," said Conrad, stretching out a bit, a very happy young man. Glancing out his open window at someone in the car next to them, he impulsively grabbed the rejected steering wheel and worked it as if driving. "*Oh!*" he cried, tossing the wheel over his head into the back seat. "This car is breaking up! I may crash!"

The passenger in the next car stared aghast at Conrad as Kai pulled them out of view toward the Brandenburg Gate, just ahead. "I'll turn after the Adlon Hotel," said Kai, "and the Metropol Theatre will be just to the left."

"Splendid."

"Yes, that was a charming joke you just made, that makes one feel amused and affectionate." Kai laughed to himself. Then he reached over and ruffled Conrad's hair. It was their first overtly physical contact after a busy autumn of boat and bicycle rides, picnics, and a couple of UFA premieres, because of Conrad's employment. *Friederike,* too, was a premiere, at seven o'clock sharp, with Lehar himself conducting.

"Who sings tonight?" asked Kai, as they entered the theatre. "Who is so extraordinary that he can present Goethe on the stage?"

"Richard Tauber," said Conrad. "Kammersänger," he added. Of highest merit by official citation. "Surely you know him from opera."

"Ja, der Tauber. He is perhaps too superb. Too passionate."

"Here is a story," said Conrad, showing their tickets to the man at the door. "They criticized Tauber for wasting his talent in operetta, and he said, 'I don't sing operetta. I sing Lehar.'"

Kai smiled. He said, "It is admirable to defend what you love."

He was affable at the first intermission. Content. But Conrad felt disappointed. This was not the Lehar that he liked, exotic and bizarre, filled with tango and parade. *Friederike,* set in Alsace, was a humorless bucolic tale whose one spot of color was a live sheep that simply stood there during someone's solo.

The second act, at least, was more dramatic, as the heroine had to renounce Goethe to further his career, and thus staged a heartless rejection to send him to destiny. He was bewildered, then furious, and she keened in "Why Did You Kiss My Heart Awake?," at once intimate and intense. It was encored. At the second intermission, Kai and Conrad ran into the Baroness, with Alfred Kerr.

"Herr von Kleist," she said to Kai, extending her hand for a kiss.

"Madame."

Once introduced, Conrad and Kerr were able to join in praising the heroine, Käthe Dorsch.

"An actress," Kerr insisted, "who somehow also functions as a soprano. You heard how she soared at the climax of her monologue."

"This is sensitive music," Kai agreed. "But it lacks nobility. It is tea with too much sugar."

"I wish I could quote that," said Kerr.

Kai solemnly nodded assent.

"But how jarring," said the Baroness, "to see you at a Singspiel, Herr von Kleist. You and your brother are such snobs about music—everything in G Sharp Minor, is it not so? And everyone you know has G Sharp Minor politics."

"Madame," replied Kai, with a click of his heels; and he led Conrad away.

"What just happened?" asked Conrad.

Kai shrugged.

"You really know some grand people, though."

"Do you not know movie stars at UFA?"

"Not on my level."

In Act Three, Friederike and Goethe met briefly after eight years' separation. It was terribly sad to see them part all over again, but, as the heroine herself put it, "Goethe belongs to the whole world, and thus to me."

The Metropol was a big house, seating 1800, and Conrad and Kai were deeply into a discussion of the piece long before they reached the exit. "How much does one owe one's country?" Conrad ventured to ask. "Those two were so in love. Is that not all-important?"

"But how truthful is this page of chronicle?" Kai countered. "The greatest of all Germans exhibited amid gavottes and flirting?"

"Well, but it's reassuring to see the great man among us. As if his spirit watched over the land in times of peril. How we need someone like that today."

Kai was pensively silent.

"Did you like Lehar's setting of the 'Roslein' verses?" Conrad asked.

"Schubert's is better."

They had finally got out of the theatre to find the street lined with uniformed Nazis, shouting and menacing people.

"Jews out!"

"We want no Jews here!"

"Who asked for Jews?"

People were hurrying off to the east and west, polishing the sides of the theatre masonry in avoiding the Nazis. Through their shouting, one could dimly hear someone egging them on with a speech. Conrad caught some of it—about *Friederike*'s librettists and Tauber and Lehar's wife and others connected with the production, all Jewish. There was a bit about "the mongrelization of national sentiments." A few brownshirts were throwing eggs, punches were thrown, the police arrived: a Berlin cliché, as the weary law, so goaded and scorned from the first day of German democracy, turned up pretending to exist.

Kai seemed to want to stay and look on, but Conrad dragged him off to the car. They rode in uninflected silence, till they were nearly in the Grunewald. Then Kai said, "I will drive you home."

Conrad lived a good two miles out of Kai's way, so he performed the indicated demurral, glad that it had no effect. At his door, Kai said, "I am your friend, so I must try to enjoy what you like in music."

Kai gave Conrad a hug, their first, and Conrad to his horror got an instant erection and had to jump away, passing it off as nervous humor. He waved at Kai, who was but inches away. Kai smiled.

"I will go home now," he said.

Inside, Conrad's mother came out of bed to ask how it went. "You must order the records and play them for me," she said. Quoting a phrase of the day, she added, "A Tauberlied is a Zauberlied." Tauber's music is magic.

"Mutti, there were Nazis outside the theatre. Because of Tauber. You told me they were going away, and they haven't gone."

She said nothing. At that date, there was nothing accurate to say.

Conrad's family was Jewish, but only they themselves knew it. Four generations earlier, a forebear had emigrated to Hamburg from Frankfort-am-Main, changing his name and accepting Lutheran baptism. Regarding himself as the founding patriarch of an irreligious Jewish dynasty, he laid it down as absolute that the males of the line cannot be circumsized and the females must be married to men of Christian confession.

And that no one in the family could ever, under any circumstances, reveal the secret to anyone outside the blood line; and that everyone in the blood line must be told the truth. This would occur, at parental discretion, sometime in late adolescence. Thus, all the Thomamüllers would would bear two identities: one known to others and one carried within the self.

Conrad, an only child, now fatherless, had none but his mother to depend on, and he attended dutifully when she warned him to be careful around Jewish people.

"They cultivate an occult sense of kinship," she explained, "and will prod you with seasoned questions. Unmasking is an obsession with them."

"But why?" Conrad asked.

"I do not know."

She was wrong: it was far more the Christians who relentlessly sought to unmask Jews. Certain of them seemed to pelt everyone they met with questions;

any secret they uncovered made them joyous. Privacy is the best thing to steal, because it is irreplaceable.

Such people would steal anything. At school, there was a student named Caspian who flattered the popular boys and bullied the others. One day, Professor Ohlendorf ordered an inspection and discovered a number of missing items in Caspian's desk. These included a jacket belonging to Hans Wentrepp, universally admired because it was modeled on those favored by aviators during the war. Everyone in the room knew whose it was except Professor Ohlendorf, who detected a nicety in one's knowledge of Latin gerundives but who confused one student with another.

"Who is the proper owner of this jacket?" he called out.

Everyone waited to see what Hans would do. He did nothing. He was such a fine fellow that he would protect a thief rather than bring sorrow to another human being—which is why Conrad wanted them always to be good friends.

"You have news," Hans told Conrad at their next meeting.

"Truly? How do you know?"

"Kamerad, you are like those signs outside a theatre, where one reads so many details. You are completely a notice of yourself."

"Well, I honestly do have news. I met ... a new friend."

"A gutspurt?" That was Hans' term for a merry young man one can count on for occasional sex. Hans took the phrase from the name of an aphrodisiac popular with his elderly clients. "Have you ...?"

Conrad shook his head.

"Tell me three things about him," Hans urged.

"He is my age, but seems much older. He has a family business, very mysterious. He is very sincere."

"I mean physical things. Build his picture."

They were at the Romanisches Café, a feature of Berlin's arts world. Conrad always felt he was too proper to enjoy life, so he tried to keep company with those who did: with their stubble and shirts without collars and scolding laughter.

"There's Brecht," said Conrad, aiming Hans with a look at the playwright. "And Arnolt Bronnen with him, no?"

"They're skinny as thieves," said Hans, as the waitress brought their order.

"That is a correct appearance for two such radical artists, I think."

"I love that you are meeting very sincere young fellows with a mysterious family business." Hans loved it even more when Conrad told him how romantically they met. "Put that in one of your movies," he suggested.

"It is a problem that I feel immature around him. Like a knight's squire."

"But you have that fine black hair and favorable smile," said Hans, a bit puzzled. "Don't they give you authority?"

Conrad blushed into his pea soup with wurst.

"Watch out, though, if he is not a gutspurt. Like Horst, that swindler with his collection of personalities! He had such fun one night, my Horst, imitating one of his commissars giving a talk. The workers! The shackles! Our right to live! Then he imitated a Nazi orator—and he gave exactly the same speech, except now with 'Versailles' and 'Jews' in it. The *same speech,* old fellow. People like Horst, they are not morally fixed. Because they have no beliefs except in themselves."

"Sometimes you seem so smart," said Conrad.

"Just sometimes?" joked Hans, finishing his lemon cake.

"On sale in Berlin," said Pfuikeck, suddenly looming above them with what was supposed to be an affable expression. "Two luscious morsels at the Ro*man*. And how much—two marks? three?—for the pair?

"Leave them alone," said Jimmy, gently, with her irritating smile.

"Just right," said Conrad. "Leave us alone."

"After a taste of that irresistible apple tart," said Pfuikeck, reaching toward Conrad's plate.

Conrad grabbed his fork and would have stabbed Pfuikeck's hand had the cabaret manager not drawn back in mock-horror. Everything he did was satire. He was brilliant and unlovable.

"Come, will you?" said Jimmy. "I see Brecht and that Bronnen of his."

"With the foul breath?" as they moved on. "A writer who won't clean his teeth is capable of anything—reviving the alexandrine, quoting Eichendorff …"

Watching Pfuikeck and Jimmy go off, Hans said, "Yes, it is a glamorous world here, my friend. But some have such biting personalities."

"They are theatre, the arts, the divine spark. Without them, we are animals."

It was now routine that Conrad spend Saturdays with Kai in the fortress, and, on the first cool day of the new year, 1929, Conrad found its front door thrown open by a stranger. He was perhaps two or three years older than Kai, with light brown hair and the darkest blue eyes Conrad had ever seen.

"You must be Kai's brother, no?" said Conrad after a moment, for the stranger was looking at him without speaking.

"Gunnlaug," he said, not bothering to shake hands as he pulled Conrad inside. "Kai had to stay an extra night in Cologne, but he just rang up from the station and will be with us very soon. Now you have met me and we will be good friends, as Kai predicts. He says you are a good listener, you learn from living. Most admirable. Unfortunately, I have duty and must leave you—some boss needs ferrying. But it will not be long."

All through this, Gunnlaug unbuttoned Conrad's overcoat, took it off him, hung it in the hallway, pulled out a pocket comb with which he smoothed Conrad's hair, and took him by the hand upstairs to a room Conrad had never seen. The door had always been closed.

"Sit where you like while I change," said Gunnlaug.

Completely nonplussed, Conrad took a chair by a table while Gunnlaug collected clothes from an armoire, laying them out methodically on the bed. As he stripped, he said, "So, you are my little brother's new confidant, first-class. You teach him operettas and he teaches you Beethoven. One evening, we'll have a musicale. I will sing Schubert and Brahms for you and you will bring us the mischievous tunes of the boulevards. It is enlightening. Refreshing. Ja?"

Nosing into the armoire, Gunnlaug hummed some vaguely familiar old strain. "I am very protective of Kai, and he has probably complained to you about this."

Gunnlaug was now shamelessly nude, and Conrad, wondering where in the room he might properly look, could not avoid noticing a small tattoo of lightning bolts and a letter code under Gunnlaug's left arm just before he pulled on a singlet.

"It seems as though you two are your whole family," Conrad observed.

"There are many von Kleists," said Gunnlaug, donning the dress shirt as one who takes the best tailoring for granted, who judges others as fiercely as he praises them, who thinks he knows how humankind works: a close and comfortable fit, Gunnlaug in the world. "The others are reticent on country estates."

Silence. Gunnlaug gets into his shorts, rigs his tie. Socks, pants, boots, jacket, cap, swastika band. Gunnlaug is in the SS Leibstandarte "Adolf Hitler," at that time little more than a bodyguard of a few hundred. Inside the armoire is a full-length mirror, in which Gunnlaug gives himself a quick, thorough inspection.

"Kai says everyone is afraid of you," says Conrad. "But who is everyone when you live so alone? Where is Mutti, or for example silly cousin Helga who eats all the strudel? Who is this everyone besides Kai and sometimes me and your blazing eyes?"

A stirring below signaled the return of Kai. Conrad jumped up and started for the stairs, but Gunnlaug took hold of him—not roughly—and turned him so that they both faced the mirror, Gunnlaug behind Conrad, his hands on Conrad's shoulders, the two of them gazing forward. Now it was silent downstairs. The old wooden monster of a wardrobe creaked and its mirrored door trembled.

"Are you afraid of me?" Gunnlaug asked.

"No," Conrad lied. "Shall we greet Kai?"

They didn't move. Footsteps heralded the arrival of the wonderful Kai.

"Yes," Kai said in the doorway. "You are meeting my brother."

Feeling relieved—spared, even—Conrad went up to Kai for a handshake and got a fast hug with no embarrassing side-effects. "How was your trip?" Conrad asked.

Kai replied, but to Gunnlaug. "It is the same problem as in Duisburg and Dortmund. Our friends are agitating for support and contributions. It is more difficult now because they are so much better organized."

Gunnlaug nodded. "I have my Party business, but I should be back for dinner. Otherwise, I'll meet you at the theatre."

"We are taking you to the opera," Kai told Conrad. "It's *Der Freischütz*—the Reichvolksoper." German Opera Number One.

"I'm not dressed for the opera."

"Kai will put you in his clothes," said Gunnlaug, slowly fitting his arms around his brother to hold him with a tenderness of such ferocity that it spoke sense to Conrad that they were a family of two.

Carl Maria von Weber's *Der Freischütz* tells of a rural sharpshooter who bargains with the devil for magic bullets. As the most important line in the libretto warns, "Sechse treffen, sieben äffen." The first six shots make you, the seventh destroys you. To the neophyte Conrad, the performance seemed capable enough; it was the piece itself that fascinated. At supper in Fürstner's, after, Conrad outlined how Germanic the show had been:

"First of all, the occult and the nature stuff, and the way the two interact. You know—the stroke of midnight in the Wolf's Glen. Magic in the forest. Well, and all those male choruses. That strange habit of humiliating the loser after a contest. The Schadenfreude, no? That uniquely German feeling that someone else's failure is my success."

Gunnlaug glanced at Kai.

"Now consider the unpredictable violence—the seventh bullet that flies for hell. At your sweetheart, your friends, your people. Then, also, this picture of Germans maintaining a purely German society even in Bohemia. It could have been Hesse or Thuringia, or Switzerland or Poland or even Russia along the Volga, because it was Germans who settled Central Europe."

Another look between the von Kleist brothers.

"And God is constantly invoked, yet His laws are ignored or defied. How German that is, with the ageless rivalry between Emperor and Pope, and the Faustrecht." The law of might is right. "And there's the social hierarchy—the people obey the Head Forester, who bows to the Prince, who reveres the Hermit."

"Conrad," said Kai, "you speak with such clarity that you might be an archivist making a study."

"How's your omelet?" Conrad countered.

"It is quite useful. But after such wonderful music, it hardly matters, I think."

"One last thing," Conrad added. "This opera shows that everything depends on whether you throw your lot in with the creative force or the destructive force."

"How often does one have a choice?" asked the doubting Gunnlaug.

"It is in the Wolf's Glen," said Conrad. "In cities as well. In art. In science. Really, it is the historical temptation of the German people always to choose between the one who builds and the one who wrecks."

Silence as they ate.

"Thank you for the opera," said Conrad at last.

Gunnlaug replied, "Thank you for explaining the world to us. Let me give you some more wine."

They were well past the wine that night in Hermann Göring's house in Badensche Strasse, where the former aviator and now Party Reichstag deputy was treating industry Bonzen and their wives to a feast. After the ladies had retired, Göring passed around the cigars and brandy and called off his assembled prizes.

"Coal," he said. "Steel. Pianos. The press. Iron ore." A bow to all. "Reserve your share of the new Germany with a contribution of one hundred thousand marks a head to the National Socialist Party."

Göring showed them his pirate's smile and rubbed his palms together.

Breaking an awkward silence, Steel ventured to say, "This is hardly the time to …" He faltered.

"… Yes," the Press began, unable to continue.

Pianos, toughest of the bunch, put in, "One cannot suggest the amount of a voluntary contribution."

"But, meine Herren, who said 'voluntary'?" Göring answered, laughing. "Who *said* such a thing to you?"

There were coughs and subtle inquiring looks in another pause. Then Göring told them, "I would hate to think of any of you excellent fellows bearing the weight of the Party's resentment once we are in power." A puff of smoke. "And our time of power is getting surer every day, despite what you may hear. No, it would go much too badly for you." The ironist's smile. "Not to mention your families."

It was too late for Conrad to think of getting home. He phoned Mutti to say that he would stay over with Kai, and that he had been promised Kai's nicest pajamas and a fine breakfast supervised by Gunnlaug. "Venison, perhaps, if our bullets fly truly."

He sounded merry, but Conrad was nervous about the sleeping arrangements. There was no guest room at Schloss von Kleist, for there were never any guests. Lying next to Kai on his narrow bed, Conrad reflected that he had dreamed often of this moment, yet had neglected to prepare a scenario.

Now he had one: Conrad is alone when the shadow of Kai falls across the floor. It is the theme of the double. "Can I come in with you?" His hair in an uproar and his breath heavy, as if he'd been running through the woods. Then—

"What a satisfying evening," says Kai, suddenly, with a great yawn. "I am always proud to be seen with my brother. He is such a heroic figure. And you looked so handsome in my clothes."

Conrad prattled about the opera for a bit. He noted the brilliant swindle of the magic bullets, giving the Devil's fool the notion of invincibility till the seventh shot tears the world apart.

Kai yawned again, shifted position, and silence took the room.

Conrad couldn't sleep. He kept waiting for The Thing to happen, whatever It was. It seemed absurd to lie awake, so he borrowed Kai's robe and went downstairs.

He found Gunnlaug, wrapped in a blanket, puffing on a pipe, and reading newspapers on the kitchen table. Looking up, Gunnlaug said, "See how different each of these reports is. Yet it is all Berlin, one set of events. How can the truth be split into competing versions of itself?"

As Conrad sat beside him, Gunnlaug opened one paper. "Here. The *Morgenpost* tells of an incident in which a motorcar ran onto the sidewalk in the Friedrichstrasse. Three people injured, driver charged. Simple? But then the girls' magazine *Lustige Blätter* frames it with a piece on 'The Perils of Shopping' and demands protective measures. The Center papers, as good Catholics, see it as a spiritual parable of materialism overtaking piety—why were these pedestrians not attending mass? The Communist press considers the persecution of the workers by automation, and the Nazis expose the driver as a Jew on a murder spree. But there are not all these sides to a story. There is one side: what happened. Everything else is lies."

"Then who's right?"

"No one. Life is an endless struggle for primary access to space, food, water, military power, colonies, oil, silk, trade markets. You see? This is nature. This is struggle. How can one group be right? The strong overwhelm the others, and it has always been so."

"But it is happening in the streets. It happened to Kai and me."

Gunnlaug nodded, resting his pipe in a saucer. "It is the wild crime of revolution, ja?"

"Zu viel auf einmal brächte Reu!" Too much at once is perilous!

"Or is there too much order?" said Gunnlaug, with a sad smile. "Too much politeness, operettas, novels. It tames people, makes them secure. But they are not secure, because there is not enough on earth for all. Not enough work. Not enough sleep. Not enough happiness. Some must outlast and some go under. Are you cold?"

"I ... yes. What?"

"You are shivering. Come under the blanket with me. Quick, now."

Gunnlaug pulled Conrad in front of him on the bench, wrapping them both in the huge old cover, patriotically dyed in the Kaiser's colors.

"Ach, that tattoo again," said Conrad. "What is it for?"

"It is my group. And my blood type. You are wondering, Is it the strongest group? No. But the Republic is too weak to survive. It will go under. Listen."

Gunnlaug held Conrad under the all-enclosing blanket and told The Tale of the Barking Dog:

"Beneath a man's window there was a dog that whined and howled all night. The man sought out the dog's owner, who said dogs will do that. But this noise fulfilled no useful purpose and caused discomfort, so the man shot the dog. The next day, the owner tied a new dog outside and let him whine and howl all night. The man shot both dog and owner, and so he had peace.

"Problems," Gunnlaug went on, "demand solutions. Not debates. But that is the Republic, debating and not solving. It is like the newspaper stories. The Center considers whether the dog had a soul. The Social Democrats argue over remedial legislation that will not be passed. The Communists await orders from Moscow. And meanwhile the dog owner laughs at everyone. So I shoot to kill and there is no more problem of a barking dog."

Conrad was asleep. Gunnlaug hefted him up, carried him upstairs, and put him to bed with Kai, who stirred in his sleep and smiled.

Pfuikeck ran his cabaret by constantly replacing or revising numbers rather than creating a new show, but audiences could invariably expect The Act: Pfuikeck's Hitler imitation. Lately, The Act offered a new tune, "My Hitler":

> Oh, how I love my Hitler!
> My Hitler!
> My Hitler!
> I wind him up, my Hitler,
> And so he goes boum-boum!

The staging was the usual Pfuikeck frenzy, with the chief in his Hitler moustache marching and heiling like an automaton while the other performers hoofed and can-canned. For a climax, Jimmy was pulled across the stage on a wagon, posing as the Chariot of Victory atop the Brandenburg Gate, complete with cardboard spoofs of the two pairs of horses on either side of her. "The Quadriga!" the cast called out as she passed. "Berlin will stay Berlin!"

"It's too much Hitler stuff," said Pablo, at rehearsal. But the writer Erich Kästner was there; he strongly disagreed. "Hitler is a great danger that must be diligently opposed," he argued.

"The public is sick of it," said the others. "Hitler is finished."

"He is Nosferatu the Undead," said Pfuikeck, helping Jimmy out of her paper architecture. "Never finished. Besides, he goes so nicely with the Lehar."

This was the new piece, a lengthy takeoff on *Friederike* called *Fredericus,* after Frederick the Great. In the Pfuikeck version, Jimmy played Goethe, in the notorious blue frock coat and yellow vest affected by Werther, while Pfuikeck shamelessly frisked and emoted as a smitten Frederick, complete with flute. Stefan, another of the troupe, played a secondary character, Dubistder Lenz. *Friederike*'s Lenz was the one who sang to a sheep; Pfuikeck's Lenz *was* a sheep, in ratty old carpeting that smelled of spoiled food.

"Deft as ever" was Kästner's caustic view of the sequence, though he did enjoy the ball scene. In the Lehar original, the characters barely knew the minuet; in Pfuikeck's *Fredericus,* they introduced "The Nazi Charleston":

> The Nazi Charleston's quite the dance!
> The Charleston!
> Krupp and Bechstein love to prance

> This Charleston!
> It's the country's big romance,
> And even Hindenburg may chance
> The Charleston! The Charleston!

"Krupp and Bechstein could sue for libel, even so," Kästner warned them.

"For being called Nazis?" Pfuikeck blandly replied. "It's a political party, what more?"

"Anyway, Hindenburg loathes the Browns. You've unfairly—"

"No! *Idea!* All listen!"

Eyes half closed, Pfuikeck oozed about the stage as if in private conference with the muse. "Oh. Yes. Please." He threw his arms wide. "No, it's *too* revolting, so I *can't* resist! We must have Faust in our play, I kept thinking. Then—not Faust. The *Devil!* But! What if the Devil! *Is!* Faust! Pablo can dress as Goethe, but with horns and a tail until—"

"You cannot combine the two!" Kästner cried, appalled. "They are the outstanding opposites of German—"

"Don't be absurd, Kästner," said Pfuikeck. "'Zwei Seelen wohnen, ach, in Meiner Brust,' or however that runs." Alas, I have two souls in me. "The opposites are one, you see? Faust ... and Pablo, that steamy Latin lover, hoorah!"

"We want to divert and comment," said Kästner, "not ... Hello."

A man had risen from the audience. No one had noticed him before, though he was conspicuously dressed, in a cape over what could have been a costume from the last revival of *Götz von Berlichingen*. He was lucid, gallant, brilliant, sometimes restless and sometimes sentimental, and as much scientist as artist, with a wicked sense of jest and a heavy dick. He said, "You ought not to confuse the ambitious Faust with the nihilistic Devil. So many men mistake intensity for authority. Who writes the present piece?"

After a moment, Kästner said, "The members of the company improvise at rehearsals, and sometimes I ... or some other ... order it as a text."

"I used to fine my actors ten groschen for extemporizing," said the stranger, unfastening his cape as he came forward. "In art, there can be but one author."

Kästner meant to reply, but couldn't seize the words. He simply stared as the stranger came up on stage. Pablo took his cape.

"Writers must punish the people with truth," the stranger told Kästner, with a hand on his shoulder.

"If I may break into the awestruck silence," Pfuikeck began, "just who are you in the first place? Really, you police spies are—"

"I am Goethe."

That gave Pfuikeck at most two seconds' pause. "Right. And I am Frederick the Great, as you can see. We'll have Martin Luther and Bismarck up for skat, make an evening of it."

"You are most unfair," said the stranger, smiling nonetheless. "It is I who should be offended, at this pasquinade on my life, my writings ..." Taking them all in, he said, "We've clearly come a long way from *Hedwig, the Bandit's Bride*. Karl Theodor Körner's potboiler? Useful in emergencies, though I imagine it's out of the repertory by now. Long forgotten, even."

"Puff," said Pfuikeck, with a limp mime of his fingers.

"Well, we hardly remembered it at the time." Roaming the stage, the stranger reached Jimmy. "I'll say she's a pretty Goethe, in the end," he said, admiring Jimmy with embarrassing boldness—embarrassing to anyone but Jimmy. "Yes, what eyes." Turning to Pfuikeck: "And you are the capocomico? What is the argument of the piece?"

Jimmy touched the stranger's hand, drawing him from the fuming Pfuikeck, and told him of Lehar's operetta. He was bemused. "Stirb und werde," he murmured, ironically. Die to become better.

"Will you join our troupe?" Jimmy impulsively asked.

"What nerve!" cried Pfuikeck.

"We need an extra man—you said as much yourself yesterday."

"I had in mind, *dear heart*, someone *young*."

All looked at the stranger. He was not young.

"Someone of a certain momentary charm, perhaps," Pfuikeck added.

There was nothing momentary about the stranger, but he did have charm.

"Someone with far less command, in any case. An apprentice."

Here was no apprentice, but Jimmy extended her hand with one of her less ruthless smiles, and the others applauded as the stranger kissed it.

"It's settled," said Jimmy.

The company ignored Pfuikeck's noises of protest as the stranger enthusiastically took charge. "We'll need French themes!" he told them. "Culture, esprit, genie! We want subtle references and mockery—never scorn. Too easily hatred replaces intelligence."

"Pardon me, *Goethe*," Pfuikeck sarcastically put in, "but I've read plenty of scorn in—"

"The creative vision delights in contradiction," the stranger quickly explained, reclaiming his cape from Pablo with a flourish. "It's a source of vitality. Where will I stay tonight?"

Jimmy smiled again, with a telling shrug.

"How lucky," said the stranger. "Seeing that I haven't even had a chance to change my money."

"Overflow" is what the Baroness called it: the relentlessly expanding demands made by someone who needs you less than you need her. Overflow was "Can I stay over one more night? It's so nice not having to share a toilet down the hall." Overflow was the request for taxi fare—"because you always get so anxious when I'm late." It was the moue of tender blackmail, the goading of one's own apparently limitless humiliation, all hot and begging for a piece of criminal mischief.

The Baroness went into the "secret" guest room, and was appalled but not surprised to find Jimmy lying in bed next to Horst Pack. The covers were thrown back off their rude animal flesh and the room stank of sex. Jimmy stirred, stretched, winked at the Baroness, then rose and crossed the room to kiss her mouth with a facetious pull.

"Can you taste Horst there?" she asked.

"What happened to the Parisian cityscapes that—"

"Not so loud," Jimmy murmured. "Horst wanted to steal them, so I put them under the bed."

Jimmy cupped her breasts with the Baroness' hands.

"Don't let Horst see," Jimmy told her. "He's so jealous."

The Baroness drew her hands back. She would not share Jimmy with the shadow of Horst.

"He is jealous even of the old man staying with me now. But Horst would like to perform a trio with you and me, because he is so impressed with your house."

I have never known one more beautiful, sensual, faithless. She cheats for joy. Lap her up, flying together in that lovely blur, and she is already considering her next customer. Woe to us all.

"Horst says a trio will arouse greatness in you, which he would love to tear down. That's how he talks. But German men are the worst lovers, really, because they don't care what women think. Touch me here, please. Deeper, quickly. Horst is so selfish."

It should be sudden, the break, a lightning stroke. A goodbye and no.

Jimmy turned the Baroness around and started to unhook her dress, saying, "You must know Horst now." But the Baroness veered to the side, and whirled back with "Take him out of here! Fast as sin, or I'll have the police on you! Yes, it's true, with your face of surprise. That's your warning, so let us see what choice you now make!"

Horst was looking up in a daze and Jimmy was stunned, but the Baroness had already jumped for the door and fled. She gave orders to the staff and locked herself in her personal domain, alone with her chambermaid, Duscha.

"*Now* what?" said she, as the Baroness burst in. "I heard the noise and unhappiness."

"No rebuke, Fräulein. Just help me out of—"

"Madame is on fire!" Duscha pushed the Baroness onto her sitting-room couch and began undressing her. "Now we see what comes of letting the rogues of Berlin into your house. No, do not reply, Madame, if you please. With your sweet nature, anyone can—"

"I am willful and wayward, Duscha."

"If Madame so wishes," said Duscha, blithely. "Tea and bed?"

"No. Well, tea, anyway."

Duscha pulled one of those cords that communicated through Berlin's oldest houses, a servant appeared, and before long the Baroness and Duscha were enjoying a Klopsbrot, meatballs and bread with potato salad and relishes.

"Remorse makes one so hungry," the Baroness observed. "Have you a boy friend, Duscha?"

"Madame! Is that for you to ask?"

"You're young and pretty, so you must have a young man. Though you're not from Berlin, with that accent. Maybe not even from Germany."

"You're wrong, Madame. I'm from Brandenburg, after all. The Spreewald."

"Yes, distract me with lively nonsense. Tell of the Spreewald, of its mysteries and terrors."

"There are no terrors, Madame." Duscha covered a slice of dark bread with minced pickle. "Our customs unite us, and there is the strong family feeling. You know, we Slavs were here before you Germans."

Duscha's people, the Wends, had been inhabiting a wilderness of rivulets cutting through woodland back when there was no civilization but theirs. Some fifty miles to the southeast of Berlin, the Spreewald remained primeval and isolated, folkways without a history and people without politics. One might have said that time stood still there; but time had never started up in the first place.

"Is it beautiful there?" the Baroness asked, sipping her tea.

"There is a stillness as we glide along the water that feels like the end of a fairytale. And how jolly not to risk your life trying to get across the Potsdamer Platz. It's just weather and family and Christmas. We call it by the older name, of course, from before. Is that beautiful, Madame?"

"That's Silesia, as much as I remember it. But how reassuring this tea is. It almost ... well, makes one forget. There's something in it, ja?"

"Herbs, Madame. And such. Er birgt, was Heil dir frommt." It's what you need just now.

"So why did you come to Berlin?"

"Oh, you know how city folk like a rest in the country. They became so dazzled. You'd think they never saw a tree before. We rent out spare rooms and run the boats and look after them. And one summer, my cousin Iljen rented to a musician. A violinist."

"The name?"

"We just called him 'Sir.' He came to us with a young assistant and a piano. The tall, thin kind for poor people. But such wonderful music, practicing for his concerts in all of Europe! It made me realize that there was nothing in the Spreewald. Just Wends and the life of Wends. The violinist was extra nice to me. He told me of Berlin—the concert halls and opera houses, the plays and films, the restaurants. And music everywhere, he said. There is no music in the Spreewald, just uncles and boats. So I came here."

"You are a lovely thing, and I hope you are happy."

"I am in Berlin!"

Erich Kästner brought Goethe to the Baroness' that night. When he introduced him to Bella Fromm he called the old man simply "Mask and Shadow's latest adherent," supplying no name.

"They have termed me 'Der alte Herr,'" Goethe explained. "They take me for a mountebank for my curious outfit, Hessian accent, and extravagant claims to greatness."

"He's a ghost," Kästner offered.

"I'm a redeemer."

The three writers talked shop. Bella was "social correspondent" for Ullstein, the biggest publisher in Germany. "I attend parties for the *Vossische Zeitung*, essentially," she told Goethe. "I lure diplomats into faux pas and write how pretty their wives looked."

"It is much more than faux pas," Goethe replied. "Anyone can see that these are serious times, revolutionary times. Vacillating counsellors, savage mobs, wicked slogans, scapegoats. Even the music is vulgar."

"They play one group against another," Kastner said.

"So easy to do," Goethe agreed. "Does the dachshund care what happens to the Alsatian? Then, one day: all dogs forbidden!"

It was not as crowded as usual tonight. Even the Baroness had not yet appeared.

"I can assure you, sir," Bella told Goethe in her typical forthight way, "that I deal in more than faux pas. Being Jewish, I am well aware of—"

"Kiss the hand, I beg, dear lady," Goethe quickly put in. "I had no intention—"

"My column unfortunately does not allow—"

"I did not wish—"

Kästner, seeking a way through this impasse, blurted out, "Nietzsche said that every German he knew was anti-Semitic."

"He didn't know me," said Goethe.

"General von Schleicher," said Bella, as that worthy sailed up. The former Colonel had been promoted and now had ingress to the places of highest power in German politics.

"Frau Bella."

Before Kästner could get everyone introduced, there came one of those insidious commotions in the form of an ugly silence: Josef Goebbels, the Nazi Gauleiter of Berlin, had entered with two adjutants, all three in the black of the S.S. Everyone in the room froze, stared. The Baroness' guest lists had included a few Nazis, but never in uniform—and never this implausible runt with the snapping crocodile mouth and the clubfoot. Goebbels took his great lovely time in doffing his gloves, feigning nonchalance. But the lack of welcome reminded him that, outside the Party, he was small and ugly. He whispered something to the Nazi on his left. He whispered to the right one. And, when still nothing happened, he called out, *"Where is the Baroness?"* in the tones of a potentate known for depopulating regions on whim.

Here was the Baroness, summoned by frantic servants behind the scenes. "So, a premiere," she said, simply.

"I would of course have waited for an invitation," said Goebbels. "But it might have been months before we met."

"Years," she added, with disarming serenity.

Over in the corner, Bella asked General von Schleicher, "Why does the ugliest little monster in Berlin travel with two handsome young men?"

"What have I missed?" asked Fritz Lang, of Kästner, as all watched the Baroness finessing Goebbels.

"Oh, it's Lang. May I present the journalist Bella Fromm? General von Schleicher. And this is ..." Kästner shrugged. "Goethe."

He looks it, anyway, Lang thought. Aloud, he said, "What an honor—here, in Berlin."

"In Germany, I am everywhere."

The Baroness led Goebbels to the buffet, the two adjutants following at the usual bodyguard's grace of twelve feet. Some conversation: "Have you seen *The Threepenny Opera*?" she asked. Goebbels laughed with "Yes, a delicious Red shocker, isn't it? A Bolshevik valentine decked out in insolent nigger-Jewish tangos." He grinned with that keyboard of a mouth. "I wish the Party faithful were as facile. But our operas, too, will come. You will hear our arias and poets."

"The Nazi leadership makes odd pictures," von Schleicher observed, as they all watched. "This one is like a dummy from a music-hall act. He has escaped his maker. He is on the rampage." Von Schleicher was trying to hearten Bella Fromm, who was geuinely upset to find Goebbels in this place. "And have you seen Göring lately?" von Schleicher added. "He looks like a prize pig playing Prince Danilo." Struck by a thought, he cried, "What a romantic film they would shoot, these Nazis!"

"Film is not romantic," said Lang. "Each work of this art is integral and complete. Romance is the art of the unfinishable."

"That is mysterious enough for a university chair," said von Schleicher.

"See, one sings and one plays," said Bella, for Goebbels' adjutants had taken over the Bechstein. It was Goebbels' parlor trick: to ticket the Nazis' cultural credentials, he filled his suite with the gifted.

"At the piano, Günther Helke," Goebbels announced, his left arm beating time in the air to his emphases. "In song, baritone Gunnlaug von Kleist. A short program of the best in German art. Völkisch!" Blood and Soil!

The pianist broke into the insistent pit-a-pat of Schubert's "Fischerweise," and Gunnlaug set to. He was a broad, unsubtle singer, but a sound one, relishing the words and keeping the rhythms sharp. The singer of Lied is, by rule, versatile, and Gunnlaug followed the jaunty Schubert with Schumann's turbulent "Schöne Fremde," a vision of an ancient paradise with a golden future:

> Here, under the treetops starting,
> In evening's shimmering light,
> What fancy are you imparting
> To me, fantastical night?

Rubbish, the Baroness almost said. Treetops starting and fantastical nights—the costume jewelry of whoring poetry. Yes, whoring itself to music as women whore to men in love with themselves. Like this von Kleist boy in his bully's dressup.

The von Kleist brothers were relatives of the Baroness' late husband; she had liked them as earnest, inseparable little orphans but did not care for the imperturbable paragons they had become. And to see such well-bred young men in the Nazi horde, with the screamers and cutthroats.

In an undertone, Bella asked von Schleicher if Hitler could ever get into government.

"Right now, the Nazis are a noise. But one more inflation and Stalin himself will be chancellor."

The Baroness was imagining Gunnlaug with Jimmy, in one of those pounding fucks men enjoy when they're drunk and honest. Yes, sing away, lad. Then put on your tie, watching, in the mirror, the corpse of Jimmy amid twisted sheets. The beautiful cheat. Oh—and now he's on to *Die Schöne Müllerin*, Schubert again, and singing directly at me, is he? He flatters his hostess with the sweetly gloating "Mein!":

> The enchanting miller-girl is mine!

He closed his set with a flourish, a little punch of his right fist, curious to see. Anticipating a Nazi salute, the guests did not applaud but stood eloquently silent as the Baroness came forward, acknowledging the music in her own enigmatic way. All the same, Goebbels peacocked about with his two young men, taking champagne and even interesting von Schleicher in a diplomatic tete-a-tete.

"Look at Goebbels' eyes," said Bella.

Goethe nodded. "They forgive nothing forever."

He liked my film of *The Nibelungen*," said Lang.

"How do you know?" asked Bella.

Fiddling with his monocle: "One hears these things."

The Baroness had vanished: to change clothes and sneak out on her own party in search of Jimmy. She would pass from club to club, embracing her degradation as the condemned angles his hood to oblige the hangman. So this is love.

We turn in relief to Conrad and Kai, theatregoing once again, now to an American war play, *Rivalen*. The rivals of the title were Sergeant Quirt and Captain Flagg, intimate antagonists in a private war for the same woman.

Conrad found it funny, mad, and disturbing. He was silent on the way back to the fortress till Kai said, "I think those two wanted to be with Charmaine at the same time. They excite each other."

Conrad said nothing.

"It would make a fine movie at least, ja?"

"The Americans already did it, two years ago."

"With a moonlit scene for the two soldiers? They are bathing, with gleaming skin?"

Conrad did not reply, so, for a while, Kai made conversation for both of them, deliberately getting Conrad's ideas and diction wrong, to tease his friend out of his sulk.

Conrad stared out of the open window of Kai's motorcar. He finally said, "I really like you, you know."

"No, you seem very disagreeable to me, Captain Flagg."

Conrad nodded, vacantly.

"What's wrong, Conrad? Why won't you joke with me?" After a bit, he asked, "Are you my rival, after all?"

The Baroness caught up with Jimmy at The Gypsy Baron, where Jimmy felt like slashing her Schnapsfreundin with a helping of truth. As the beautiful always do, because they can. "Slimy money-bitch," Jimmy called the Baroness, turning a shoulder to her. "Horst says the Kozis will take your gang to the guillotine. He wants to be there for the fun."

Now the awful concessions, the apologies from the one who was wronged, and *crack!* came Jimmy's hand across the Baroness' face.

"Now do you see?" said Jimmy, with icy calm. "Do you realize at last that I do not care for the touch of you again?"

Hand on cheek, astonished, the Baroness started to reply when *crack!* came Jimmy's hand again *crack!* enjoying herself with these avid slaps, a fool for scandal as all the bar *crack!* takes a look. And even now the Baroness wants to beg for reconciliation. Just as Schnapsfreundin—just that much. Just to see you every so often. But Jimmy shoves her so violently that the Baroness is knocked down. Then Jimmy strolls off.

A few sensitive souls help the Baroness to her feet and offer to see her to a cab. Gnä' Frau, Gnä' Frau. She mustn't be seen so. No, too kind, I can manage.

That Jimmy, they all say.

Leaving the club, the Baroness discovers that she has hurt her right ankle so badly that she cannot walk. There are no cabs in sight, but she doesn't want to leave in any case. What if Jimmy comes out? Oh, too much more of this hunger and one loses one's freedom, identity, self. The Baroness is free or she is no one.

And that may be reason enough to break out in wracking sobs. To hug oneself and rock away while sitting on the curb. To feel that feelings as hurt as these can never be wholly soothed again.

See what comes of love!

In the fortress, Kai cheered Conrad with a midnight feast of omelette and fried potatoes. Then he asked what the sulking had been about.

"Well, I wasn't sulking."

"Ha! You *were* sulking, and now I will rough you up as a lesson to be always in a good humor with me."

As Kai pushed back and rose, Conrad said, "I got a promotion in employment yesterday. Now I am assistant producer."

Stopped in mid-jest, Kai tendered his congratulations, but then, wearing a wicked grin, he slowly paced around the table toward Conrad.

"No," said Conrad.

"I will show you who commands."

Conrad edged along the table away from Kai.

"It is no use to escape," Kai warned him, now feinting and rushing as Conrad dodged away, keeping the table between them.

"This is too much like the play tonight!"

"We give the scene they were afraid to write," Kai told him, pushing some chairs around to block Conrad's way. He caught his friend, dragged him protesting into the next room, and held him down on the couch, the two of them breathing and waiting, each unsure of the other.

"It is a joke, yes?" asked Conrad

Kai slowly shook his head.

"But you will let me up?"

Kai did so, and, after trading inquisitive glances, they reached for each other and held on carefully, tight.

"You are hard, too," said Kai, into Conrad's ear. "It was not an accident that we were at such a play this evening, and it is not an accident now. No, we are not rivals, because we see the world in the same ways, although you are so creative and fascinating with your interpretations and I am more direct. Yes, because it suits a man of business, giving orders to employees. But you and I are equals. So it is correct, what happens."

Gunnlaug came up to the Baroness, there on the street, in time to catch the last trickle of her weeping. He sat next to her and said, "Yes, the famous nonconformist. Nevertheless, it is odd to find you like a beast in the road."

"Sind die Tiere hier nicht heilig?" Aren't the beasts worthy here, too?

Gunnlaug laughed quietly.

"And why are you here, young von Kleist, at such a time?"

"Mm. It is fate, perhaps. Or I am following you."

She gave him an ironic look through her snuffling.

"Or I may have dropped off Herr Gauleiter of Berlin Josef Goebbels and am free for the rest of the evening."

"That disgusting outfit," she said, only then noticing that of course he was still in S.S. uniform.

"You're doing that quite unsuccessfully," he said, taking the handkerchief from her.

"You're too young to be understanding," she complained, as he took her by the chin and gently cleaned her face.

"Who has the power to break so strong a woman to her knees, weeping in the street? I must meet such a man, and challenge him."

He looked at her as intently as when he sang at her piano.

"I prefer not to be overwhelmed," she told him.

He got up, taking her with him, and signaled to a passing cab; when the golden boy needs one, they line the road.

"I thank you," she said. "Good night."

"I'm taking you home," as he bundled her inside. He wasn't trying to overwhelm. Men like him don't have to. They don't bend you to their will: they attract with it. They have a wild magic, and everybody loves them.

So Gunnlaug rode the Baroness to her palace and took her upstairs past the servants and told Duscha to run the bath and bring some wine, and all was done as he demanded.

Kai was running down to the river, stopping here and there to pull off his clothes. Drunk on his own youth, he shouted joyously at Conrad, who followed with misgivings. It is too cold. There are fish, perhaps eels.

At the water's edge, Kai flung away the last of his clothing and dove in with a "Hopp!" When he broke the surface, shivering and laughing, Conrad was still getting undressed. "Ja, ja, anything to please you," he said, and at last he dove in, too.

"It is timeless!" Kai called out, grabbing Conrad, swimming around him. "It could be in any age what we do, it is before history and bedtimes!"

"You are so beautiful like this," Conrad marveled. He pulled Kai out of the water, stood on the shore admiring, but Kai slipped back into the Havel.

"You come here!" Conrad shouted, almost as free as Kai now. "You!"

There was stillness.

"Kai!"

Nothing.

Suddenly, Kai leaped up to catch Conrad by the leg and pull him into the deep. Conrad fought back, and now it was Kai dragging him onto the strand, back toward the grass, and they wrestled for dominion, mouths all over each other, fighting and running off hoping to be captured. Then a neighbor's light came on, and Kai warned Conrad with a *sst* and they sneaked into the trees at the side of the house, giggling and shushing each other with great tenderness. Conrad grew uneasy then. But Kai solemnly brushed back his hair and told him, "You will not be afraid. I have done this before."

Gunnlaug was washing the Baroness by hand in her antique lion tub, ever changing position and shedding another article of dress. He got at her neck with a deep, nagging pull, sucked heavily on her breasts, played with her fingers, kissed her about the eyes with the bliss of an aficionado in a master's workshop, and, finally nude himself, got into the water too cull her sweetness and she how she would feel then. His fingers discussed her till he cried to him.

"Pray for mercy," he whispered.

Her back was arched, her eyes half-open.

"You're a cat, steaming hot," he said, gobbling her up. "Weeping again? Oh, the taste of those tears!" He drew back, to take her in, boyish about the eyes as his hands controlled her, to cast a spell.

She knew. "Stop that!" she ordered, tracing lines in his face, his hair. "You are too good to me. It breaks my heart."

"Wer ist gut?" Who's good, lady?

"Don't enchant me," as he spread her back, legs atop his shoulders, to feast like a monster. Sometimes he looked up at her even as he lost himself in her savor. "It is absurd like this, in the water!"

"You are here as well, my sweet," he told her. "The servants took one look, knew what we were up to, and fled."

"They're discreet."

"They're terrified," he said. "Now I fuck you."

She let him pull her out of the tub. "I will give you nothing, ruffian!" she warned.

"Ja, that way is better," never letting go as he took her into her room. Pinning her to the bed on her back, stealing quick deep silly kisses. Then: "I want you so much that I will take you apart and put you back together with what I do to you."

"And I'm supposed to enjoy that?"

"Tell me after."

Conrad said, "Yes, we're both exhausted and thrilled, but how long do we have to lie on the grass like this?"

Kai's head came up. "Have you no sense of occasion?"

"Where's Gunnlaug tonight?"

"In town."

"What will he ... never mind."

"Say about us?"

"Can't we go inside?"

"All right."

As they go up, Conrad looked doubtfully at the clothes strewn about the lawn.

"No, leave that," said Kai, an arm around his shoulder to take him back to the castle. "I want to be pure in the moonlight. Like young knights. We are fearless and incorruptable, especially in the sequence when the Black Sorcerer tempts us. He shows us a vision of Germania giving herself to vampires."

"That doesn't tempt me."

Kai stopped moving. Into Conrad's ear, he whispered, "I won't be sure of you until we have saved each other's lives at supreme risk to our own. Swear!"

"I'll do anything to get inside at this moment."

"Swear!" Kai repeated, holding Conrad by the sides.

"All right, I swear—but only because I am so overcome at the sight of you. I must change into something greater than myself."

"Before moon and stars, we are united!" cried Kai, taking Conrad by the neck, pulling him close.

"Yes, and now we can go indoors." As they broke, he added, "And if you bring a sacred oak into it, I'm taking the first train to Dresden."

The Baroness was bucking, and Gunnlaug kept trying to ease her down. "Surrender!" he told her; she wouldn't. It was unhappy and appropriate, a terrible combination.

"I defy you," she told him, but he only laughed, his mouth wild on her breasts as he drove inside her with a tenderness made to break her. "Sei mein!" he growled. Let me have you; he didn't care how she would feel then. She had her hands in his hair, her face right up at his—she would look; she would know—and he forced her back so lavishly that she screamed for joy despite herself. "Sei mein!" he repeated. Let me own you. They swung into it, past the duelling, and the potion rose between them on the upward slide till they hit the summit, she first and he, greedy and understanding, in answer, with one last "Sei mein!" Let me love thee.

They crashed apart at once as if separated by an unseen hand, and lay tumbled and silent till the Baroness, with the knowledge of having made an unforgivable if unavoidable mistake, said, "Dein bin ich von je." I was yours to love from the first.

Gunnlaug chuckled. Into her ear, sweetly gloating, he whispered, "The enchanting miller-girl is mine!"

Late on the night of October 3, 1929, Alfred Kerr paced his study in despair. There had been yet another murder of one of the rare statesmen with the authority, intelligence, and public following to hold back the radicals—Gustav Stresemann, the foreign minister. This one they didn't shoot: they killed him with vexation, grinding him down throughout the decade with their slanders and sabotage. Now he was dead, and, surely, with him, the republic. The Nationalists and Communists will tear it apart.

Sitting at his desk, Kerr tried to concentrate on proof sheets for Arnolt Bronnen's new novel *O. S.*, sent to Kerr weeks ago. Wasn't Bronnen a Red at one time? He certainly wasn't now: the novel was a shrill defense of paramilitary conspiracy. They say Bronnen is one of Berlin's most accomplished opportunists. Could he know something the rest of us don't?

Hearing a ruckus outside, Kerr threw open a window to find a drunk staggering along the road shouting, "Heil Hitler!" at intervals. He now ran, now bumbled, crashed to earth, and heaved himself back up to stagger along with his heiling. Kerr expected to see other windows shoot up, hear the outrage of respectable citizenry; there was nothing but the drunk and his shouting, dying away as he passed along.

Are they not listening? he wondered.

Paul von Beneckendorff und von Hindenburg, the President of the Republic, was a hippopotamus: slow as opera, dim and unpredictable. He could meet a statesman he had known for decades and confuse him with a groundskeeper, then break into parade alert, all memory retrieved, along with the prejudices and resentments typical of all Old Generals.

Close to von Hindenburg through friendship with his son Oskar, Kurt von Schleicher nevertheless had to tussle with Franz von Papen for the President's favor. The old man had the habit of agreeing with whomever he last spoke to, so, to keep von Papen from taking control, von Schleicher coached the hippo in how to rise peremptorily, saying, "The interview is now completed." This sometimes worked, though he was just as likely to rise and say, "The German Army cannot surrender!"

Today, on a lovely spring afternoon, von Schleicher was guiding von Hindenburg through a line of visitors in the Chancellery garden. One has to emphasize: "And I present the *Chancellor*, Herr Heinrich Brüning, the *Chancellor* of the *Republic*, sir, Herr *Brüning*, as you see." Then someone mentions Adolf Hitler, and von Hindenburg explodes as if actually alive. "That Bohemian corporal!" he shouts. "He is not fit for government! Not fit for Germany!"

"He is an Austrian corporal, in fact," says von Schleicher.

"The German Army cannot surrender!"

Suddenly exhausted, the president must sit. A chair! The hippo rests. "The interview," he gasps out, staring obsoletely at the gathering, "is now completed."

When he was off duty of an evening, Gunnlaug would come to the Baroness and, accompanied by some hireling, sing to her. She forbade him to appear in uniform. "There are too many Nazis as it is," she said. "It used to be just those irritating little brown men invading even the nicest restaurants with those stupid little collection boxes. Now they're surging at the polls and showing up at dinner parties and fucking you with love of such seductive hunger that you throw away your freedom to feed it."

They went dancing at the Adlon Hotel and never talked politics. Gunnlaug was very young; the young are very silly. Surely he would soon enough grow sensible and leave the movement. She said as much to him once—lightly, in order not to offend.

"Verderberin!" he replied, just as lightly. "Weiche von mir!" Away, temptress!

At the Adlon, Marek Weber's band played medleys of the latest American musicals, bits of the classics in dance tempo, waltz kings, and Latin spice. Gunnlaug wanted never to sit down. "One more," he would say, leading her into a *Traviata* fox trot with a violin solo that turned the Adlon ballroom into a gypsy encampment. Gunnlaug was impulsive, and she loved him for it.

It was rumored that Weber's saxophonist supplied drugs of pleasure to clientele straight out of the Gotha. "Let us meet him," said Gunnlaug, and they summoned him to their table when the band was on break.

It wasn't Weber's regular saxophonist, though. It was Pablo, of Mask and Shadow, a moonlighting substitute. Pablo liked the attention, and although he didn't peddle drugs he was a devotee of opium and offered to share a pipe with them when he got off.

So they went back to the Baroness' and puffed on dreams till Pablo suggested they sample the delights of love, all three together.

"No," said Gunnlaug. "Because there is too much insubordination and not enough reward for sacrifice. Because I have already perverted this lady's nature with my love. And because I am given nothing to admire but death."

Pablo looked at the Baroness pleadingly. "It is all the rage here. The latest thing from Paris!"

Gunnlaug laughed.

"Life is too modern these days" was the Baroness comment.

They fell asleep on their couches like exquisites in some ancient chronicle, and when they awoke Pablo was gone.

"Willkommen, Fürstin aller Nächte!" said Gunnlaug to the Baroness, most grandly. Hello, Princess of the Night! Gunnlaug had the recollection of Pablo kissing his eyes during sleep; that must have been the opium making movies.

Ernst Josef Aufricht had a motto: when all else fails, revive *The Threepenny Opera*. In November of 1930, he put it on once again, with Lotte Lenya now in the lead role of Polly, and Pfuikeck dropped in especially to see her. He had to pester Aufricht for a pass, but then nobody gave anything to Pfuikeck if he didn't nag.

Conrad and Kai were there that night; Pfuikeck spotted them at the second interval. He stared and wondered. The taller boy had the patrician's brisk, easy formality; did he know that his companion was a common little rag of the clubs? How Pfuikeck longed to smash their cozy evening. He hated those who seemed content. They make it look so effortless, too, with their tight little stomachs and spidery long fingers, studying each other with furtive smiles, and the manly hand on the shoulder as they move down the theatre aisle. I would be Herod with such boys. I would be Attila, Torquemada. Into the crocodile pit!

After the play ended, the streets were all but impassable, swollen with screaming Nazis who had just disrupted a showing of the American film *All Quiet on the Western Front* with stinkbombs and mice. They were hot for more turbulence, and someone—Goebbels himself, it was said, to Bella Fromm, and by someone in Goebbels' office—had sent them on to the infuriating Jewish-Bolshevik classic, for well over two years now Berlin's most wicked pleasure. Surrounding theatregoers with menacing gestures, the Browns went into their favorite war cry:

> Germans, awaken!
> Jews, we will kill you!

The street was an overstuffed chaos of people, and Kai and Conrad were dragging each other away, either one taking the lead whenever a few inches gave them progress as they head east for the Weidenhammer Bridge. They could hear police sirens and the Nazis' infernal chanting—Berlin's new music—and they found themselves growing furiously impatient with the people around them, who were simply not getting out of there fast enough. Pfuikeck had been trailing Kai and Conrad as best one could in the melee, and now he pushed up to murmur to them, "A secret way! A car, escape! Follow me!"

"You go fuck a dog," said Conrad, tearing away with Kai through a sudden opening in the crush. More and more, they found room to travel in, till they came upon a half-dozen Nazis tormenting an old man they had backed against the side of a building.

"Yiddle for us, Meier," one of them ordered. Two others, grinning at some secret joke, broke into one of their anthems, and the rest joined in as their leader slapped the man's face on the strong beats. They were light slaps, for show, but then the Nazi punched the man's face so hard his head hit the wall. The Nazis cheered as the man fell with a hoarse cry. One of them sang out:

> Meier, Meier,
> Ready for the fire!
> First you're scragged with piano wire!

"How many of you shits does it take to hurt a helpless old man?" Kai called to them, storming up to their leader and kicking him right in the genitals. With surprise on his side, Kai turned and felled another, and Conrad, hating this but having no choice, rushed in after Kai. "Schiffbruch!" Conrad shouted. Disaster! The two friends had been so frustrated by the unmoving crowd that the tension was crashing out of them in crazy war, and they fought and ran as one, panting and ashamed and disturbed till they got over the bridge under the cover of a squad of policemen. Nobody was following them, it seemed, and they walked for a long time in silence. A cab took them home.

"Your dress coat is ruined with blood stains and your left eye is swollen shut and that gash on your forehead won't heal for a month," said Gunnlaug, cleaning his brother's wounds in the kitchen. "Brace yourself, now."

"*Ow!*"

"Good." Opening Kai's shirt, he took off the collar and checked his torso for bruises. "It is no worse than you deserve."

"They are most honorable wounds," Conrad put in. "I am embarrassed not to need medical attention."

"Conrad fought by my side," said Kai. "We are blood brothers and knights of the devious moon!"

"My brother," Gunnlaug told Conrad while bottling the merbromin, "was always fighting in school, till they sent him home for all time. But where does such a cultured boy as you learn his warfare?"

"The fight coaches at the studio taught me a few tricks. And Kai and I would sometimes ... we would try things out, or—"

"Dangerous children's games," said Gunnlaug, rigging a bandage on Kai's left wrist. "Did you fight nobly, you knights?"

"No!" Kai cried. "We kicked their eggs in and ran away. What else could we do, so outnumbered?"

"Na und," said Gunnlaug, washing Kai's face and tickling his ears. "And how was the play?"

"I am displeased with everything tonight," said Kai, shaking off Gunnlaug's fingers. "With the theatre especially, a bitter piece fit for defeatists." Kai looked angrily at Conrad. "I was polite before, but now I speak. It is very complicated in Germany. It is not a community any more, so we are at the mercy of our enemies." Turning to Gunnlaug: "And there is the problem again of the business. Most particularly in Duisburg. As I told you it would be, but also in other places. There is always that blackmail that they specialize in, so—"

"Who is 'they'?" Conrad asked.

"Ask my brother. Ask Odysseus and try to get a straight answer. Ask my destiny. Ask the ridiculous people tonight, so busy moaning and worrying and not efficiently making their escape so *we* were slowed up."

"Well, but who is 'they'?" Conrad repeated.

Kai answered without answering: "The difficulty is that every solution to our problems creates new problems." He got up, buttoning his shirt. He took a deep breath, one of exasperation, knowing it was a waste of time to say this. "The Treaty of Versailles is destroying us. We must be freed of it. The Republic revels in Versailles. So we must be freed of the Republic."

"By your 'friends'?" Conrad cried. "The blackmail, and the violence we saw tonight, and that is your friends?"

"Defeatism!"

Conrad was furious. "Why is it always surrender or conquer? To compromise is—"

"Oh yes, to *compromise!*" Kai turned to his brother for support, but Gunnlaug was silent, even blank: waiting and watching. Turning back to Conrad, almost weeping with vexation, for this lack of understanding from his friend was all but unbearable, Kai tried to master his anger.

"Here is compromise," he said. "All over this middle of Europe, there are cities made by Germans. We create these places, build them and staff them, and over the centuries they grow with industry and art. Let there be such a city to the east, where many Poles live in the surrounding places, and they come to the city to find work. And they stay. And their generations stay, and soon there are more Poles than Germans in this place. Yes, it is most true—and now this Treaty of Versailles tells us that this is a Polish city. It is as if a German cooks a dinner, and eighteen Poles come to eat it, and suddenly it is a Polish dinner. *This* is compromise!"

Feeling Kai's sorrow, Conrad started to move toward his friend. He hesitated. He said, "But these people are violent because they are violent. They need to destroy, not solve problems. And do not tell me I'm wrong because I am not wrong."

"Sing to us!" Kai begged his brother. "I will play Schubert's *Swan Songs* for you and we will have something beautiful to believe in."

They use the music as a weapon, Conrad was thinking. Their shield, at any rate. They believe that no one else can hear what they hear.

However, Gunnlaug sang to Conrad as ever mother sang lullaby, till he reached "Der Doppelgänger" and the lines

> I dread it, when I his features witness—
> The moon reveals what I am to myself!

Oh yes, it is the theme of the double, haunted by night and death, the music a Dies Irae and the poetry Heinrich Heine's.

"A Jewish writer for Schubert," said Conrad, as the song ended. "What would the Nazis make of that?"

"Every schoolchild knows Heine," said Gunnlaug. "What can they do, ban the classics?"

Kai banged his hands on the keyboard and jumped up. "The cycle is not finished! One song remains!"

"One song always remains," said Gunnlaug, taking his brother by the sides to pull him from the piano. Then they stopped and stood looking at each other in that worrisome privacy of theirs.

"We should sign Gunnlaug up at UFA," said Conrad. "There's no one like you in films yet. We should schedule a test scene, and you could put aside that hateful uniform."

Considering Conrad, then lightly brushing the boy's hair back, Gunnlaug said, "That is quite enough from two chicks who are tired and cranky and heading straight for bed."

He prodded them upstairs to Kai's room, no stalling allowed. "Yes, put me in my coat and tie in Duisburg," Kai grumped, as he and Conrad undressed, "and I have responsibility. But when I return home, I am no more than a sweet to be filed in the candy box."

"Quick march," said Gunnlaug, tossing them pajamas.

"In the Ruhr, they treat me as a man," Kai went on. "I am young, but I have the authority of the family name. I have education. I have Prussia, whose jurisdiction extends from Finland almost to France."

"You have a Mona Lisa smile, which must be useful at pompous and confusing board meetings," said Gunnlaug, pulling down the bedclothes.

"What if they knew that my brother treats me as a child? Would they sign the contracts we so badly need? Would they let me direct those meetings?"

Gunnlaug pushed the two boys into bed, threw an extra blanket over them, pulled a chair near to the bed, and sat. "Listen to The Tale of the Chosen Heir," he said.

"*Lectures!*" Kai snarled, wrapping the pillow around his head. "I will not listen!"

"In a land surrounded by other lands, there lived a king who was intelligent and strong. But he was an old man, and childless. His people were enjoying good times, living in harmony with their neighbors. Still, the king knew he must leave his people with a leader to take them through the inevitable bad times. He must choose an heir."

"A pack of cliches!" Kai muttered. "Narrative algebra!"

"How can you tell, as you are not listening? The old king narrowed his selection to three candidates. The first was wise, the second artistic, and the third a criminal—a worse one even than my brother, whose offense is that he has lost his manners."

"If you do not treat me with respect," Kai warned, coming out from under the pillow, "I will smooch my Conrad right on the mouth before you. Then we will see what you think of my Mona Lisa smile."

Gunnlaug riffled Kai's hair.

"You see?" Kai almost shouted to Conrad. "He has so many personalities that it is impossible to shock him!"

"Now came the test of character, as the king asked each candidate what he would do if bad times came and neighbors began to menace one another. The wise one said, 'All peoples must share, even if they end in living on half-rations.' The artistic one said, 'We must put on great fairs for inspiration.' The criminal said, 'We will take what we need to live.'"

Gunnlaug paused for dramatic punctuation, then: "Who was chosen to follow the king?"

Kai leaped out of the bed and held his brother: rather, was held by him.

"You would die for each other," Conrad observed, accidentally. He had meant only to think it.

Conrad's professional life knew good times. Promoted again, he was integrated into the studio hierarchy enough to accompany a deputation to the latest hit of the musical stage, *The Flower of Hawaii*, in the company of two producers, one scriptwriter, and one star, Renate Müller. A zesty musical-comedy heroine in her early-middle twenties, Müller was brighter than actresses are supposed to be, with beauty and an easy manner.

The Flower of Hawaii had had its premiere in Leipzig in July of 1931, but it was too cosmopolitan for any place but Berlin, with its jazz band orchestra, its dips into English and French, its use of a white performer in blackface, its very setting in an American colony. It was a smash, and now that sound had found its way into cinema, popular stage musicals were of great interest to the studios.

Renate Müller loved the show, but, as their driver sped through the town dropping everyone off, the two producers expressed irritation.

"A woman performing a drunk scene!"

"Louche carryings on!"

"Is it even music? Or nigger belly dances?"

"I liked the man in the white suit," said Renate Müller. It was *The Threepenny Opera*'s Mackie Knife, now in a polka-dot tie. "He is like the conferencier in a Paris revue. He owns the stage the moment he enters. And the Hungarian girl, die Barsony ... didn't you like—"

"Mongrel theatre," said one producer.

"Jewish trickery," said the other.

"There would be no German operette without Jewish trickery," said Conrad, quite calmly. "Many of the composers and performers and all of the librettists and managers have been—"

In genuine bewilderment, Müller said, "Just a year or so ago, one would not have heard such language from producers at UFA. Have you perhaps had a drink of water from a foul spring?"

Silence. Then: "It will shoot well, true," one producer sighed.

The other: "Sarongs. Palm trees. Ships ride the spray."

"It will make a terrible film," said Conrad, "because it is nothing but song and dance spots. Good films are good stories. This show depends entirely on the communication between the stage and the public, the ... vitality." He turned to Renate Müller. "As in those Parisian revues. To film this piece would be to hunt shadows."

"Young man," said one producer, "you are far too smart."

Renate Müller got out first, followed by the writer. As the first producer left the car, he repeated, "Far too smart."

In the presidential election of April 10, 1932, the incumbent von Hindenburg retained his office while Chancellor Brüning finagled secretly to restore the Hohenzollern monarchy to Prince Louis-Ferdinand. Von Schleicher, who sought the chancellorship himself, exposed the intrigue, and Brüning was replaced by the giddy von Papen, who hissed innuendo into von Hindenburg's left ear while von Schleicher flattered and goaded into the right one.

At Mask and Shadow, every new political crisis inspired a sketch, a number. Claire Waldoff joined the troupe to sing a duet with Goethe filled with risque double meanings, and they were the rage of Berlin for two weeks. "Knallenefekt!" cried Pfuikeck, reserving for himself a choice morsel, "My New Best Friend." It began with a lazy verse:

> Hymie Grünbaum went out walking
> One fine autumn day ...

Hymie makes the acquaintance of Buster Keaton, and the lively refrain strikes up a celebration:

> I'm Keaton's new best friend!
> I'm Keaton's new best friend!
> He's going to shoot a movie with me!
> I'm Keaton's new best friend!

In the second verse, Hymie meets Marlene Dietrich, and, in the third, the Cannibal King himself:

> I'm Hitler's new best friend!
> I'm Hitler's new best friend!
> He's going to cook nice kreplach for me!
> I'm Hitler's new best friend!

By the summer of 1932, however, Mask and Shadow dropped the political satire, for Nazi violence had so escalated that any opponent, any critic—even any doubter—was in real danger. Nazis rioted in courtrooms and threatened judges, smashed Jewish store windows, joyfully murdered in the streets before dozens of witnesses. And with so much of official Germany either Nazi or concordant, prison sentences were nominal when there were any at all. The new religion was coming, with or without the new god.

Hans Wentrepp saw a Nazi gang board a streetcar, drag out a couple whose looks they didn't like, and begin beating the man to death. The woman threw herself on top of him, but the Nazis pulled her off and threw her headfirst into the path of an automobile.

Hans backed into a doorway, but Horst Pack had spotted him. Blood ran down his S.A. uniform as he sauntered over to Hans, taking out his Nazi collection tin. He shook it at Hans; it was empty, silent. The murderers had fled, but other Browns were still around, watching Horst talk to Hans.

"Ja, here is my old friend," said Horst. "You will give something?"

After a bit, Hans asked, "What happened to the working class?"

Horst broke into a short burst of laughter. "Things are changing so rapidly today," he said, suddenly serious. "Anyway, it's the Nationl *Socialist* German *Workers* Party, see?"

Hans tried to go, but Horst pressed against him, his breath filling Hans' ear. "I would hate to think that you might talk about people. That you would tell stories."

"Whom would I talk to? I don't know your friends. Let me pass."

Horst didn't want to, but his comrades shouted to him to hasten along. He stepped back, nodded out a polite "Auf wiedersehen," and melted away down the street with his new kind.

Erich Kästner felt so discouraged that he took a vacation to the quietest place in Europe, to visit the writer Hermann Hesse in Switzerland. Hesse had emigrated in resistance to the Kaiser's inauguration of the Great War. "I am the genius that schoolteachers mark for persecution," Hesse fretted. "I ask questions, I have projects, I am different."

Hesse had settled in Montagnola, near Lugano, on the Italian border, and he was used to visitors. Kästner showed him some poems and Hesse spoke a bit about the epic novel he was contemplating, *The Glass Bead Game*. He never smiled. He was a polite conversationalist but not a good host. Not even a glass of something. Oh, perhaps coffee later, if he didn't get too caught up in his patter.

"I cannot read a German newspaper," he told Kästner. "They are like English mystery thrillers—who will be the next chancellor? The next Kaiser? The next Hitler?"

"Governments fall so easily now," said Kästner. "The Nazis could easily be in and out inside of a year. Most in Berlin expect it. It was Brüning, then von Papen, now von Schleicher. Then Nazi Hitler. Or Nazi Gregor Strasser. And then—"

"So you will enter?" said Hesse.

"Enter?"

Hesse just looked at him.

"Enter where?" asked Kästner.

"The madhouse. Germany."

"Von Schleicher has found the solution," the Devil tells Hitler. "He will divide your people with a wing loyal to you and a wing loyal to Strasser. And thus crumble you both."

Hitler broods. He is low, suicidal: the End of it All. He has played this act so often that Göring likens it to Garbo in *Grand Hotel*. ("What is all the posing?" Göring asks. "You want to die, die. Don't talk. Do it.") Hitler says, "If we let that Schleicher halt us when—"

"I told you, Yankel, leave von Schleicher to me. He's signing bills to insure magnificent employment opportunities, all of which you will take credit for when you're in office."

"I trust no one," Hitler whines, then helplessly lets off a tremendous barrage of shitting noises and noxious smells.

"I forgot to warn you. Treat with the devil and you take on a wee bit of sulphur."

The Devil suddenly seems about twenty feet tall, with a tank of a tail that coils around Hitler, pulling him so near that the Devil parts his hair with infernal breath. The shock of it—"*Hopp!*" squeals Hitler, as farts of excellent variety tear through him: the card shuffle, the ack-ack burst, the *feh!*, and the dainty-yet-fatal Diplomat Stinkerette.

"The mark of hell," the Devil shrugs. "What I love is, as soon as you totalists take over, the first thing you do is kill the Jews and the homosexuals. Why *is* that?"

"I have friends of music," Hitler pleads, and the Devil releases him. "Friends of national sentiment," backing away. "Friends of monetary contribution ... but true friends?"

"There's always Himmler."

Hitler gestures in hapless agreement.

"No, he really is. Do the imitation, will you?"

Hitler shakes his head despondently.

"Do it or there's hell to pay," the Devil merrily warns.

Adopting Himmler's chinless tenor, Hitler intones, "When the dead speak to us ... the beautifully fallen warriors of true German land ... when the dead awaken and other such medieval notions that I'm too demure to bring up on a working day ..." The spoof thickens as Hitler draws his lips together in kiss-myself idiocy. The voice as high as the Jungfraujoch: "A folk without a present has no past." Ten seconds, then: "Ja."

Dropping the impersonation, Hitler snorts, "*Loon!* A folk without a *past* has no *future!*"

"Stalin has a future in the famine market. He's killing millions of Ukrainians of starvation. Millions!"

"Why?"

"Because with Stalin, anything is possible. With you, *everyehting* is possible—and that's why we're buddies."

The scene changes to a desert isle where tea is taken in coconut husks.

"Yes, revolution," the Devil blithely goes on. "It's sheer destruction that pretends to be creative. Like the operas of Marschner. Oh—here's one they're telling in the Kremlin: What happens when the Soviet Union takes over the Sahara Desert? Nothing for five years. Then there'll be a shortage of sand."

Hitler's body erupts in a Verdun of farts and belches.

"Maazel tov," says the Devil.

The scene changes to a Tunisian waterfront café. The devil flirts from behind a dirty menu. "Try the rugelach cookies," he urges. "What, no appetite? But you've a witch's own hunger for Germany."

"Enough of these promises!" Hitler cries, though he is careful to keep his voice down. "Will you stop the scheming Schleicher, ice-cold, now?"

A dancing girl steams it up around the table, irritating Hitler. But the Devil is amused. "Play 'The Wedding of the Painted Doll' on your finger cymbals," he requests.

"Is it or not?" Hitler asks, in a momentous whisper.

"I'll take care of that half-start Gregor Strasser, never fear. He goes out of history tomorrow."

"And I will be chancellor? You will give me this?"

The meadow primeval, miles up in thin air, in a world in which nothing has happened yet. No cities, no science, no music. Morality has yet to make its Christian witness. Eerie figures float in the distance, as unevolved as clouds.

"*I* give you this?" the Devil asks. "The *world* will give you this. France is terrified of losing its young male population once again in war. England can't afford to fight, and her ruling elite find your racial policies ... intriguing. Spain, Italy, and Russia are Communazi like you. America looks away. Africa is nothing. China is busy with Japan and Japan is busy with China. Everyone will give you this."

A breeze tickles the meadow. Sweet, green, windy warm. Two of the floating shapes approach. Hitler stares as they slowly take form—a big red-bearded dolt with a lean little monster of a hammer and a maiden with a fascinating necklace: Thor and Freyja.

"Are they coming to us?" Hitler nervously wonders.

"They're curious. You're their heir."

Another of Hitler's intestinal disputes savages the serenity of the place, and Struwwelpeter is now among the company with his loony black hair. He sniffs about, sees Hitler, starts toward him. And he is one dizzy baby. He is out of control, on his quest. He is ugly. He is modernism.

"We must go somewhere else now," Hitler tells the Devil.

"No," the Devil murmurs, "see him come."

"Save me from this awful monster!"

Instantly: the Baroness' salon. The great room is empty but for ghosts of the Great War dead of all nations. They sit immobile on the Baroness' lush leather divans, eyes on Hitler. The Baroness' paintings of German history are different today: Teutonic knights dismembering Slavs. A Crusade invading a ghetto. Frederick the Great getting fucked by his favorite, Hans Hermann von Katte.

Turning away in disgust, Hitler finds himself unescorted in the Romanisches Café.

He is instantly recognized, there in the haunt of those he would destroy—artists, thinkers, experts in the art of being different. They could fall on him now, bang him apart and save the world unspeakable grief. But democrats fear violence: which is why it is easy to take them down with it.

But now the Devil reclaims his customer, mumuring, as they vanish, "Hindenburg has finally given way. You have been appointed Chancellor! It begins!"

"Did I just see Hitler?" one diner asks another.

His friend looks at him. "In the Ro*man*? Really, now!"

"Perhaps it was Pfuikeck doing a turn. I'll have to tell my housekeeper. She's such a fan."

"Of Pfuikeck?"

"No, of Hitler. She says, in Germany, he is everywhere."

The Nazis held a torchlight parade that night, to celebrate their leap into power. It was January 30, 1933, the beginning of a helter-skelter reign of terror that lasted for months. Thousands of the different were herded into makeshift concentration camps to be tortured and killed, newspapers were closed, universities and government offices purged, homes invaded by mobs. Paris was like this once. Mask and Shadow was sacked, and Pfuikeck ran for his life. At first, he stayed with Goethe and Jimmy, but Jimmy found him tiresome and sent him away.

Hans Wentrepp, too, was in hiding. The Nazis had come to arrest him, but he was not at home and his mother was able to warn him.

"Why you?" Conrad asked, in disbelief.

Hans didn't know.

"Could it have to do with ... well, the clubs and such?" Conrad asked.

"What does it matter? They're all closed, anyway."

Conrad arranged with his mother for Hans to stay with them; that was the easy part. The hard part was Hans' thanking Conrad. It felt painful to accept gratitude from one's moral superior. Worse, Hans actually said, "Thank you, Conrad"—the sound of Conrad's name, coming from one who always took friendship so lightly, touched Conrad. It alarmed him. He invented games for the pair of them, pulling out his long retired toys and even treating Hans to a show in Conrad's puppet theatre. Here were old friends: Helen of Troy, a monkey, an astrologer in peaked blue cap with yellow stars, a witch. But Hans was distracted and could not enjoy the piece.

Horst Pack was drunk every night now, vomit-in-the-gutter drunk, his pockets full of highway robbery. Berlin was a Horst dream now: you menaced anyone, took what you liked. Nobody fought back.

No: Jimmy fought. Oh, did she resist him, the dirty tease, finally getting what he owed her from the start. She knew how it would be the moment she spotted him, waiting in front of her building. Some of them whimper and beg. She tried to kick him down, and she was fast, too, but Horst wasn't so stinking wet tonight. He got his arm around her and his knife at her throat. So they glided inside and up the stairs, keys and all, smooth, lovely.

"Take your coat off," he told her. "You scream and I'll kill you." This was very true, she was sure. He himself got his jacket off, but he remained in uniform, pushing her to the bed with "This is the best way" and that knife and as if he might cut her open like a package. Does one call this kissing?: he tasted her like a cannibal, love and hatred all one.

She went limp, bearing it. It's over soon enough, she kept telling herself as he hammered her with savage wordless shouts and a flood of his dreary ooze. She felt it fairly, felt it take, even in that moment. She would bear issue of this. It made her thoughtful and suddenly thirsty—but then the door banged open and light blew in from the hallway. Der Alte Herr was back.

He stood, an outline, unmoving in the square of the doorway. Horst, dim and spent and still clutching the knife, saw light on the wall, looked around, saw the old gentleman, and rolled off Jimmy.

A moment of nobody moving. Then Horst slowly rose a few feet in the air, spread out and face up as if still in the bed. He hovered, just wet enough not to say anything yet.

Jimmy was going to speak. She was on her way to "He raped me," but for some reason she couldn't hear the words.

"I know," the old man said.

Then Horst pitched forward as if shot from something. He seemed about to slam into the wall but fell in a heap on the floor without getting there.

"It doesn't always work," said Goethe.

But now Horst was flung about the room as if a great wind was drunk on him, and he shouted at each contact, wrestling with Jimmy's clothes cupboard as if to right himself. He grabbed at the knobs, and a drawer slid out as he flew. He tried to smash the old man with it, missed, let off a few oaths, struggling in holy grip.

"Juchhei," said the old gentleman, quietly, stepping deeper into the room. Horst was now pinned against the wall, and the old man took the knife from the bed, moved quickly, and cut across Horst's left cheek with a driving bite, the handle ploughing the flesh with the blade so a scar would take hold there. Horst was screaming, so Goethe made him silent. The neighbors.

"Give him tea and show him the door," said Jimmy. A line from some charade.

Horst's clothes crisped away into nothing, for some reason.

"That comely face now reads of shame," said Goethe. He turned to Jimmy, but she waved him off. "Whizz," she said. "Quick," pulling the bedclothes around herself. "A fuck. A child. Whizz him away with your bold magic in my dream. Or what?"

Goethe whizzed Horst to some anywhere in the city. Naked in the cold: let him work it out for himself. Jimmy came pouring out of the bed with a miserable smile, shaking her head, yes, no. She went into her dance, faking an American ditty she called "How That Nazi Could Love!" till she sank senseless to the floor, the very breath battered out of her. Goethe carried her to the bed and fed her a golden broth.

"Who made this?" she asked. "What is it?"

"Honey and sunlight."

As she tried it, he said, "At this moment, you are at your most innocent."

"How did you do all that?" she asked at last.

"I've been experimenting."

"Yes, and why are you here?"

"It was an emergency. Germans weren't listening to—no, eat. It will restore you."

"It's good. I hurt, only not as much."

"That hurt will be love, by and by. Just wait."

"Does your brother know about … us?"

Kai and Conrad were lying in bed late one Friday night, touching at the sides and yawning.

"We are devoted young knights blazing a path. He would know something."

"You always make us sound like adventurers inventing. But I think others like us are all around."

"What others?"

"We don't have a name, but we are a people even so. I notice it so much now." Conrad stretched from neck to feet, folding his arms behind his head. "There are others just like us. Not young knights. Just a folk who are made differently. We live in secret, hiding in jests and creative acts as at the studio or on the stage, till one day we lose an oar in the Havel and Kai appears all white and blue ... I am losing the theme ..."

"It is a chance turn of events. An oar lost, yes, and—"

"No—*there* is my theme! It is not chance. This is how we do things, our kind. No"—for Kai was too eager to disagree—"No, I have it now. Listen to The Tale of the Different People."

"Oh, you are just like my brother, telling stories to shut me up."

"There was once an alien tribe living among the folk of some country."

"What country?" Kai asked.

"The Land at the Center of the World. The king's councillors said, 'We should kill these people,' and when the king asked why, they said, 'Because they think they are superior to us.' The king only laughed at that."

"Why did he laugh?" asked Kai.

"He laughed because Kai is jealous that I can tell stories, but no more interrupting. Now the councillors said, 'We must kill them because they are becoming irreplaceable. They perfect agricultural technique. The invent indoor plumbing. They produce the best movies.'"

Kai asked, "But who *are* these people?"

"You," said Conrad. "And I. And many others all over Berlin, including all those innocently relaxing in a café who were all taken away by the Browns three days ago. Because the café was known to be frequented by ... by us. Do you see?"

"Ha! You believe that the affection between us is ... No, finish the story."

"Now the councillors said, 'We must kill them because they are so unlike us that they understand us as we can never understand ourselves. In their effort to fit into our ways, they have learned everything about us.' And the king said, 'We must kill these people at once.'"

Kai, silent for a long moment, took Conrad's right hand, holding it in his own hands. "Did you know anyone in that restaurant you just mentioned?"

"Not that I'm aware of. But I have a very good friend, who is staying with my mother and me. He might easily have been there. He loved the sauerbraten."

"And he is ... one of this people? Does he invent indoor plumbing?"

Conrad laughed quietly. "Some of us are not creative. Some of us just look nice."

Hitler spends the evening of February 27 with the Goebbelses, thrilling the little clubfoot. Göring is the ruthless arranger and Hess the food taster, but Goebbels is the smart one, and Hitler knows it. Still, Goebbels is never sure just how close he is to his master. What, for instance, of this persistent tattle of a faked assassination attempt on the Fuhrer's life, to be followed by mass roundups and martial law? Why has Goebbels not been let into the news officially?

Goebbels shyly asks his lord about it. Hitler only grunts distractedly.

Keen enough to know when not to push, Goebbels offers to ring up the Party Press Secretary, Ernst Hanfstaengl, to come around and play piano Wagner for his boss. This music always revives Hitler.

Goebbels phones; Hanfstaengl says he's too tired. Goebbels lets the Führer know how little he trusts the Secretary's commitment. "Especially now that we are where we have worked so hard to be, all those years of planning, the dreaming, the reverses. But you have shown them all, mein Führer!"

How Goebbels beams. Hitler snorts. He is *not* where he has worked so hard to be, not yet tyrant of Europe, warbringer, earthstormer. Then the phone rings. Hanfstaengl. He wants the Führer.

Goebbels demands to know what it's about.

"Just put him on!" Hanfstaengl cries.

"He is too tired."

"Fine! Tell him the Reichstag is burning!" And rings off.

"That Hanfstaengl and his brainless jokes," says Goebbels, rejoining the Führer in his brooding silence. But no conversation is necessary. It is good just to be near him, to share the radiance of his power. Germany awakened? It is history reborn. It is legend penetrated.

Magda Goebbels blunders in, with the most peculiar expression on her face. "The Reichstag," she says. "It's the Reichstag."

Goebbels goes to her, showing his chief the loving husband. He'd like to shake the truth out of her, all at once; but he must coax instead, as if unwrapping Christmas love candies.

"The Reichstag is on fire," she says.

Hitler jumps up as Goebbels speeds to the telephone. What if it *is*? A moment of reckoning! The Red Jew has set the very nation on fire—but we'll put a stop to his pranks, just wait.

Hanfstaengl answers. "No more of your stupid jokes," Goebbels barks out. "What is happening?"

"Come and see for yourself. Come as fast as you can."

"Is it—"

"I *told* you what it is. The Parliament building is burning down and the very sky is made of flame."

"The Reichstag is on fire!" Goebbels screams, and Hitler: "I *have* them!" He, too, is screaming. "Come to the emergency, we make a start, ja?"

"Not you," says Goebbels to his wife, pushing her back to clump off after Hitler. "You'll hear all about it from the maids."

Their car tears down the Charlottenburger Chaussee right up to a police cordon. Fire trucks, the great roar of the flames, hissing in the watery rush, like a movie, like poetry.

Göring is there, booting around as he improvises orders for the roundups. "Now these swine will know Germany," Goebbels puts in, gazing here and there at the last moments of republic. Hitler is looking away, lost in thought. He knows whom to thank.

"Cut them down where they stand!" Goebbels cries. "Drag them from their beds, that's the way! A rope on every lamppost! No limits!"

Göring had to laugh. "Leave all that to us, Herr Professor." Turning back toward the Reichstag as something came crashing down inside it, Göring chuckled. "Why didn't *we* think of this?"

On an emergency decree signed by President von Hindenburg the next day, Hitler ordered mass roundups for the protection of the people and the state. Anyone in Germany could be arrested, kept incommunicado, treated a la carte; even the most prominent people in the land were without defense. Erika and Klaus Mann, still in Munich but with their bags packed, telephoned their father, the world-famous writer Thomas Mann, to warn him to prolong his sojourn in Switzerland. The *weather*, they most carefully said, was not favorable at home.

Thomas, who didn't realize that phones can be tapped, was not getting the message.

"There is such chaos here now," Erika patiently explained, trying to convey her subtext with emphatic pronunciation. "What with ... the spring cleaning."

"In early March?" Mann asked. He was never a good listener, too absorbed in his stories to attend to anyone else's.

"Let me try," Klaus urged her, but now Erika simply shouted into the receiver, "Stay in Switzerland! Just *stay* where you are! *Now* do you understand?"

The literary, music, theatre, fine arts, and film worlds were all under attack. Typewriters banged out lists of those to be fired, closed down, picked up. Fritz Lang was called to an interview with Goebbels himself.

Lang has encountered Goebbels now and again, and he has seen the tiny ghoul put on his inept charm. The film director has arrived without his monocle, fearing that Goebbels might find it an arrogant nicety. One must appear powerless—however talented—before the powerful. Yes, he loved my *Nibelungen*, and rises behind his desk with a Nibelung's smile as Lang appears.

Lang sees everything as movie shots. From Goebbels' smile, Lang cuts to a stunted crocodile chased from the swamp by its fellows and breaking into the village to redeem his blunted pride by eating humans.

"The Führer is most interested in film production," says Goebbels. "As am I. And we want you ..." Goebbels pauses, enjoying the suspense ... "in a very superior position of leadership in National Socialist cinema."

The crocodile lunges through doorways, cracking people in half with a single bite, chasing screaming children up and downstairs in the tempo of Charlie Chaplin.

"My mother was Jewish," says Lang.

Goebbels knows that, idiot. These mischances can be rearranged with a certificate. What matters is film: as pacification, inspiration, evolution.

The crocodile eats office buildings, granaries, castles. It is insatiable; the more it eats the more it hungers. It goes into a long speech on the power of film. Hollywood, Eisenstein, newsreels, the magic fire of the twentieth century, seeing is believing, body rigid and left arm swinging, eyes like loaded pistols. Or is he an actor, miscast as a human being?

We cut to clockfaces. Ticking clocks everywhere as Lang sweats out the minutes. If Goebbels doesn't shut his snout soon, the banks will close and I'll have to flee without my money. What a sequence! Shadows stalking me, the train's many curious occupants, all spies. Terror mounts as I near the French border ...

At last the crocodile closes its Fressenmaul and waits for Lang's reply. Lang is humbly evasive. Think it over? Yes, my thanks. An innocuous exit. Is he being followed? It's the first of April, the day of the Boycott. All Jewish stores. As Lang moves along the street, he sees the warnings painted on store windows, the Nazis standing in doorways.

"Move off, you lump!" a woman tells a Nazi, as Lang passes a marked store. "I don't like Jews any more than you, but they gives the best prices in the street and I'm going inside!"

"What if I'm being followed for real?" Lang wonders. Now he is Peter Lorre in *M*, and Berlin is a city of manhunters. Lang pauses before a grocery, considering whether to turn around or proceed. What would the shot reveal, if someone is watching him? It's a Jewish grocery: no one inside but the proprietors. Lang can see them but sees also his reflection in the glass. A trick shot. Lang pulls down the corners of his mouth with his fingers, like Lorre in the movie. *I live in what I create.*

From inside the store, a woman calls out, "Ernst, your coffee's ready." The Nazi in the doorway turns and says, "Thank you, Frau Scheimer." He takes the cup from her.

If I filmed such wicked nonsense, they would laugh me out of Berlin; and Lang hurries home, grabs his passport and the available cash—the banks have closed, after all—and heads for France by the first train. At the border, nothing happens. Lang is free.

He tells himself that he was growing fat on success, that a change of air will sharpen his gifts. But he knows that, cut off from his mother culture and its mythology of heroes testing death to give meaning to life, he will be good for nothing.

Seven weeks later came the Bookburning, in every city in Germany. Students—book readers—threw paper to the flame. Erich Kästner felt drawn to the Opernplatz to see the Berlin edition, the most lavishly staged in all the land.

It was simple curiosity. Will there be a public for this? Or will it be like one of their torchlight parades, with the band music and the screaming but with true Berlin inside, behind its doors, refusing?

There was vast gathering in the square; Kästner had to edge his way through noise and rabble to hear the happy students chant their robot slogans.

"Against the defeatism and Jew corruption of Heinrich Heine!" cried one group of boys, throwing books onto the bonfire. "For the end of decadent Jew sensualism and the rebirth of purity in German art!"

The boys laughed at their own solemnity. Their professors indulgently pointed a reproving finger, heiled, chatted. It was a holiday, as Arthur Schnitzler, Sigmund Freud, and Ernest Hemingway went to the fire.

"Will they dance around it, do you think?" said a voice in Kästner's ear.

It was the critic Alfred Kerr. He and Kästner had never liked each other, but it seemed logical for them to comrade up tonight.

Bertolt Brecht blazed in the pile. "For the murder of traitors." "Against the useless lives of the gossips called 'artists.'" "For the overwhelming of all resistance."

"The Communists created this," Kerr murmured to Kästner. "They wrecked the election to defeat the liberal Marx. The Communists made Hindenburg president, and Hindenburg made Hitler chancellor. Now you see."

Kästner nodded as he watched.

"In our ancient history," Kerr went on, "when German warlords defeated Roman legions, they would strip their prisoners, dip them in oil, and lock them in the hay cages. Yes, did you know this? Made of wicker bars and bottomed with kindling and straw, to be lit by torches from below. They would haul the hay cages into their air for their banquets and feast to the screams."

Kästner looked at him.

"Germania," said Kerr. "Ach, there's Bronnen."

He pointed. The former Communist and now Nazi writer was helping the students collect the titles for the next wave of burnings.

"Jewish," said Kerr. "He thinks his enthusiasm will ... exculpate him."

"Heinrich Mann!" cried the students. "Erich Kästner."

Kästner flinched involuntarily, but Kerr dolloped out, "My dear Kästner, what a compliment!" Kerr mock-scrutinized him, as if surprising genius in the journeyman. "They themselves are so empty, and so angrily so, that their enemy is anyone with content."

"For the end of liberty!" the students shouted, their voices growing in number, filling the square. Some in the crowd were shouting responses, others helping the students, giving glory to the fire.

"Run, Kastner!" Kerr suddenly whispered. "Go!" For Kerr has noticed a woman staring at them. At Kästner's unknowing hesitation, Kerr added, "Who knows what they'll throw to the flames next?"

Now Kästner saw the woman, an actress who knew him. "Dort steht ja Kästner!" she shouted, pointing. There he is!

As people turned to look, Kästner slipped away. But Kerr stayed till he heard them shout his name, too. In the cult of the tribe, the individual is a freak.

Asserting ever more control over the population, the Nazis revived the ancient Nordic custom of Sippenhaft. Clanship. If you were guilty, your family could be punished in your place. When Hans Wentrepp learned that his father and brother had been arrested on his behalf, he gave himself up. Then brownshirts extorted money from Hans' mother for his protection while in custody.

Hans was taken to a camp north of the city and placed in a cell so small that prisoners had to sleep standing up, though it was too noisy to sleep. Guards laughed and shouted, prisoners screamed and wailed under torture, and a phonograph played only one song, a military march, sometimes all night long. One wall of Mietskaserne—tenements—overlooked the camp courtyard, but no one ever gazed out of its windows, not even children.

Horst Pack was assigned to this camp, where everyone called him "Spidercheek" because of the scar on his face. He had tried to drop in on Jimmy and the old man with the spooky tricks to let them know who was running things now, but they had moved away. It was Horst who devised the camp game of Kopfbruch: a prisoner was bound to a wooden log and gagged. A second prisoner was brought in and handed a huge smithing hammer. If he smashed open the bound prisoner's head, he could return to his cell. If not, he would be next on the log. Of course, once a prisoner's head was broken apart, his killer was promptly bound to the log and gagged in any case.

Said Horst, "It has such logic, you can smell it!"

The Browns played Kopfbruch almost every evening, laying bets on who would and who wouldn't. You could never tell by looks. A jittery little poodle of a man might crack the skull like an egg with one blow. A cold giant might burst into sobs.

Horst was thrilled when they led Hans in for Kopfbruch. Instantly placing the boy as one who might recall Horst's pungent escapades in the crazy bars of night-Berlin, Horst pulled him out of line and took him over to the pulley post. Horst thought he might have liked Hans in the before, but he couldn't remember why. So much had happened in the last few years.

In the camp office, Detective Inspector Heinrich Müller, of the S.S. security service, was explaining the world to the camp commandant. Müller was the sort who thrives in any regime: resourceful, secretive, aggressive, unquestioning. "In Munich, where National Socialism is most authentic, we find that the most severe punishment is the only useful punishment …"

When Müller paused, it was not to let anyone else put in a pair of words, but to take a pose suitable to the next statement. Now he brought his folded hands up under his chin, parked them on the edge of the commandant's desk, and leaned forward a bit.

"This is a corrective phase in their existence, and it must be conclusive. I have learned this from Soviet police methods … such very effective methods …"

Müller presented a thin smile, sat back in his chair, and continued briskly.

"When the war for survival comes, we cannot treat the enemy leniently. Killing the foe is not an expedient. Killing is the subject matter. It should be carried out as brutally as possible, to crush the spirit before destroying the flesh. We want no echo to remain of those who opposed us ... no trace, you see ..."

Müller looked off into the future for four seconds, then turned back.

"Crush the spirit," Müller quietly repeated. "Then destroy the flesh."

The pulley post was a kind of gallows, on which prisoners were suspended by a rope drawing their arms up behind them. The pain was indescribable, and prolonged torture—especially dropping the subject from his height, then hauling him up again—usually resulted in the practical loss of the limbs.

Why would anyone want to do this? Hans wondered, as Horst's fellow Browns bound him, laughing and nodding at each other.

"Will you try not to scream at first?" Horst asked Hans. "Yes, I think so. Don't worry—you'll be up to stay."

"Look how he's weeping!" said one of the guards. Not for himself: for the world. When they pulled him up, Hans let out the plundered screaming of the truly innocent.

And Horst, looking up at Hans, exulted, "Like this, I feel that I am God!"

PART II

THE FREE-SHOOTER

Dear Cristel Pack would read bits from the newspaper to her Horst each morning. She controlled the news as she controlled the marriage, over a proper National Socialist breakfast of porridge and plain coffee.

"Sugar and cream," says Cristel, "is a weakness in your cup."

She was six foot two and built heavy. She carried her housekeys on a chain around her waist. She cooked in a giant oven, a special model calling for vast ladles and baking pans big as sledges. Cristel was a slightly well-off widow when Horst met her, at a Party festival, and he married her for the security of being bullied for life. "The Führer's Reich and my marriage," ran his little joke. "They both last a thousand years."

Cristel had a son from her first marriage, Wilhelm, for the departed Kaiser. He was in the army; she never mentioned him. But then, Cristel didn't talk much about anything. In place of conversation, she often maintained a thin smile.

"Another report of the first month of Herr Göring's four-year plan," Cristel read out to Horst. "All goes well."

That would make this the autumn of 1936.

"Ja, just like Red Russia," says Horst. "They make plans and we go without things."

"Warning," says Cristel, amiably ominous.

Horst shuts up.

It was rumored that Cristel had been the first woman in Berlin to join the Party, and she arranged for Horst to join the Gestapo and for herself to assist the neighborhood Blockleiter. In fact, it was really Cristel who did the spying and reporting, the collecting for Party causes, the questioning of citizens.

"Here is another article on the film *Lucky Kids*. Quite a National Socialist success, it seems. 'Delectable Lilian Harvey and her happy partner Willy Forst' ... und so und so ... 'The audience laughed most heartily' ... und so weiter ... 'The editing deserves commendation' ... Even the editing!" A mirthless laugh. "Do you notice how every film gets a fine notice now? 'It is set in New York City, amid the headlines and scandals of American life' ... A kidnapping at the opera ... an heiress loves a boxer ... Oh, and see—Lilian meets Willy in a night court! Do they have such things in America? It's so romantic, ja?"

Cristel looked at Horst over the paper.

"Just like you," she said. "Romantic."

Cristel's favorite charge in denouncing those who failed to live up to National Socialist ideals was "endangering the defensive power of the German Volk." That covered just about anything, though it centered on the Andersdenken and Einzelgänger: those who thought or lived Differently.

"It is enough news for you," said Cristel, folding the paper up. "Or you will be late to work."

"Why should I work when you have so much money?" asked Horst, getting up. "I am always wondering this."

"Ja, so ambitious, my Horst. Back in the before days, you were a good-for-nothing because the Jews had it all. We take it from them, and you're still a good-for-nothing." Opening the apartment door, she asked, "What's your excuse now?"

Jimmy was nesting with der Alte Herr for the traditional protection, not least of her son, born on November 1, 1933, named Josef, and known to all as Joschi. The Old Gentleman's interest in Jimmy, too, was traditional, at least for the Old Gentleman. Jimmy was as comely as ever, though the crushing experience with Horst on the Nazis' Night of Power had tamed her hedonist style. The Old Gentleman bought a used gramophone and a box of discs; together they stayed in and listened to music. At other times, the Old Gentleman read to her—Shakespeare and Calderon de la Barca, of course, but also living names, for he was eager to learn what Germany was writing nowadays. Still, what fascinated him above all was the cinema.

Is this the poetry of the age? he wondered, leaving the Ufa-Palast am Zoo to head right for the Capitol and the next feature. If the stage was an intellectual experience, film was a sensual one—the lasting art, its every gesture recorded by a marvel of science.

Jimmy never went along to the movies. If she had her way, she might never go out, like a dragon in a cave, or like Frau Kraus from next door, with her eight-year-old twins, Gustav and Herta. They and Joschi were inseparable. Joschi wanted to do everything they did—eat their dinners, wear their clothes, learn their prayers. They were Catholic, so Joschi decided he was Catholic, too, though he had no idea what that meant.

Jimmy, who had known no religion, thought it amusing. The Old Man advised caution. "All Christianity," he said, "is no more than a Jewish heresy painted in ladies' cosmetics. Right, Joschi?"

Joschi, toying with a little model car, solemnly nodded.

Jimmy was doing the washing up. They had supped on beets and fish; the windows were open despite the autumn chill to disperse the fish smell, and the Old Gentleman was looking out onto the street.

"Look at the hands flying up," he murmured. "Half of them heiling and half crossing the road to avoid meeting a friend and having to heil again." He turned back to Jimmy and said, with a smile and a bow, "Grüss Gott. Grüss Gott."

"Glaubst du an Gott?" Jimmy asked. Do you believe in God, then?

"I believe in moderation and a clear sky."

They all accepted him without question as der Alte Herr, even Alte Hans. Jimmy called him just "Herr," except when they made love. One night, as he soared high in her, he cried, "Eternal woman is our inspiration!," and she scolded, "No dirty talk, Junge. Just fuck me."

Junge. Schuft. Kerl. Those rascally endearments of Jimmy's wild nights, the one souvenir of all she had been. Or no: Joshi was a souvenir as well. Mothering was easy. "I hate you!" Joschi would cry when thwarted, and Jimmy would say, "Well, I still love you." Joschi never knew how to reply to that.

His was not an easy birth, and National Socialist mothers were not permitted painkillers. Jimmy would sometimes tell Joschi of how she had screamed for deliverance, frightening all around her.

"I did that to you?" Joschi would ask, wonderingly.

"It only made me love you more," Jimmy would say. "Because it must have hurt you just as much."

Then Joschi would enfold himself in Jimmy's arms. They were shamelessly physical with each other, and while it interested Old Hans as something one might write about, he wasn't writing much: because he had already written everything. True, sometimes he would annoy Jimmy by springing out of bed at night to deliver a pregnant thought of its proper issue.

No, what the Old Gentleman was doing was learning the movies, as somewhat more than an extra at UFA. He was all over the lot at Babelsberg, listening in on meetings and watching shootings.

"How do you get in and out like that?" Jimmy asked him.

"I vanish. I pass through obstacles. I am always there."

Jimmy laughed. Such eccentricity. But he was entertaining and worthy of love.

Best of all, his authority was breathtaking. One Saturday afternoon, the Blockleiter came by, collecting for the Winter Relief Fund. He was startlingly mild-mannered for a Party worker, which is presumably why Cristel Pack came along. She did all the talking. Jimmy, Old Hans, Frau Kraus, and the three kids were enjoying a meal of klops, noodles, and cucumber salad while listening to music on the wind-up.

"Heil Hitler!" Cristel called out amiably, heaving her horrible big body into the room. "And how about a little Suppentopfschnüffelei?" Snooping around, even in the cooking pots.

Apologetically, the Blockleiter tried to explain Cristel's presence, but she told him to shut his snout and gazed keenly about. Frau Kraus was about to protest, but Jimmy restrained her with a look. Anger a Block Leader or his confederate and one got an invitation from the Gestapo.

Pulling open drawers and even reaching into the children's pockets, Cristel said, as if to herself, "Everyone's hiding something from me, if I know where to look." Shutting a drawer with a bang, she told her partner to take contributions. "Since they're having such a party, you see," she explained, with an eerie grin. "They'll want to think of others who are not free to be dancing about and being idle."

As the Blockleiter shuffled helplessly through the place with that irritating little beggar's box, Cristel took note of the musical program. "What kind of playing ..." she began, moving to the gramophone. Unfortunately, the current selection was a Polydor medley of tunes from Ernst Krenek's forbidden "jazz opera" *Johnny Strikes it Up*. Cristel didn't know the piece, but she recognized Different music when she heard it. Shoving back the playing arm with her great paw, she took up the disc and smashed it against the gramophone's side.

"That nigger-Jew music isn't all the rage any more," she told them.

This is when Old Hans steps forward, scrutinizing Cristel—just looking, deeply, deeply. She looks back, strangely quiet, immobile. Old Hans turns his gaze to the Blockleiter. *He* flushes a deep red and starts for the door.

"Oh," Cristel moans, fighting it. "We will not leave." Yet she, too, moves to go, all so unwillingly. "We will come again," she insists. "We will smash your faces in!"

But they are gone. As their footsteps die away, everyone lets out a thrilled noise, and Joschi hugs the Old Gentleman. Jimmy is proud.

She has chosen a right man.

Gunnlaug and the Baroness enjoyed love in the aristocratic tradition: separate living quarters, a fluid rendezvous schedule, a disdain for social niceties. The Baroness shut down her salon and withdrew, somewhat, from the great world.

I have become what I always feared to be, she thought: a woman in love with the idea of a man. How much easier it is to love in brute animal appreciation: of skin, colors, the unforgivable beauty of the parts. But this one is no Jimmy: this one conquers with his imagination. Ach, it is sin to be so finely made! Primitive people gave such as Gunnlaug to the gods. They explain one's dreams, forgive one's father, and answer one's prayers, all together. Before, one was floating through life. Now one has a theme.

The Goebbelses' union was a genuine Nazi marriage: of two fanatics who loved everything in the Party except each other. He would caw brutal dismissals of her before dinner guests; she would stare at his club foot.

Goebbels was at his best as the public man—making speeches in his cold, rat-a-tat fury or energizing Party dinners with the club toast, "Sterben Juden!" Death to Jews! As Minister of Propaganda, Goebbels was keen on reinventing German cinema till it rivaled the Hollywood model that so captivated his people.

And how to blame them, when the Americans were so entertaining? Their films were not about life but adventure—gangsters, reporters, heiresses. They were movies about movies, and even Goebbels was enthralled. Night after night, he would screen a Hollywood hit while an adjutant translated the dialogue in whispers. An especially enjoyable film would find Goebbels muttering himself into a rage.

"Another Yiddish tutti-frutti about nothing!" he cried, partway through *Swing Time*. "The entire cast is penniless and unemployed, yet they have plenty of time for gambling and stealing each other's trousers!"

Effeminate Eric Blore had him shivering in repulsion, and when Ginger Rogers shampooed her hair while Fred Astaire sang "The Way You Look Tonight" Goebbels cried, "It makes no sense to see her like that!" Then came Astaire's blackface number, "Bojangles of Harlem," and Goebbels was reduced to a disgusted whisper. "They flaunt their Rassenschande in one's face!" Their racial integration.

By the fadeout, Goebbels was back up at full tantrum. He stormed through the room, ripping the work to pieces as realism, as propaganda, as national art. "And yet," he said helplessly, "it has such ... charm." He paused there, stupefied by a simple riddle.

Important films were premiered dramatically, with Party Bonzen arranged along the first row of the balcony and curtain calls after. This could be embarrassing if a movie failed to please; more than a few were greeted with jeers, even whistling. Goebbels was helpless to control this first-night public, but he did ban criticism of all German films by reviewers, who were now to discuss themes and praise talent. Then he called the major producers in for a harangue on what they were doing wrong: everything. The propaganda chief illustrated the talk with scenes from his favorite titles; Conrad heard about it the next day from his boss, Rolf Kümplers, who had been among those summoned.

"Those hands of his," Rolf was saying. "Slicing away as if ... as if he was angry at the air ..."

"What scenes did he show you?" Conrad asked.

"There was a nice one by Georg Jacoby ... *Die Czardasfürstin*. Of course, Dr. Mabuse had to add that the music was 'by the Jew Kalman.' So there was no composer credited, you see. It was the final scene, in a railway station. A thespian troupe was waving farewell to its beloved heroine as its train pulled out. So ... sorrowful. She was waving, too, from the platform. She has ... found love. And they must go touring. Or something in that line."

"The director shoots from the train as it slowly pulls out," said Conrad. "The heroine recedes into the distance just as she will disappear from her friends' lives. And all in time to the loving music."

"Yes, I should guessed that you ... well, yes. Yes, like that."

"It's a beautiful shot. There's too little of that sort of thing in our movies."

"That's what Dr. Mabuse said last night."

Rolf, in shirtsleeves, had perched on the edge of Conrad's desk. "Herr Doktor also encouraged us to find work for his South American discovery Rosita Serrano."

"La Chilenita," said Conrad.

Rolf smiled. "What is she like, at any rate?"

"Blond. A bit heavy for her age. She can sing, though—especially Latin dances with crazy high notes."

"Let's imagine: *Rhumba in Santiago*. I wonder if he has fucked her yet. Of course, the one he's wild for is the Hungarian girl ... Baarova. He gets so hot when he's around her that his ears sharpen to points. Although how this affects the career of Baarova's actor boy friend ... What's his name, the one with ..."

"Gustav Fröhlich."

"Jawohl!" cried Rolf, beating his fist on the desk. "I like my staff *informed*."

"What is Goebbels like, anyway?" Conrad asked.

"Ruthless ... vindictive ... slippery as a ... very ardent. The one true believer of all the head Bonzen. Göring's a pirate for hire. Hess? A ghost. Himmler is Pandora opening her box. But Goebbels ... incredibly smart. And very, very good at his job."

Walking over to a table laden with scripts in trays labeled according to each title's stage of production, Rolf said, "Germany is in the grip of an iron chaos. Ministers of state battle over territory and important posts go to the politically reliable man, no matter how cretinous he may be. Blackmail and racketeering on the most spectacular level. A gangster kingdom. Essential government business is delayed while the Führer sleeps till noon, screens a few operettas, dines on his vegetable plate, then harangues his secretaries with nostalgic monologues. Who runs the country? No one. But if anyone could, it would be Goebbels."

Conrad was never sure how to take it when Rolf spoke so honestly of touchy matters. Rolf trusted him, and they were behind a closed door at the end of a long corridor. Still, nowadays candor was a criminal act.

"So ... how do we give Dr. Mabuse what he needs?" asked Rolf, aimlessly picking through the scripts. "He doesn't want Party cinema, you see. He wants Hollywood hits. *No more armband films!*"

"He couldn't have said *that*."

"He meant to. Oh—he's cutting out that song you liked so much." Rolf was at the scripts again. "In that operetta about ... the marching number. That the mother sings."

"'They Were All Out of Step But Heinz'?"

"Herr Doktor calls it unpatriotic."

"How are we to give him good films when there's so much we cannot do?" Conrad got up and came over to Rolf. "You aren't getting my scripts out of order, I hope."

"What are we weak in?" Rolf asked. "Good stories?"

Conrad shook his head. "There are only three, anyway—*The Iliad, Romeo and Juliet,* and *Don Quixote*. Oh! How about *Der Freischütz*? That opera about—"

"No fantasies. Dr. Mabuse calls that 'Jewfilm.' And he's banning all the old titles with Jewish actors in them. No ... he wants ..."

Conrad was wondering who his boss was when he was off the lot. Rolf never spoke of his personal life. Conrad didn't even know if Rolf was married, though a fellow in his—probably—early middle thirties would have to start a family to get ahead in this government.

"He wants inspiring tales of love and honor," Rolf went on, "disguised as racy comedies."

"You need racy actors first," said Conrad, straightening out his script baskets. "Ours are mostly uncles and vamps."

"Well, but—"

"Look at Hollywood's actors. Those exciting personalities. *There's* love and honor. But this regime doesn't trust exciting people. It likes a kind of distinctive mediocrity."

"Uhu," said Rolf, taking that in.

"Then there's all the writers and directors we lost," said Conrad, heading back to his desk.

"They did know how to entertain, didn't they? They get smart from ... Yes. Smart." Different. "Dr. Mabuse has an official commission for us—our very own National Socialist version of that Hollywood piece about the crazy people on a train."

"*Twentieth Century?*"

"It's set on a steamer coursing the Rhine. With all those hilltop castles in the background and the water traffic passing. Very kinematic, he says. A view of Dirndlmädchen getting nationalistic with flowers ..." Rolf laughed. "Can it be done?"

"Anything can be done. Can it be *good?*"

Rolf leaned on Conrad's desk again. He was not handsome but tall and trim, with an engaging smile.

"The whole thing is the train," said Conrad. "That's what America is—speed. It's the 'screwball comedy.' Masquerade, practical jokes. How do we place all those comic scrambles on an amiable tourist cruise?"

"Dr. Mabuse sees it as a musical entitled *Behave Yourself, Wilhelmina.*"

"For Renate Müller, perhaps?"

"Die Müller has a Jewish boy friend in England, and she won't ... One thing Goebbels will not tolerate is resistance on the racial question. Which is very much a pity, young Conrad. We must not underestimate Dr. Mabuse."

Conrad was wondering just then if one could fairly call a man "dashing" if he wasn't traditionally good-looking.

"You're dreaming," said Rolf, very quietly. "You mustn't be dreaming these days."

The terror of Berlin holed up at Number 8 Prinz-Albrecht-Strasse, in Kreuzberg, Gestapo headquarters. There Heinrich Müller was developing control techniques. "I like Soviet methods," he often said. He let his superior, Reinhard Heydrich, do the screaming. Muller cultivated finesse.

Claire Waldoff was surprised at his lightness of style. She knew what terrible things happened here. All Schöneberg, where she lived, spoke of a local boy, barely fifteen, who was caught distributing resistant literature. His interrogation consisted of being beaten and stomped upon; when he left the hospital, Gestapo agents were waiting to pick him up, right there at the door. This time, he was crippled for life. "A display piece," they called it.

Waldoff went in fearlessly. The Nazis had closed the cabarets, but she had her love and she had herself. It was a slow day for Wilhelm Müller, so he took on Waldoff himself. Sitting at his desk, unmoving and alert as he liked to be, he went right to content: Waldoff had been heard to say, when they started rationing lard, "Just wait, there'll be more of that to come." Was she glad to say this? Is the regeneration of the fatherland not worth a sacrifice? Questionable persons have been spotted entering her house—are they members of an outlaw group?

Müller laid his forearms, palms down, flat on the desk before him. After a pause, he said in quiet tones, "This is your warning. Intelligent people do not promote a second invitation to this address."

Excused, Waldoff rose, trying not to react to the cries of distress that seeped in from somewhere down the hallway. Müller, still sitting, just looked at her. On the wall behind him hung a framed photograph of Heydrich. He must be the worst of them all, Waldoff thought. I didn't get that kind of placement in my biggest run at the Metropol.

On the way out of the building, she passed a repulsive little ball of a man with a Hitler brush. A nondescript Gestapo operative in the typical fedora was leading him into a room, carefully using the door to shield its insides from view.

Two teenage boys were being tortured for the visitor's amusement. He was Julius Streicher, Gauleiter of Franconia and publisher of the Führer's favorite newspaper, *Der Stürmer*, so coarsely anti-Semitic that it was hidden from public view and sold under the counter during the 1936 Berlin Olympics.

"Hakenkreuz!" cried Streicher. Swastika! Horst Pack and two assistants were running this interrogation, and Streicher approached with the wonder of a connoisseur, muttering as he examined the instruments of persuasion, steel circles placed in the two boys' mouths, then ratcheted to force them open ever more widely.

"Just the thing for these stubborn youths, "Streicher announced. "These dirty young fellows who treat maidens as their personal toilet. Hmm. So, so, the winding pin," he said, feeling it. He stared at the youth before him, then broke into a shouting rampage with *"You thought you could get away with it, didn't you? When they get out the testicles press, you will see what you got away with!"*

Huffing and puffing, Streicher paraded around the room, staring at one prisoner, at the other, and back again. He screamed and pranced. He was the Stormer. The sound of his breathing thickened the air like smoke.

"Do you see where your knavery has landed you, you young fuckers? Do you still want to rape a helpless blond Mädel and kiss her luscious white breasts? Do you kiss

while you fuck, you whelps, you young stinkers with your tricks from some whoring sexy Italian comedy?"

Turning to the Gestapo men, Streicher asked, "What is their crime?"

"Their father is a malingerer," said Horst. "He has evaded arrest, and these two will answer for him."

"*Na und!*" Streicher cried, turning back to the prisoners. "So the blood is tainted *right from the source!* Oh, but they should be *whipped,* with workshy fathers and uncontrolled longings ... *Hakenkreuz!,* but I would teach them respect if we were in Nürnberg! Violating sweet young ... Oh! The *maggots!* Quick, turn the winding pin on this one, let him see what it is, raping and fucking our virgins. Yes. Yes. Yes, oh *now* he loves rape, I wager! Such a sentimental boy, always hard for a Mädel. Shout when the cream flows, is that it? *Do you cream now, my fine young rascal?"*

The Gestapo would gladly have blocked Streicher's visits, but as a Führer favorite he had power. He was swaying slightly now, his eyes fixed on one of the victims, and he murmured incomprehensibly in a gurgling fuzz. Then words formed: "I commend you, Herr Pack. The fatherland need fear nothing with sturdy policemen at the ready."

With a "Ja?," Streicher clapped Horst on the shoulder and rested his hand there. "A fine example here. A true National Socialist youth."

Streicher felt the back of Horst's neck.

"First class," Streicher said.

Horst thought, These old freaks are all alike. Always shouting about girls, but all they want is to eat up my stick.

Taking a last stern look at the two prisoners, Streicher said, "My readers demand to know of these uncontrollable longings, the ruin of German manhood! What good, solid punishment for these young sensation-mongers! These *sensualists!* Hiking trails and the jolly comraderie of the campfire aren't goddamned *good enough for you,* is that it? *Animals! Do you think we will let you dedicate yourselves to such luxury? Such hedonism? Is that what you young charmers think?"*

He was raving again, pacing and pointing, running his hands along the outline of youth, skin, terror: the monster made officer in the backwash of revolutionary flood, as the other monsters join him in the halls of command. Cretins shout, It's ours now! as the mouths of the two tormented boys form the wide-open O of a silent scream, the cry of Germany racked on the Hakenkreuz.

Conrad's great-grandfather had planned his dynasty's future with intense precaution. Like the Rothschilds sending sons to foreign capitals for commercial security, Conrad's family was carefully dispersed, with branches settled in Sweden, Italy, and Switzerland as well as Berlin, where this grand organization was first designed.

It was decided now that Conrad's mother would go to live with the Swiss Thomamüllers. Though the attitudes of National Socialism did not penetrate Grunewald villa culture as thoroughly as they did life elsewhere in Germany, whenever Conrad's mother went into town she was bombarded with signs of Nazi aggression. Berlin was a place of golems. One afternoon, Frau Thomamüller chanced upon a procession, two lines of Browns escorting a handful of civilians with placards hanging from their necks. One read, "I laughed at a newsreel of our oppressed national comrades in the Sudetenland." A beautiful young blonde, her head lowered in shame, wore "I gave birth to a cripple." Behind her was another girl; her sign read, "I am a Jewish pig."

Conrad and Kai decided to make a holiday out of taking Conrad's mother to Zürich. The relatives there were very formal and uninteresting. "They say we Prussians are stiff," Kai murmured to Conrad during the first minute. "Ha! They make us look like wild Spaniards." Still, they had a huge, comfortable house in the finest quarter of the town, and they had that air known only to Thomamüllers of bearing profound beliefs in discretion and loyalty. Best of all, Conrad's mother had been very close to Zürcher cousin Maria when they were brides.

Himself, Conrad was to move into the von Kleist fortress; he had been virtually living there as it was. On the way back to Berlin, Conrad accompanied Kai on business visits to Köln and Münster, but Kai insisted on tackling his meetings alone. "It is hard enough," he said, "without my young friend along and the senior officers sniffing at a scandal like dogs at a toilet. They would gladly embezzle the whole works from me, you know—only my brother's political connections hold them back. Yes, it was planned that way from the start. Weren't we clever? Also, I corrupt one man at each plant with enormous secret bribes. So any conspiracy can be unveiled immediately."

"Why do I still not know what it is you manufacture?" Conrad asked.

"Bricks?" Kai replied. "Ball bearings? Fabrics? What difference does it make? Do I ask about your films? What matters is how we feel when we are together, and how we say to each other things of such tender honesty that no one can know us. The truth would shatter a world."

As always, when Kai got back to Berlin Gunnlaug fussed over him till Kai had to escape and then pout when Gunnlaug failed to pursue.

"Just for this, I will not give you the business news," said Kai. "Maybe we go bankrupt."

"If I stretch you out for a whipping, I expect this news would be told auf eins, zwei," said Gunnlaug. He moved into the kitchen, the two boys following. To Conrad, Gunnlaug said, "Should I treat him roughly, or soothe shocking revelations out of him with lullaby bliss?"

"That is his outrageous idea of comedy," Kai told Conrad, even as he held on to his brother and almost wept for joy at the touch of him.

Conrad said, "Really, I give up on comprehending you two." He didn't mean it. The more he saw of them, the more he knew.

"So," said Gunnlaug, breaking the embrace, "you shall tell me about Switzerland. Then we will plan the concert."

Conrad and the brothers had invited people over for music. It was Conrad's idea: the guests would come to the fortress for von Kleist-style rough-cut sandwiches and potato salad, the best meal in Berlin. Then Gunnlaug would sing classic Lieder to Kai's piano. Coffee, dessert, and homeward all.

Conrad asked Renate Müller, his favorite actor at the studio, and also Reinhold Schünzel, who had directed Müller in six titles, including *Viktor und Viktoria*, the best musical-comedy film produced since the Nazi takeover four years before. Conrad also asked der Alte Hans, because they were always running into each other on the lot, and he seemed quite a friendly sort. Very cultured—and surprisingly vigorous for an older man. He asked if children were welcome to hear these classic German songs. Who could say no to that?

Müller and Schünzel came on their own, but Gunnlaug sent a car for the rest of the party—Jimmy and Joschi, Frau Kraus and the twins, and Old Hans. Herta brought along her stuffed bear, Quisli, and Jimmy wore a new dress of the sort that would have been laughed off the stage of Pfuikeck's cabaret as virginal, even bourgeois. Frau Kraus was so excited to ride in a private car that she accidentally left the quilts airing on the windowsills. "But I dressed the children in their very best Sundays," she told Jimmy, at least three times.

"It is good for children to hear our concert," said Kai, as they were setting up chairs around the piano. "It is a way to become smarter, hearing the inspiration of poets."

"Again, who is the Old Man?" asked Gunnlaug. "This is a point on which I am not clear."

"He works at the studio," said Conrad. "But, really, he's a most remarkable fellow. I call him 'the Cloud Gatherer.'"

"Why?" asked Kai, bringing in two pint-sized rocking chairs.

Conrad shook his head. "He seems so ... well, powerful."

Gunnlaug said, "He is some admirable Altvater, I suppose."

He impressed the von Kleists, in the event, though they were unsure of his relationship to Jimmy. Then when they figured it out, they thought it a most amusing scandal.

Conrad had the feeling that he knew Jimmy from somewhere; she was enigmatic about it in a most charming way. Renate Müller captivated everyone and was especially agreeable to the children, prompting Old Hans to praise the eclectic nature of the gathering. "Nur alle Menschen machen die Menschheit aus," he observed. Humanity means *everybody*.

After lunch, the company went outside to enjoy a river view in the cool of a bracing Berlin April. Gunnlaug offered a bit of family chronicle to explain living in a fortress. There was a great deal of German history in it, but none of the grauitous assualts on liberals and Jews, the English and the French, and the Czechs and the Poles that one inevitably heard these days.

"Now the music," said Gunnlaug, initiating a walk back up the lawn to the house as Frau Kraus told Kai, "The children are so thrilled at this."

"It is important for them to enjoy different experiences," Jimmy put in thoughtfully. "I want Joschi to be smart, like you and Herr Thomamüller. You know the names of many things, and what they are for."

Old Hans, bringing up the rear with Conrad, smiled at this. "You are an impressive young man, it seems."

Blurting out a diversion, Conrad asked the Old Man about his interest in cinema. "You always seem so informed about the schedule," Conrad noted. "Even projects still in the works. Do you fancy going somewhere in the Filmwelt?"

"About one hundred fifty years ago, I must have said yes. But now I save my energy for other things."

At which Conrad, who figured he must have missed something, let out an innocent laugh.

The music began with classic Schubert. For the second group, Conrad set up his puppet theatre and dramatized the songs as Gunnlaug sang. For Schumann's "Conversation in the Forest," the Helen of Troy marionette played the "beautiful maid" and the Astrologer the lone rider. When he realized that she was a cruel enchantress, Conrad flew in the witch puppet in Helen's place. The coup de theatre inspired gasps from the public, and Gunnlaug was especially fiery singing the final line: "You will never come out of this wood!"

Brahms' collection of folk songs came next, lightening the hall with the raffish "Och Mod'r, ich well en Ding han!," in Kölnisch dialect. A young woman yearns. Her mother asks why. A doll? A ring? A dress?

A husband. Herta was so taken by this number that she impulsively rished up to Gunnlaug and, not knowing what else to do, held Quisli up before him.

"What is this bear?" he asked, with a smile.

"Please, Hertl," young Gustl said. "The program must continue."

In fact, Gunnlaug had never sung to so avid a house. Closing with Mahler's comic "In Praise of Good Judgment," he and Conrad made this singing contest decided by a donkey so vivid that the kids leaped up as one and marched around the room in time to the music. At the last grandiose "Hee-haw," the applause was intense, and everyone had an appreciation to share.

"So the ignorant sit in judgment on art?" Schunzel remarked. "That is very apt today."

Renate Müller went up to the piano to thank the von Kleists most warmly, while Conrad showed the children how to work the puppets.

Handling the Astrologer, Gustl said, "With magic, I could complete my Abitur in two weeks and never go to school again. I will become an aviator in the Luftwaffe and be photographed for the gazette. Joschi will train with me," he explained, putting his free arm around Joschi's shoulder, "and Hertl will wait eagerly at home to hear of our adventures."

"I will be a cinema favorite," said Herta.

"Can Mutti come?" Joschi asked Gustl.

"The children are making dreams out of the music," Frau Kraus observed.

"If you would know the world," said the Old Gentleman, "you must know the arts. Will we have a *bis*?"

Yes: the encore was Schubert's "To Be Sung on the Water."

"My brother loves this one," said Gunnlaug, as Kai returned to the keyboard. "It gives him many notes to play, and he thinks he is the song."

"It is the rippling of the waters," said Kai, breaking into this immortal cameo of man and nature at one. To the lapping of the current in the piano part, the voice glides in delicate conquest as if it, too, were a boat:

> Until I on higher, more glorious wings
> Myself vanish from the transformations of time.

There was a long silence when the music stopped, till the Old Man said, "Thank you." No one else spoke.

Finally, Gunnlaug made a little speech. "I think traditional music is best," he said. "So much music today seems antagonistic to us, or imposed upon us. It *dares* us to understand. Should music do this?"

"Ja, Sansculottismus," said the Old Man. "Revolution is never good. It is about personalities, not ideas."

He rose, approaching the piano as if congratulating it.

"Still," he went on. "New things invent themselves. They are not imposed. They *happen*. The new music, with its sarcastic use of classical techniques. The bitter political cartoons. The cinema, science married to theatre."

He bowed slightly to Müller and Schünzel.

In a healthy society, art is ever in motion. Ach, if you knew how quickly my staging of Kotzebue's *The Zither Player and the District Court* went from sellout to quarter-houses. And those? Almost entirely on invited entry!"

He smiled.

"But there was talk of dessert, café ..."

Everyone laughed. The kids and Conrad took charge of the puppets to lead the company into the kitchen, and all sat around the table as Gunnlaug started the coffee and Kai set out the pastries. Joschi couldn't decide between a secretive pear Torte and the always beguiling chocolate layer cake.

"Ei, this is no time for half-measures," said Kai, serving the boy both of them. Joschi, wide-eyed, looked at Jimmy. She brushed his hair, saying, "It is a special day. To hear this lovely music, so German yet so necessary to the whole world. Or no?"

"*I* think so," said Gunnlaug.

"It would be painful, gnädige Frau," said Schünzel, "to have to go out into that world and lose what is here. It is not readily available elsewhere."

Sadly, he had already planned his departure. Schünzel was part-Jewish, and had been allowed to continue directing only because Goebbels could not replace him. He would be off to America within days.

"Sehr nett" was Gunnlaug's review of the afternoon, when the three were cleaning up after. Very nice; and he meant it.

"You were glad for a new audience to show off to," said Kai, rinsing dishes in the sink.

"*Now* what is he resenting?" Gunnlaug asked Conrad, drying for Kai.

"I do not resent. I accompany the magnificent baritone, and then I preside over company board meetings in the Ruhr with austere expressions. This is necessary in one so young. But I notice that *on my name day* there is no—"

"There's a Saint *Kai*?" asked Conrad.

"He has middle names," said Gunnlaug, cleaning the table with great energy. "Today is—"

"So you did remember."

"You are disappointed that I did not leave a keepsake on your pillow."

"As once always so!"

"There is no time for this now," Gunnlaug replied, hanging the table rag on one of the wooden pins by the sink. "They keep me moving. Some are calling me 'The Flying Adjutant,' like the Dutchman." He handed Kai a stray plate from the table. "When they want to make an impression, you know. On foreigners, especially."

"For your singing?" asked Conrad, restocking a dish in the cupboard.

"For his looks," said Kai.

After a moment, Gunnlaug said, "This regime believes that one's appearance tells what one is. It is disconcerting. Are we to be strong or pretty? It cannot be both."

Taking the next dish from Conrad and shelving it, Gunnlaug went on, "I did not tell you this before. Last month, they reassigned me to General Schlöchtenfeld. A primitive type, *typisch* of this new Germany. Five years ago, he was running whores in Wedding, and now ... *General* Schlöchtenfeld. He has an Alsatian, takes the dog with him everywhere, without a lead. A great, lumbering fool of a dog, like all those big ones."

At the sink, Kai and Conrad had stopped to listen.

"The general beats this poor animal at every opportunity. What has it done? What is its remedy, beyond crawling off to howl in its helpless pain? A fine general of the S.S., and there you see it."

Gunnlaug evened up the chairs around the table, one after the other. Kai turned off the water. Conrad just stood there.

"So, boys. Then what? This Schlöchtenfeld becomes so annoyed with the dog's piteous noise that he orders Lieutenant Von Lamm to secure the animal with rope and douse it with petrol from the spare can in the boot of the auto. And set it alight. Ja, I tell you. Ja, 'Rid us of this nuisance, will you, Lamm?' He says it in quite a friendly manner, in front of some half dozen of us."

Gunnlaug sat at the table.

"What did the lieutenant say?" asked Kai.

"He said, 'Jawohl, mein General,' what else?"

Silence.

"But ... *did* he obey?"

"Yes."

"He burned the dog alive?"

"Yes."

Kai sat at the table.

"How could the lieutenant do such a thing in public?"

"He was ordered to."

"This is some monstrous deed fit for the dungeons of Gilles de Rais! Couldn't he refuse the order?"

"That would be unthinkable."

"Wait," said Conrad. "Wait, now. That animal was—"

"Burned to death in all living torment on the whim of a sadistic freak, yes. I demanded a transfer, not to serve under such a creature. But think. We are ever more on a war footing. It is coming, this war."

"With whom?" Conrad asked.

"The world, perhaps. And think well on this—in war, are not the most ruthless officers the effective ones? Es muss auch solche Käuze geben." These men, too, have uses.

Now Conrad, last of all, sat at the table. And he said, "When you enter the terrible place, you become part of it. All of it. You will never come out of this wood."

"I will come out," said Gunnlaug.

Fools thought that the Goebbelses must be very much in love to make such beautiful children over and over. It wasn't love: it was the explosive hunger of the man whose second favorite work was evening the score with enemies and whose favorite work was fucking, especially starlets. Goebbels liked to audition them in the carriage house of the Goebbelses' villa. It was like having sex with a mad bologna, but those who balked could find themselves permanently At Liberty.

La Chilenita, with South American fire, insisted on greeting Goebbels at her own place. All was ready: the faintly scented air, the throw pillows, the distant music. Küss die Hand, Madame.

"I have wondered when we would meet, senor," she told him. "I have prepared long for this moment."

"I, too, my dear," replied Goebbels, thinking, Another of those moronic Dingsda accents. "And that couch seems to beckon to us," he added, in a murmur. He held out his hand, but, smiling enigmatically, la Chilenita pulled on a cord, a curtain fell away, and a cast of tens came out.

"My duenna," said Rosita. "My orchestra, my tango master, my dancers."

Da! Da *da!* Da! *Da!*

"On Rio Negro," she sings, "there stands a cottage of blissful dreams ...'

It's Rosita's big number from *Maske in Blau*, her Berlin stage hit from last year. As she sings, the dancing girls glide and dip around Goebbels and Rosita as if cameras were turning. "Pan!" Rosita cries. "Edit! Ay, close-up! Love trot! Ole!"

The instrumentalists crowd them with smiles, beseeching a chorus from Goebbels.

"I could gladly have you killed for this," he tells Rosita.

"Please, not before my duenna. See, they await your solo."

Everyone looks expectantly at Goebbels; the dancers now bear *Maske in Blau* likenesses of Rosita as they weave fantastic designs around him.

"It is Fred Astaire,' Rosita tells them.

"Ay, que rico tango!" from the duenna.

"They implore you to sing," Rosita tells Goebbels. "Please. Por mi?"

Goebbels considers the question of young women shoved to the gallows in nothing but Rosita masks, their pink nipples against white-hot skies and honey spilling forth as they drop like fucking till I can't pump hard enough to kill the whole world. Till my Hackendick fucks Paris, Russia, Magda trash and every ballerina twirling to be fucked by movies. They could call me Hangman because I hop on the noosing stool to glorify the whoreflesh so lovingly before they drop Freja screaming out, "You are my god!" to the chorale of the guitars vamping for my solo. Yes. Why not? What do I get for all this?

Rosita hands him a lyric sheet while a fiddle sizzles eagerly. Goebbels shyly intones:

> Tirana, come
> To our rendezvous!
> A secret place ...
> Yes, it's made for two.

Cheers from the company as the Rosita masks draw Goebbels into a private chamber where he can have them all.

Rosita waits till she hears Goebbels coocooing. She nods; the candy has taste. As she turns to go, she gets a sarcastic look from the duenna.

"Don't you start," Rosita mutters.

Another secret place is the Baroness' palace. The sex has just ended, and Gunnlaug lies dreaming under a blanket in the Baroness' bedroom.

"See, gnä' Frau," says Duscha the maid. "He is a happy man."

"They're all happy, running the world and having the phallus contests that they call war. It is said that, long ago, women were in charge, because we kept it secret how new life was created and men were afraid that we would stop giving birth if they defied us."

The Baroness was at her night-table, going over some paperwork to a cup of black-market coffee. Duscha was kibitzing with a duster.

"Who runs that waterfront paradise you come from?" the Baroness asked.

"No one runs the Spreewald, gnä' Frau." Turning back to the napping Gunnlaug, she asked, "Is he as pretty under the clothes?"

"But how else could I have been so swept up? He carted me off in a sack like a Sabine. I, who have ... *had* ... such contempt for the way men always grab away at things. Give me a beer! I want Austria! And he'll have it yet, because the women of Germany are in love with him."

"With Herr von Kleist?"

The Baroness shook her head, looking once more upon her lover.

"No. That other one. He'll have everything yet. And why? Because he not only makes your dreams come true, he'll explain them. His radiance redeems you. Yes, the hero is always that beautiful, that powerful, whatever physical form he has taken."

"It's very confusing, gnä Frau."

"And I am Europa, raped by a god. I think of it as my Schicksalsrolle." The part I was born to play.

Duscha giggled.

The Baroness suddenly knelt by the bed and lightly swept Gunnlaug's hair off his forehead.

"It is amazing to see you so moved by this love, gnä Frau, if one may say so. I notice that your clothes are softer now. And the smoking is over. It is a lovely story, surely."

Considering this, the Baroness replied, "But the hero must die, you know. He saves us but he can do nothing for himself."

She rose.

"It's in all the sagas. Adonis. Christ. Walter Rathenau." A rueful laugh. "Or will this one surprise us?"

"*Which* one, gnä Frau?"

"Will he disappear from a world too stupid to deserve him?"

Old Hans was lunching at the Romanisches Café when a voice asked if the other chair was free. The Old Gentleman gestured accomodatingly, then simply stared: as the Devil joined him.

"I am told they do a wonderful Radieschenpfannkuchen here," said the Devil. "Yes, so you guessed. How did you know?"

"Only Hell is completely without that air of striving that is mankind in its essence."

"Oh, sauerkraut! There is no striving—no will, no choice—without me. Mein Arbeit macht frei." I create freedom.

A waiter took the Devil's order.

"I should have known you'd be around," the Old Gentleman said, treating himself to a swig of dunkeles. "In such contaminated times."

"All times are ... well, *compromised*, if you please. By Great Men. An invention of mine, if you don't mind. The Great Man seizes his times—Constantine, Charlemagne, Martin Luther, and now ... well. Fools call it 'the tide of history.' What Tolstoyan dogshit! The rant of a novelist drunk on his notices. Believe me: one individual appears and bangs the world up good, or *nothing happens*. The Great Man. I thank you."

A waiter rustled a setting into place before the Devil.

"And *this* Great Man is my best yet. I've met them without morals, without conscience, even without beliefs of any kind. Those are the best. But this one is special even among that company. This one is *without reality*. Anything is possible with such a man! He can kill without limit."

"He's doing his best to kill liberty in Germany today."

"Yes, you have to love a guy like that."

The Devil's food arrived, and he tucked in.

"He has a bunch of atheists running a holy war," the Old Gentleman remarked.

The Devil chuckled. "Just wait."

"Canaille!"

"Oh, you visionaries," the Devil got out between mouthfuls. "You think civilization has expunged animal brutality from the human condition. You dolts! You poets! The brutality is always with us, waiting for the next Great Man to unleash it once again. The brutality is implacable. Do you *know* how many Stalin has killed, over to the East of your wonderful invention of a Europe? The counters have run out of numbers! Oh, but you're not lunching, Doktor. Can I share your potatoes?"

Old Hans is still as the Devil helps himself. Then:

"There was a primitive people," the Devil finally says. "Or. *You* would call them 'primitive.' I think of them as 'unfragmented.' They worshiped a god who was content only when blood was spilled in great quantity. He loved murder, the most vicious, hurtful murder possible, and his people found this intensely romantic.

"However, in time they ran out of prisoners and members of powerless fringe groups. To satisfy their god's bloodlust, they had to kill each other, quite as horribly as they could manage. Of course, if a people go extinct, so must their god. Yet few questioned the process, and those who dared to were immediately murdered anyway."

"Who can this people have been?" the Old Gentleman had to ask.

"True, sometimes it's simple expropriation of wealth. Define 'heretic': anyone who owns when you just rent."

"Could I have said somewhere," the Old Gentleman put in, half to himself, "that there was no man I couldn't learn something from? I feel I must have."

"It sounds like you. Waiter! Another round of dunkeles here, ja? Of course, at *other* times it's simply a rebellion against progress. Against anything puzzling, abstract, tolerant. It only starts with Jews—and homos, idealists, writers, nonconformists. It *starts* there. Then it expands. You call it 'atavism'—but at least these are people with a god that means something to them. The god doesn't love them. The god gives them *content*. He tells them who they are. Naturally, they prefer him to that Quaker altar boy of a Jesus who redeems and forgives. They don't want redemption. They want murder. Fanatics are so prescient, you see. They create the next evil."

The waiter brought the beers and cleared away the plates.

Stirring his beer to dissolve the head, the Devil went on, "They say that Italians live in the present and the French in the past. Is it the English that live in the future? A most historical people. And they love Hitler."

"Everyone decent loathes Hitler."

"The English ruling class has been paying many a fawning visit to my boy, I can tell you. 'The racial ties,' they say. 'The blood, hem-hem.' They *love* him—no, you mustn't interrupt. Do you know the Brits transferred their German ambassador over to France because of his constant warnings about what the Nazis are going to do? La, they *know* what the Nazis are going to do. Now, their new man in Berlin is a different kettle of fish altogether—that English tradition of sending their worst people abroad, no doubt. This one calls Hitler's outlawing of the Jews "a great social experiment." Oh *yes*, he *did*! 'Only Jews and Communists don't like the Nazis,' he said. Yes, it's quite historical, my dear."

The Devil leaned across the table for a confidence: "He's one of mine, you know."

"There's no way to hate you, is there? You've no honor to pierce. It's a merry game."

"It's theatre."

"You make it up as you go," said the Old Gentleman, rising. "What's next—'I'm late for an earthquake'?"

He left.

"I hate when they demonize me," said the other, vanishing.

In his office on the Wilhelmstrasse, Goebbels raged away at Rolf Kumplers over the latest betrayal of that insolent defeatist clique the artists.

"This is what I get from that half-Jew Schunzel—a fine piece of Yiddish Mauscheln." Chiseling. "*Land der Liebe* was supposed to be an operetta of the Hollywood Lubitsch form—at a cost of considerably over a million marks, too! Instead, that schemer shoots *his* version of things. Peacocking politicians, strutting soldiers, jokes about propaganda!"

Goebbels glared at Rolf from across the desk.

Suddenly: "Ja, alles *schwindel!*" The whole thing's a *cheat!* "To think I could have thrown him out three years ago with the other Jewish trash!"

"Can the film be recut?" Rolf asked.

"They are so clever at their rodent plotting and spoiling, aren't they? To mock our deep community feeling, our very *no it can't be recut!* So now you see the *impudence* of this Jew!"

Rolf said nothing.

"Schünzel has fled the country—of course!—so this was no accident! I am dismissing the Tobis president, Fritz Mainz. Let it be a warning to everyone."

Apparently wound down, Goebbels swung back into high gear. "*And!* You will see what will become of a certain young vedette who thinks she can indulge her taste for race defilement!" That jagged slash of a mouth. "*Blood corruption will not be tolerated!*"

He was virtually screaming now. Rolf held his position without variation or expression.

Suddenly quiet, Goebbels explained, "A people can live only if it grows."

With that, Rolf was dismissed.

"Also läuft der Tag dem Tugendsamen," said Rolf to Conrad on his return. Another day among the virtuous. "How does it feel to be free in a slave society?"

he added, tickling Conrad behind the left ear. Conrad blushed. "Now the boss relaxes." Rolf fell dramatically into the chair next to Conrad's desk, another of his eccentric habits. Whether under the monarchy, the republic, or now, one's employer did not sit in one's visitor's chair or tickle one's ear.

"How do you treat him?" Conrad asked. "Do you—"

"Oh, you cannot fool Dr. Mabuse with false enthusiasm. You have to be good at your job, he does respect that. This next one must be wonderful, young Conrad. *Behave Yourself, Wilhelmina.* It must … and so on."

"It must have the zest that the Americans—"

"*Yes*, while avoiding … what?"

"Kitschfilm?"

"Just right."

"You know what, then?" said Conrad, rising to pace the room. It embarrassed him that he so enjoyed looking at Rolf—his hands, his hair, his eyes. "There should be a full score. Not the usual two or three numbers, but eight or nine. The music is the only thing we didn't lose when the talent emigrated."

"Recommend a composer."

"Well, Eduard Künneke. He does the best imitation of the American styles."

"Director, now?"

"Georg Jacoby. He knows how to keep the feeling of musical comedy going between the numbers. The others let it sag."

"Who for the leads? Dr. Mabuse suggested Marika Rökk and Johannes Heesters. And la Rökk is Frau Jacoby, so … no?"

Conrad was shaking his head. "Kitschfilm."

"Already?"

"Wilhelmina isn't a ballerina in Dutch-girl costumes, like Rökk. She's modern, rebellious. And the man is a prizefighter. Not the ingratiating Heesters. They should meet in the most unlikely way that makes the audience laugh. And she should fear him even as she falls in love with him."

"Does he love her?"

"Yes, but he's wary and defensive, jabbing at the world."

"Still … a rebellious female in Mabusefilm? This cannot be allowed."

Rolf surged out of his chair and went into a pantomime imitation of Goebbels pounding his desk and shouting.

"Well," said Conrad, when it was over. "Goebbels wants everyone in an invisible brown uniform, obeying. That's not movies. That's newsreels."

"So! Only democracies can operate a cinema?" Rolf asked, wryly. "A film needs independence? Like the Dietrich that won't come back to us? Der Chef foams with rage at her Hollywood-Jewish treachery. They *say*. She works for the Jews, Jews, Jews, it's all you hear. And everyone else who ... who doesn't ..."

Suddenly tired, Rolf rubbed his forehead with one finger of his right hand.

"You mustn't be so honest with me, Herr Kümplers," said Conrad, facing his boss across the desk. "You are too trusting."

"I can trust you. You should call me Rolf. And the problem with your cinema democracy is that it shares its independence with its public, and that leads to a nation of anarchists, of a ... people with incongruent programs."

He smiled at Conrad.

"That is what we have, no? You and I? A congruent program?"

Rolf walked around the desk to Conrad, opened Conrad's jacket like a tailor checking the fit, put his hands on Conrad's waist, then drew them slowly up the sides of Conrad's torso till he was holding Conrad quite close.

He said, "Conrad, what is your program?"

After a moment, Rolf released Conrad, did a bit more of his silent Goebbels imitation, then said, "Put your ideas for *Wilhelmina* into notes, however you think best. We'll pass it on to ... yes."

At the door, Rolf paused and turned for a long look at Conrad. With a taste of a laugh he asked, "What makes you so creative, anyway? Czech blood in the ancestry? Hungarian?"

"Jewish."

"Yes, very funny," said Rolf, leaving.

Renate Müller would have made an ideal Wilhelmina, but Goebbels was ending more than her career. In October of 1937, when she was putting up in a psychiatric clinic to get away from the intense pressure on her personal life, Gestapo men broke into her room and threw her out the window to her death. The newspapers were instructed to report her suicide.

"Like *this!*" Cristel Pack shouted as she threw a pot's worth of cold water into Horst's face. "It is a lovely Christmas from you, losing your job!"

"Shut your shouting," Horst replied in his sick-of-it voice, as he went for a towel.

"Not the clean ones," barring his way. "You and clean linen—that's a fine marriage!"

He wiped his face with his hands, then rubbed them on his pants, all the while looking at her with the crooked smile she used to find engaging.

"Yes," she said, nodding. "Good. What did you do to get fired—torture the Führer's aunt?"

"And I've been called up, too," he said. *"That's* a fine Christmas!"

"If the Wehrmacht is good for my son, it's good for you."

She swept through the apartment with her half-smile on, fondling the keys at her waist, looking into her gigantic oven, smoothing the folds in her dress. She told Horst to clean up the water mess on the floor, and when he hesitated she started for him with purpose and made him jump. This is her domain.

"Frau Peterschmidt says she doesn't have a wireless receiver." A quiet laugh. "I must insist, no? Listening to broadcasts makes one a part of the national community. Music, jokes, then the news. So we all know what the truth is in exactly the same way."

"Your son, your husband—who knows what wars come? And you don't even care."

"I welcome it. I give men to the Führer for his battles, like a Valkyrie." She laughed.

"A mother's heart. They should shoot you out of a cannon, there goes Paris."

"Be nice, I'm baking cookies."

Horst put the mop into the closet, silent in thought. Finally: "I have a son, too. It's funny, ja? From the old days."

"Who's the mother?"

He shrugged, closing the closet door. "Old comrades tipped me off. It was some prostitute, anyway. I didn't pay—she wanted me. Ja, some do, even if you don't."

"You're not big enough. I need to be fucked by Thor in the sky."

"Anyway, she had a kid, this whore. My kid. Why don't you go find him and send him to the Führer, too?"

"No, I'll send you," she said, taking a batch of cookies out of the oven. "See, you can feast as you like and grow fat for me, my Hörstchen."

"Maybe I should look up family, vanish for a bit."

She planted her feet wide, threw her head back, and let out a contemptuous snort, like an unwilling bride in an old saga who hangs her spouse on the wall on their wedding night. Then, turning back to her cookies, she said, lightly, "So when do you go?"

He has a manner about him that goes beyond looks. He's very smart and very tall. Somehow these two go together. The coat sits well on his shoulders, and his hair is a bit wild. Strands fall into his eyes, giving him a mischievous look. His eyes are bottle green, widening when he is puzzled. Yet he seems sovereign and protective, just as Gunnlaug must seem to Kai. I always look forward to work because he will be there.

Conrad knew that he was involved with Rolf when Conrad started concocting descriptions of him. Strangely, it did not affect his relationship with Kai. In the cinema, a treacherous lover inspires questioning, accusations, heartbreak. But Kai suspected nothing.

Conrad wondered to what extent their mutual disgust for the regime drove Rolf and himself together. There were two Germanies now, especially in the Filmwelt, staffed by Goebbels with opposing troops of the artistically capable and the politically convinced. When Conrad suggested Erich Kästner as screenwriter for *Wilhelmina*, Rolf said Kästner had been banned from writing of any kind.

"He published poems back in the … something Dr. Mabuse resented," said Rolf. "He is verboten. *Futsch!*"

Over! As he said it, Rolf mimed a wind blowing Kästner away, himself staring past the open palm of his right hand as Kästner was carried off. Rolf seemed dark and implacable as he did this, and Conrad felt a pang of enchantment at the sight.

By the spring of 1938, Gustl and Herta were often away at camp, leaving Joschi bereft and sulky. All German children aged ten were compulsorily enrolled in the boys' Jungvolk or the girls' Jungmädel, and Gustl's enthusiastic reports only fed Joschi's frustration as he imagined how he, Joschi, would fare among such spirited company. Among the Jungvolk, all rules were boys' rules. Mutti overflowed with civilizing advices, but at camp they played Fightball: one team tried to convey a huge sphere into the other team's goal while bring grabbed, pushed, and knocked to the ground.

"Fightball's where you earn your nickname," Gustl explained, with the teaching intimacy that Joschi loved about his older friend. "All the top fellows have one."

Joschi already knew this, for he was allowed to use Gustl's as long as Frau Kraus was not around. She frowned on the whole Jungvolk business, because every time Gustl came home from it he was a little less Catholic and a little more sarcastic.

"They rile them up with excitements," Frau Kraus was telling Jimmy, as the two boys enjoyed themselves running around the local park. After a hasty Berliner Blick—the quick look about, to make certain no one could overhear—Frau Kraus leaned toward Jimmy and whispered, "Gustav told me that there is a banner over the entrance to the camp saying, 'You were born to die for Germany.' Gustav asked me what that means."

"He doesn't know?"

After another Blick, Frau Kraus said, "The instructors tell the children to ask, to see what the parents will say. To learn who is short on national enthusiasm. Yes, you see? They make spies of the children."

Gustav's nickname was Gewinner, because he so often scored goals in Fightball. He gave Joschi a nickname, to be known only to them: Rohling, "which means you're the toughest boy of all, Joschi."

"I'll be very tough," said Joschi, wondering what that meant, exactly.

Herta, on the bench with the two older women, did not like being a Jungmädel. She was one of those children who thrive in small groups but grow withdrawn in crowds. The instructors were always going after her about something—making her wear her hair in braids like the others or forbidding her to pray before sleep. Herta tried to get around that by addressing heaven silently and without physical gesture. But another girl read the grace in Herta's eyes and reported her.

"It is not fitting for a girl to be away from home for so long," Frau Kraus told Jimmy. "For the boys, it's different—the little scamps have so much energy to let off. But a girl needs her private time and helping in the kitchen." Now, proudly: "Who makes the best potato salad in all the Nikolaiviertel, I ask you?"

"Who, Herta?" asked Jimmy, with a smile.

Herta smiled, too. "I want to have a bakery some day, like Frau Korlbrünner on the corner. Every week I will change the window, and I might be inventing such new treats that the first ladies of the Opera will send their servants to my shop."

"What will you call it, Herta?"

"Die Margarete."

"Why that?" asked Jimmy, stumped.

"I like the sound."

"Hei, Hertl!" Gustl called out. "Come help Joschi and me play pretend!"

As Herta ran off to join the boys, Jimmy said, "I used to play pretend. When I was on the stage. It is a bordello of lies, but the truth is worse, isn't it? Nothing is genuine except the children."

No one hated Goebbels more than his wife, but she would not give him up. It was Magda Goebbels who tore off to Hitler that summer, when Operation Movie Star Lida Baarova had become so manifest that all Berlin took note. "Die

Betrogne lass auch zertreten!" she was heard to cry. Yes, walk all over the wife, shall we!

At the same time, Goebbels appealed to the Führer, certain he would see it Goebbels' way. After all I've done for him, the coordination of arts and news and opinion, the ousting of trickster Jews and their dupes. No one has done more than I, and what do I ask? A divorce. Simply the right to love.

Hitler said no. With war imminent, this was no time for one of the Reich's first families to betray signs of weakness.

"War?" said Goebbels. "Over the Czech Question?"

"I will cut them stragiht to the heart," said Hitler. "France and Great Britain have no will, you will see. They will give and give. What's Czechoslovakia to them? Schoolroom maps! Piano duets!"

"Mein Führer, I beg of you. Give me the chance to free myself from a contract of false premises."

Oh, and here are those Hitler eyes on you, that fairground hypnotist's ruse. A twinge of contempt in the love for this man, alone to fulfill Germany's destiny. Perhaps all leaders are freaks. Who but the shameless can be hero, who but the rootless cast so long and terrible a shadow? Surviving the stink of corpses under the red clouds burning, fantasies of the past made real. The extraordinary man will change the sky. It will never look the same again.

"I say kill the swine," said Lieutenant-Colonel Hans Oster. "None of those Weimarisch hand-wringings. No legal labyrinths! Just kill him and we kill his war."

It was a meeting of Wehrmacht officers, on this same Czech Question. Hitler was ready to set the world at war, and he wanted to start it in Czechoslovakia. The army's problem was the mountainous Czech frontier, almost insuperably defensible; the tremendous fortifications along the country's western border; and the Czechs' Skoda munitions works, the best in Europe. The Czechs might well beat the thinly expanded German war machine to a standstill—and what if Great Britain and France joined in on a second front in the west? Germany was facing destruction.

"We are patriots, not murderers," said Ludwig Beck, till recently Commander of the Army General Staff. "We must put these cutthroats on trial before the nation." To Oster, he said, "Leave the Cheka methods to that lunatic and his gang."

"Emil," said Beck's successor, Franz Halder, using his personal nickname for Hitler, "does not loll about waiting for us to arrest him. He's quick as a Silesian poacher."

"A sortie in the field," Beck began, drifting off in confusion. "An expedient ..."

"If we don't pull off something and *now*," Oster emphasized, "we will face the wrath of all Europe."

They disagreed on everything. The Catholics were livid at the suppression of the Church. Others bitterly resented how Hitler had manipulated them into accepting his murderous rule under oath and wanted to redeem their honor. Hans Oster needed to avenge the Nazis' assassination of Kurt von Schleicher and his wife four years earlier, when the Party was purged of dissidents and old scores were settled.

"Von Schleicher was the last of our heroes" was Oster's view of it. "The last adversary that rabble had to eliminate to stay in power."

Oster was wrong: there was one more hero in this summer of 1938, Ewald von Kleist-Schmenzin, distantly related to Gunnlaug and Kai. A civilian but, like most of the Wehrmacht officer a scion of Prussian landowners, von Kleist traveled to England to excite support for a palace coup.

To Winston Churchill, leader of the opposition in Parliament, von Kleist said, "Just by coming here, I have fitted the noose around my neck."

To Sir Robert Vansittart, Permanent Under-Secretray of State in the Foreign Office, von Kleist said, "If Hitler is not stopped, sooner or later he will invade England."

And to the Right Honorable Lord Lloyd of Dolobran, a leader of the majority in Parliament, von Kleist said, "If Britain guarantees to fight when Czechoslovakia is attacked, General Beck will close down the current government of Germany by force."

Nudged by the Devil, however, the English ambassador to Germany discredited the Wehrmacht conspiracy to His Majesty's Government. "Unstable" he called it. Further, he refused to convey any warning to Herr Hitler from the British. Simply wouldn't do it. And von Kleist's mission failed.

The plotters continued to talk, even after Prime Minister Neville Chamberlain made the first of his three trips to Germany to negotiate with Hitler. They developed a plan for Major Friedrich Wilhelm Heinz to escort Major General Erwin von Witzleben into the Reich Chancellery, disarming any resistance. Witzleben expected to arrest Hitler; Major Heinz intended to kill him, along with his S.S. bodyguards.

The day chosen was September 28. Chamberlain had twice come and gone, and Hitler now chose to rally his Volk for war. On the afternoon of September 27 a motorized Wehrmacht division drove down the Wilhelmstrasse toward the Czech frontier. Cannon, caissons, personnel carriers, fancy motorcycle contingents, eyes high and ready. The Berlin crowds, however, watched silently.

"*There!* The pride of German youth!" Hitler crowed, manifesting himself at a window. "Yes, unhesitating! Insuperable! Don't tell me of Czech defenses! Gypsy fiddles!"

But the silence of the crowd rubbed up against the roar of the parade, and Hitler slapped his arms against his sides in exasperation. "How am I to make war with these barnyard hens?" he cried.

"You will not make war with them," said the Devil, behind him at the window. "You will make war with yourself."

Major Heinz couldn't wait to kill Hitler. Then, with minutes to go before the operation, another negotiation for peace was announced.

Heinz was so angry he could have shot someone's mother. Oster thought it the end of Germany. Halder actually said, "Emil is in league with Hell."

Hitler was angriest of all. This peaceful restructuring of Czechoslovakia—its destruction, of course—postponed his war, his Act. So he locked the door and whipped out his revolver and told Chamberlain he could eat out the ass of one of the Nazis in the room, any he wished.

"Dear me, must I?"

"Perhaps Hess," said Hitler "An old campaigner. Very authentic, Mylord."

"Yes, but ... um. La. Quite."

Hess hung back in shadows. "I met some English at the Olympics," he said. "They don't like Bolsheviks. They like Wurst with our good German mustard. They like spanking and other society vices. Even the French are not so crooked, though they eat snails and birdies."

"Oh God, not Hess," said Chamberlain. "Imagine the sinister taste."

A thousand tiny clinks sounded in the corridor.

"I hear Göring's medals," said the Devil, apparent to Hitler only.

Göring came in and Hitler pointed Chamberlain over to the grinning Field Marshal. "Yes, Mylord," said Hitler. "Taste, Mylord. Pretend it's the banquet after your fox hunt."

"Oh, dear."

Göring dropped his pants with a buccaneer's grin. "He might encounter a National Socialist caramel or two," said Göring.

"It's fine sport," said Hitler, as Chamberlain set to. "Instead of shooting little foxes. So, Mylord. Now, Mylord. Taste the history."

Silence as Chamberlain rims Göring. A footnote in the archives.

After a long while, Hitler asks, "Das schmeckt, Mylord?" Taste good?

"Yes, the aura of a real man," Chamberlain manages to spit out. "My, how it puckers. Sticks to the ribs!"

Chamberlain rims with a nibbling schnurk, then wild slurping.

"Yes, Mylord," says Hitler at intervals.

"What table d'hote, don't you see!" Chamberlain pants out, lapping away. "In school, it was sometimes necessary to apply baker's sugar. Gracious, not so here!"

"A second helping, Mylord?" Hitler asks, when Chamberlain catches his breath.

"Oh, yes. So fresh. Sic semper."

"See how the English love Germans," says giddy Hess, still cloaked in darkness. "They run shops and hostels. They practice rude address on one another because of class distinction. This is obsolete in Germany, thanks to National Socialism."

"All done, Mylord?" asks Hitler.

"Yes, thanks. That's over."

"So is Czechoslovakia," the Devil puts in.

Chamberlain, on all fours, shakes his head, trying to come to. Göring pulls his pants up and lets out a chuckle as Hess puts a hand over his mouth in bemusement.

"Bumbershoot, Mylord?" says Hitler, handing over Chamberlain's furled umbrella.

"That twittering Tschemberlein!" Hitler shouted later, alone with the Devil. "Such a Luftikus for a statesman, such a Strohkopf!" Lightweight, strawhead. "He stole my war right out from under me!"

"The French helped. And your beloved Benito. Well, he did let you take Austria."

"'INTERNATIONAL CONFERENCE PRESERVES PEACE,'" Hitler sneered, imagining headlines. "That Tschemberlein is the *stupidest* man in Europe!"

A spectacular fart rattled through Hitler, almost doubling him up with stomach pain.

"Fie, they're getting worse," the Devil observed. "You really are going to have to put your Act on. There are ... time constraints in these contracts, you know."

"I'm trying, aren't I? What does it take to make a democracy fight?"

"You don't handle the English right. They—Oh, for heaven's sake, that dandruff again! And a Siegfried-sized helping of vegetable pie on your ... Hold still, at least!" Cleaning Hitler up, the Devil went on, "The English don't like subterfuge and games. Their worst attack word is 'sneak.' You know, they had the chance to support a Putsch against you and turned it down."

"Who are the traitors?" Hitler immediately screamed. "It's that *Beck*, isn't it? The blackhearted *swine!*" Warming to his favorite subject, the world against him:

"That aristocratic East Prussian trash with the rotting estates in Kuhscheissfurt and Kuckuckdorf!"

"You're missing the point, Moischele. The English oligarchy wants to get along with you. They'd govern in the same way in England if they dared."

"What stops them?"

"The English people."

A pause. Then: "Tschemberlein and those others—they don't like Bolsheviks."

"No, indeed, they don't."

"They don't like Slavs."

"They don't care about them."

Hitler snorted: a sign of relaxation. "But they hate the Jews?"

"They don't hate them. They just want them gone."

"Even if ...?"

"Even if."

Hitler smiled. "It is so close now. To think of being so near to it ... and that blundering Tschemberlein ... that *interloper* ... *Now* do you see? I must have war in the East! With such times comes confusion, lack of information, excesses that even my enemies will excuse! *I must have war in the East!*"

"Yes, but stop shouting already. I'm not one of your crowds."

"Everything is possible," Hitler hissed out, "if the will is strong."

Conrad had an unofficial agreement with Rolf that Mondays were Conrad's after six, so that his theatregoing was protected. On other days, however, the workday could drag well past evening, for even now, five years on, Goebbels still had no effective grip on how one creates art when politics suborns inspiration, and the front offices of UFA were too perplexed to please him.

"I think we'll be working for Fritz Hippler next year," Rolf announced as he came into Conrad's office.

"In the newsreel division?"

Carefully shutting the door, Rolf continued with "The stories don't work but the headlines are top-hole."

"I hate it when you're honest."

"I did a Blick in the hall first." Rolf sat on Conrad's desk. "Dr. Mabuse has banned *Behave Yourself, Wilhelmina*."

"That's not possible! After all our calculations, he still hates it?"

"He loves it. 'Hollywood marzipan,' he calls it. But it turns out our heroine is ... a free soul. It *is* Hollywood, he said, in quite wondering tones. How did we pull it off? A dance from start to finish. A dance of American life on a steamer on the Rhine." Leaning down to get close to Conrad, Rolf finished with "How did we do it, Conrad?"

"Is he mad?"

"He's thrilled." Jumping off Conrad's desk: "This proves that we can make the movies he wants. I need ... a coffee. This is my Berlin today, Conrad. Shall we try a café? Come, my friend."

Rolf had an auto, and they ended up at a Viennese-flavored place on Unter den Linden. No sooner had they sat then Conrad began, as always, and in very quiet tones, to exhort Rolf to mind his tongue. There was peril in every statement.

"In Greece," Conrad explained, "it was the concept of 'asbeia.' Impiety."

"To the gods?" asked Rolf, lightening his coffee with ersatz. "The commissars?"

"See? You're still joking. But isn't that how they went after Socrates? To the Greek mind, one could assert oneself in the military or athletics. But in the arts or philosophy, nonconformist thought was dangerous. The Greek polis favored a fascist democracy, you know. Liberal to a point, unified above all. To criticize existing structures of behavior or thought could—"

"I'm actually quite touched that you ..." A gesture. "Yes, I ... I game with it. But only around you."

They sipped coffee in silence.

"I'm not reckless," Rolf added. "I'm bored. Yes, very touched, I have to say. So let's not talk of kino for once. No business. I'd so much rather ..." He smiled. "So. Do you have a sweetheart?"

"Yes."

"Tell me of her."

"No."

"No ... Shall I tell you of mine? No, young Conrad making a face?"

Rolf put a hand lightly atop one of Conrad's. "It's too late for you to go all the way home to the Grunewald, and I live nearby, so …"

So. Rolf's hand sat heavily on Conrad now: what if some stranger was watching?

"They can't see past my back," Rolf assured him. "You want us to be buddies, don't you?"

Conrad nodded.

"Good," said Rolf. "In the secret movie of this, for the fadeout, you must say to me, 'You will be a gentleman with me, won't you, sir?'"

At the von Kleist's fortress, after a late dinner a few days later, Conrad and the two brothers discussed the case of Prometheus. Kai thought him the greatest hero possible, because he gave mankind the power to enrich itself.

"He was not a hero to his own side," said Gunnlaug.

"Prometheus started civilization," Kai insisted. "He created Europe."

"He was the first subversive."

"That shows how vital subversives are," said Conrad, starting to clear the table. "They initiate the next era."

"Stack," Kai told Gunnlaug, handing over his plate.

"More and more is my younger brother the head of this outfit," Gunnlaug observed. "That is because he is in charge of the money. *He* is the business, ja? Vital to the national economy—yes, you will hear this said by Party functionaries."

Gunnlaug got up from the table as Kai and Conrad carried the plates and silver into the kitchen annex, to wash up.

"But to me," Gunnlaug went on as he followed, "my brother is the chosen one, in the eternal ritual of sacrifice to the gods for bringing back the spring."

Taking hold of Kai, Gunnlaug stared into his eyes, trying to mesmerize him even as he himself was in thrall. Wild magic is loose in this place.

"All the tribe is assembled," said Gunnlaug. "They gasp at the boy's beauty. Surely he is already of the gods—dawn pink and heavenly blue in color. Even the executioner-priest is abashed at the radiance of the stripling. No wonder he—"

"You dry," said Kai, handing him a towel.

"Is this whole religion about looks?" asked Conrad, at the rushing faucet.

"Yes," said Kai. "You are to be tall as Goebbels, trim as Göring, handsome as Himmler. Ei!"

"Well, the Greeks had a cult of beauty, too," said Conrad, starting to pile the dishes as he finished washing them. "But it wasn't a fetish. And there was no distaste for those who were made differently from the norm. Last week, there was an attack on a restaurant frequented by homosexuals." Conrad laid out the word calmly, for the von Kleists to absorb. "They carted everyone off and closed the place. Actually, it is amazing enough there was such a gathering place for outlaws of the regime. It was bold of them."

Running water, cleaning up, no talking for a bit.

"What were they afraid of?" Conrad finally said. "Is some homosexual going to impart the secret of fire?"

When they were done, Gunnlaug lit a pipe and read to Kai and Conrad from a book of Czech fairy tales that had been in the family for many years, thrice mended.

"The ones with the most violence are the best," said Kai. "Because it is such relief when they are over. Sometimes they cut your eyes and ears off, but they make you whole in the end. As if nothing had happened. Do you agree, Conrad?"

Conrad was distracted, fretting over his treachery to Kai. "What?" said Conrad, and Kai giggled.

"Conrad is making movies," he said.

There was some music after, and the usual early to bed, for the von Kleists maintained the hours of an outpost on war alert. Conrad fell asleep in Kai's arms to the creaking stillness of the fortress: still settling in after all this time, as if unsure even now of its place in the world's doings. Conrad imagined the foaming of the Havel outside, its meeting with the Spree and their joyous run down to the North Sea. That stormy terror! There, where so many now-great nations invented themselves out of macabre cults of bog and boulder. And, yes, the sacrifice of beautiful youth. And Conrad dreamed.

He was in company in a dark room. From somewhere there came the sound of a record; the needle had reached the label with a repetitive fooshing noise.

Someone else was there. Sitting in Kai's armchair, legs crossed, looking at Conrad. Dressed in the style favored in the pleasure bars of the old days: shirt open at the neck, close-to trousers, hiking boots. The visitor did not look angry, yet he was unhappy with something Conrad had done. Conrad was sure of it.

Conrad threw off Kai's embrace to get up and face this vision: Hans Wentrepp come visiting. He is summoned by guilt. Rolf. Subversion. Freedom. Hans, so tender and faithful. Was he heroic? Promethean?

"Verzeih!" Conrad cried. Forgive me! But now Hans was gone and Kai was awake.

"Who will forgive you?" asked Kai, taking hold of Conrad out of somewhere else. "And for what act?"

"Hans!" Conrad cried. "Hans!"

Kai shook him. "Come out of this daze."

"No, because ... Lord, don't let me be weeping now."

"Whisper, and then you won't weep. And who is Hans?"

"Shh, you must whisper, too," Conrad whispered. "I betrayed you and our friendship in a most unknightly manner, you should know this."

"How?"

"I don't want to talk about it."

"Ei, that is not like you. You always want to talk about it."

"Will you please whisper? I don't want Gunnlaug to hear."

"Then you *will* talk about it, or I will get him."

"Well, quickly I would say that I became quite close with someone at the studio. And I ... I actually ..."

Conrad stopped there.

"Went fucking?" said Kai. "Oh, that is not so terrible perhaps. Our friendship must be larger than bourgeois ownership. Where are you going?"

"A walk in the night air, I thought. To clear the—"

"Conrad, you *are* crying! No, I will not let you go! Ha, you are shaking! You are cold all over! Now I *will* get Gunnlaug!"

"No! That only makes it worse!"

"Conrad, you will make me cry, too, like this. Please! Please, my friend!"

"I will be calm if you whisper," said Conrad, mastering himself.

"You were so immediately resistant when I wanted to fetch my brother. Is this because he is in that black uniform? Never mind—let us get back into bed, at least. I do not like the uniform, either. It came of a scheme to make influential business contacts. You would be amazed how our rival industrialists became involved in that gang so long before. It was simple good sense for the family interests. Now, you come to bed."

"No."

"Yes. Or I get Gunnlaug."

They went back to bed without speaking and lay side by side in the darkness. Kai dropped off soon enough, but Conrad could not rest. Hans never made it out of the Brown prison camp in 1933. If only he had gone to Switzerland with Mutti. She would have taken him; she loved Hans because he was so polite and so true to Conrad. She never guessed about them that they were born subversive.

The very next day, on an unusually balmy evening, der Alte Hans was sitting on a bench in the Tiergarten when another older man asked if he might sit with him. The stranger had a distinguished air, one born of long success in a freely chosen field. "I believe I have seen you," the stranger said, "at Neubabelsberg."

Ah, a colleague! "But you are surely not a petty actor and helparound, like me," said Old Hans, as the stranger sat with weighty exhalation. A personage, to be sure.

"A composer," he says. He slyly hummed a snatch of *The Song Is Over*.

"A classic!" Old Hans enthused. "I have just been assisting on *The Stars Are Shining*—you will spot me in the restaurant crowd for "Have You Seen the Latest Hat That Our Miss Molly Likes To Wear?." Bien entendu, it is not a hat but a crepe that most picturesquely falls on her head from a balcony. The cast is agog."

"Unfortunately, I will miss it," said the composer. "I am heading across the ocean, to New York. Or perhaps even Hollywood."

"A difficult voyage. To pursue the artistic life in a foreign culture."

"I find it more difficult not to be able to speak my mind."

That was a test statement: the Brown would blaze, the neutral grow inscrutable, and one's fellow non-participant sympathize. But the composer did not wait for a reply. "I've been making some farewells," he said. "I'm nearly sixty. I may never see my friends again. Of course, friendships in the theatre world have greatly altered in the last few years."

Nodding, Old Hans said, "In *my* youth, now, there was no political concensus among the actors and playwrights. True, *The Zither Player and the District Court* or *The Landslide at Goldau* would not inspire feelings of a political kind. But then ... a *Don Carlos*! A *Wallenstein*! And each of us saw them in a different way!"

"Yes. That is why I look forward to New York. It is how Berlin used to be."

"I wish you luck, Maestro Stolz."

Consternation greeted the Old Man when he got home that evening. "Geliebter, Beschützer, Vater," Jimmy purred at him. Lover, Protector, Father. She purred when she wanted something, a holdover from her greedy youth.

"Na und?" he asked, noting that the children had been sent to play next door, a sign of serious doings.

"Your help is needed," said Jimmy, holding on to him and making her little sounds to enslave all men. He liked her like this, with a touch of sin about.

"I was foolish," said Frau Kraus. "But Herta was having such a terrible time in that Führerklub. She would come home in tears, saying her life was being ruined. Imagine such words from a child! But you must be tired, and here I am, all concerned with my own—"

"Go on, now," Jimmy urged her. "He lives to help and helps to live."

"The Old Man smiled at Jimmy. "Nice sentiments for the Mietskaserne." The slum tenements.

"I thought I could have her exempted," said Frau Kraus, "as she has a touch of asthma, my Herta. So I took her to the clinic. It used to be run by the Church—very strict, but they took care of everyone and didn't care if you were Catholic or not." Dabbing at her eyes with a frail bit of lace, she added, "Of course, the new Germany chased all the nuns out, and now."

Weeping, with Jimmy trying to soothe her, Frau Kraus had to sit down and collect herself. She only got more upset, though, the more she had to say. "'Your daughter's health does not belong to you,' they told me. The doctor, I mean. 'It belongs to the National Socialist state.' Can you *imagine?*"

"Where is Herta?" the Old Man asked.

"I don't know. When I came to pick her up, they told me ..." Frau Kraus broke down suddenly, but quickly collected herself. "She had been transferred, you see. They told me that, short and good—and I won't describe the noise I made then, right in the clinic before them all." To Old Hans: "I beg of you, mein Herr. I cannot learn where they have taken my Herta. It is no more than a taste of asthma, and I exaggerated it to get her out of that—"

"Do we know anything else?" Old Hans asked, coming close to take her shaking hands in his. "Was there a name? Or one of those spurious code phrases with which this regime paints over its shames?"

"They told me nothing," she almost wailed. "I said I would not leave until ... the lack of *feeling!* They pushed me out like an old dog sniffing in a notions shop!"

"Could someone in the Filmwelt help us?" Jimmy asked the Old Man. He looked doubtful.

But "I know someone," Jimmy said. "She's important. Probably could telephone Herr Generaldirektor Wasistda on the spot." A shrug. "You know how it goes among the very wealthy. Would she be glad to see me? Here's a dainty moo of a laugh. "Sometimes one last glimpse is appreciated."

"Who is this?" the Old Gentleman asked her; and Jimmy told him a bit of it in her forthright way, as Frau Kraus went to see to the washing of her face after so much crying.

"The Baroness, in truth," Old Hans said at last. "I've been her guest once or twice."

"You!" Jimmy cried in delight. "Is there no grandee unknown to you? Will you untie all the secrets of the age, while you're at it?"

An impish look from Old Hans, and Frau Kraus returns with "This is what comes of spying on the Mass and closing down the Church schools!"

"All religion is witch-cult," said the Old Man, more out of habit than to disconcert Frau Kraus. "But now, let us find Herta. Can we visit like this, ungroomed? Especially you, dear Jimmy, in that tarty frock with your hair down."

Jimmy stretched like a cat. "She'll like me like this."

The servants were reluctant to admit them, but Jimmy asked to pass a note to the Baroness, writing simply "I plead for a mother oppressed by the Browns" and signing her first name.

The Baroness came almost immediately.

Jimmy told her about Herta. Did the Baroness know someone who could tell them where the girl was being held? Could she have the girl released? Could they go this night to fetch her?

The Baroness stared at Jimmy, an old ache stirring inside her. Am I never to choose my lot, ever to be swept away by inspiring performers? I am finished with it, we say. We are never finished with it.

The Baroness bade them wait while she contacted some people. It took time, but she eventually learned of certain events transpiring in a medical installation near Rüdersdorf, to the east.

"She is here," said the Baroness, handing Jimmy the address. "Go quickly. Tomorrow without fail."

Jimmy fell to her knees and kissed the Baroness' hand, then turned and left without a word. Der Alte Herr gave a formal bow and followed her. So Jimmy, too, has gone over for a man, the Baroness thought. And so classic! He looked familiar.

Heading home, the Old Gentleman made his plan; he would start for Rüdersdorf at once. "I liked that final touch," he told Jimmy, who was quietly outraging their tram car by leaning against his shoulder with a wicked smile. "Küss die Hand, then exit. There's business like that in *The Queen of the Pirates and the Battle of Corfu*. It never missed an ovation."

"I used to be queen of the pirates," said Jimmy, yawning.

"Now you're the battle of Corfu."

"Will you stop with that dirty sex talk again?"

Old Hans reached the clinic at Rüdersdorf in time to join a touring party of students, teachers, and S.S. men and their wives. A doctor and nurse led the visitors through a ward of the insane, the patients strapped into their beds. Morose and distracted, they seemed to have given up wrestling with their demons to wait to be overwhelmed by some unnamed terror, for once something outside themselves.

"Useless eaters" the doctor called them. "They can't even visit the toilet without fouling themselves. Why prolong their agony?"

"How are they eliminated?" asked a student. "By injection?"

Smiling, the doctor replied, "A humane solution that would nevertheless encourage the world-wide Jewish propaganda war against us. We don't kill them. We stop feeding them. They die of life."

"Der spricht auf gut Deutsch!" cried another student. That's the German way!

One of the S.S. wives asked, "Are they all mentally ill?"

"Here it is mostly the physically handicapped. Especially the children."

The next ward was all young boys; they, too, were fastened in bed. One youngster, perhaps five years old, had managed to work himself free of his bonds, and raised his head to address the party as they entered.

"Mutti does not know I'm here," he said, "and she is looking for me. She would give me a candy surprise when I get home."

The nurse wordlessly reinvested the boy's restraints.

"Could you tell Mutti where I am?" he asked the nurse.

"We have enough to do without your Mutti," she said, and murmurs of agreement ran through the company as Old Hans marveled at this evil dream. A dream of Europe going crazy every so often as a cult of vindictive mediocrity rages against the gifted. The Inquisition interrogates Shakespeare.

"Doctor!" shouted a medical man, rushing in. "Quick! There's an enema riot in the Lithuanian ward!"

Both doctor and nurse looked confused; she even began to say, "There is no Lithuanian ward." But the newcomer let out a *snap!* of his fingers, and the two fluttered into the air like dolls on sticks. Then he blew at them, and they floated away.

"Another touring party, aha!" the newcomer cried, slapping his thigh with a grin. "That's Führer style, yes. Let's *all* do it!"

Helplessly, all but Old Hans did as told, slapping thighs and grinning.

"You must work toward the Führer, yes. Now ... *sleep!*"

They dropped peacefully to the floor; the patients dozed off, too. Only Old Hans was awake, and the Devil threw off his disguise with "We meet again, mein Herr."

"Rette sie!" Save her!

"Really, how do they explain these deaths to the relatives? 'Died of an abscess'? 'A stroke'? Oh—'Pneumonia,' that's it. Strictly experimental for now. Won't be official policy till next year."

"Tausend Donnerwetter!" The Old Gentleman grabbed for the Devil in a fury, but touched only air. Running, now, through the building, he passed from ward to ward till he found Herta, sleeping with two other girls on a makeshift cot in a corner. Picking Herta up, he turned to see three orderlies bearing down on them, but he was inside his powers now and bent them all to his will, forced everyone from his path, stamping along with the girl like some hero of ancient epic with nothing to lose but death itself.

"Künststück!" the Devil called out from somewhere, as Old Hans strode to the exit. Music-hall magic act! "Your strength is only as great as your word, and no one reads you in this Germany! You *shadow*! You *haunt!*"

His footsteps echoed through the silent halls, faded, were over.

Ernst vom Rath died of his wounds today," the Devil concluded, whispering. "Welcome to Hell's Berlin."

The Old Man and Herta were nearly home, heading up the Oranienburger Strasse from the Hackesche Höfe. Though exhausted, the child did not complain and kept pace with the Old Man's quickmarch. How strange the wide street seemed in November's early-evening darkness, so empty, yet steeped in disquieting faroff rumbles. From the river came shrill whistles. Signals? Some men raced up the road, staring at the Old Man and Herta as they passed, all but examining them. But the men moved on.

"Old Hans," Herta asked, "do you know those people?"

"They don't know me, at any rate."

More whistles, and shouting.

"We must hurry," said Old Hans: but the way was blocked by another gang, rushing around the corner as one of them hurled a wooden stool into the glass front of a small grocery. *Crash!* And "Now storm break loose!" they shouted, pouring inside.

"Quickly," said Old Hans, taking Herta along as a woman screamed from inside the store, wordless screams, desperate, to the noise of everything being broken up and pitched about, the laughing like this they feel that they are God screams and breaking up all about them. Quickly.

Cristel Pack was at her oven, fondling the chain of keys at her waist, listening happily to the commotion outside. More! More! Horst was taking part in the

People's Action Against the Jews. What knickknacks might he bring back? Ja, she had promised fresh apple bake, real lard in the crust.

Horst, as always, was the last one over and the first to take cover. The whole thing was stupid, anyway, he thought—because were we to wreck everything or hunt for loot? Cristel told him, "The Jews have everything in gold." And "Look for fine underthings, don't be shy." As if he could find anything that would fit that monster!

The fire fighters were ordered to save only buildings adjacent to Jewish ones, should the fires spread, and the police were to keep Party enthusiasts from torching Christian churches, which some would dearly love to do. As the operation was especially intense in Oranienburger Strasse, the Old Man and Herta had to work their way through a huge crowd, gathered to watch the burning of the great domed synogogue. One woman, deeply angry, said, "There is such a thing as private property," adding, "And I'll box the ears of any who contradicts me."

"I'll contradict you," said Cristel Pack, heaving up from behind the group. She had set her pastry to cool and come out to see the fun. "Ist sie eine Judenfreundin?" Cristel asked the others. She favors Jews, this one?

"I don't like arson!" the woman answered, and Cristel's affectless smile twists up with "I denounce babblers, asocials, confusers and defeatists. Idlers, prolongers, and doubters. Like *you!*" as she grabs the woman's hair to force her hand into her struggling victim's mouth. "See how I rip out your tongue on this night of nights!" Cristel bellows.

"*Shameful!*" a man shouts. He separates the two by shoving Cristel, quite hard. She staggers a bit but throws her head back to roar out her fierce laughter, another of this day's sound effects of ecstatic rage. The woman Cristel was wrestling with flees, but the man stands before Cristel, staring at her.

"Yes, you like these treasons?" she asks him, her voice low and toying, as others nearby move away a bit. Her eyes locked on his, she chants:

> Friends of Jews in a Jewish stew!
> March in line or go down, too!

"Quatsch," the man said. Rubbish.

"My Horst has gone to market," said Cristel. "He'll fetch me some Jew prizes at the holiday pogrom. Oh, look!"

For The Old Man was passing by with Herta.

"Heil Hitler!" Cristel called out to them. "Such wonderful citizens! Where is the old schemer making off to with such a tasty Mädchen? After them, good people!"

No one molested them, although Herta wanted to know who the big woman was. "I remember her from before," she said.

Greatly perturbed but trying to keep up Herta's spirit, he replied, "That curious bear Quisli might tell us."

"He would always know!" cried Herta, delighted in this worrisome day to hear about someone she could be certain of. Then she fainted.

The Old Gentleman carried her for the last few blocks. Gustl and Joschi, watching for them from the window, let out whoops and raced downstairs, though both Jimmy and Frau Kraus tried to stop the boys from venturing out into the violence.

Two doors away, Horst's unit was terrorizing a Jewish family. Helping himself to a pair of gold rings for Cristel, Horst went outside; the noise gave him a headache. So he was standing right there as Gustl and Joschi greeted Old Hans and Herta, and he was staring at Joschi. Old Hans was looking at Horst, trying to recall where they had met and noting an uncanny resemblance between Horst and Joschi.

Horst noted it, too. Did he realize that Joschi was his son? He had taken a step toward the boy when his fellows suddenly poured out of the doorway—more of that infernal stupid noise!—with the man from the apartment. The Old Man herded his children inside as insult your betters, will you insolent Jewish slime, dousing him with gasoline meant for some synogogue joining hands to dance sing tschingerassa-bum whacking him bouncing dribbling till one lights the match squealing little Jew dodging around and along as he howls his way down the street better than books and dogs this fire in medieval blood riot. Reichskristallnacht, National Broken Glass night.

When Neville Chamberlain heard of it, he broke out with "What can one *do* with such a people? They *will* get in the way so, d'ye see?"

Shortly before Christmas, Kai treated Conrad to a trip to the opera. Yes, life goes quite merrily on. They took in a new work, an adaptation of Ibsen's *Peer Gynt* by Werner Egk. The opera focused the play's picaresque into the adventures of an opportunistic emptyhead who ends up as he had started: with nothing.

Conrad thought the music surprisngly bold, with reminiscences of now banned composers and even a reference to the cancan from Offenbach's *Orpheus in Hades.* Jew music. At one point, these words were sung: "What war ever turned out well?"

"Jazz, satire, and defeatism," said Conrad to Kai after they had left the rest of the audience behind them and could not be overheard. "It must be true art, then—free of crippling decrees. Have the Browns run out of ways to control us all?"

"They never run out," said Kai. "They accumulate."

"Yes, so now the Jews cannot attend the theatre. It is forbidden."

Kai said, "Can there not be a single day without this? Always the Jews, the tinder box of Europe. Someone points at them, and suddenly it is arrests and killing, and not only of Jews! Do you see how extremely stupid this Jew hatred is? It does not solve problems. It creates them."

Kai was truly angry, stomping over to the auto, slamming his door closed with a ferocious smash, and not leaning over to open the passenger door for Conrad, as he always would.

"What right have you to be angry with me?" asked Conrad, as he got in. "Did *I* do this?"

They drove in silence till Kai said, now in an airy tone, "Herr mein Führer saw the *Peer Gynt* premiere. He liked it, they say."

"Well, who cares what he likes?"

"Do you care what I like?"

Conrad was tiring of these games.

"I like you," said Kai, finally, "because you love my brother."

"No. I love you."

"I am my brother."

They had reached the Tiergarten, the trees balding in an unnaturally frigid autumn. The leaves weren't coloring or falling: they were gone, as if there had been another decree.

Kai started up again. "When we are close together, without secrets, skin against the skin, then I am Conrad and you are Kai."

"No, Kai."

"Ei, I am pressing you with guilt. Is it that you are still sometimes having it off with that man of the movies?"

"No. Well … I mean yes, sometimes. But no, you must not play these word tricks that confuse things."

"It is good that you have a friend at work. But you can love only Gunnlaug and Kai. Why do I say this? Can you guess?"

Conrad ventured a look at Kai's profile as he steered the auto in a turn, the street lamps backlighting him like a Hollywood iconographer.

"Is it because you are so handsome?" Conrad asked.

"That is no reason. Ha, you saw the opera tonight, telling of this man without an interior. There are very many like him, harmful to others. They look for an interior in a movement they can join. It tells them what to say, how to spend time, whom to despise. It gives them life. Peer Gynt would make a good Nazi, ja? My brother Gunnlaug says the interior of the Nazis is apocalypse. Hitler cannot control the world in the end, so he will destroy it.

They were nearly home now.

"Ha," said Kai.

Inside the fortress, Kai embraced Conrad almost shyly, as if fearing a rebuff. "It is so shocking when we fight," he said.

"We didn't fight," said Conrad, easing out of the embrace. "You did."

"I am troubled, and that makes me fight. Even with my double."

"Now that is ... *Kai!* I am your comrade. I am your admirer. I am your sweetheart. I am not your double."

"We must have a snack after such an intense exchange," said Kai, leading the way to the kitchen. "Even if there are shortages in the shops, they cannot run out of bread and cheese."

As they kitted up and took their places, Kai said, "It was pleasing music tonight, ja? We are fine smart fellows at the opera. Everyone wonders who we are. The business goes well. Tomorrow evening we will read aloud from the *Oresteia*, to make us wise. And yet I am afraid that it is my brother who will make Peer Gynt's journey to the end of nothing. This is why I worry. What do you think, Conrad?"

Tears were running down Kai's cheeks. He wiped these away with a sportsman's smile, yet more flowed.

"It seems I am a fountain," he said. "If wicked things were to happen to my brother, I would not want to go on, my dear Conrad."

"Oh, Kai, you must stop weeping."

"Yes, how I know that. But I will sit here awhile with you and pretend I am back in the business world of the Ruhr, where tears reveal immaturity and failure to rule with good sense. Na und? I recover at once."

They looked at each other across the kitchen table.

"Their interior is apocalypse, Conrad. Isn't it always so with these fellows who hector us with spectacular manias? They should be objects of amusement on street corners, but we, reckless as gods, give them coronations. What comes next? A kiss to quicken the dead? Or a new age in brutality?"

They sat in silence, not moving.

Then Kai said, "Who will be happy, when this age at last is over, but Gauleiters and Commissars? You see? And so we are trapped in history."

"What about the Pope?" says Hitler. "That type always wants to make trouble."

"And this one plans to," the Devil answers. "That gala pogrom of yours got him blazing. He plans to retrieve the moral authority that his office hasn't known for a thousand years."

Hitler sneered out, "I'll whip up a tasty brew for that Vatican almond cookie."

"Have you heard this one? What happens when the Soviet Union takes over at UFA? Nothing for five years. After that, there will be a shortage of Rosita Serrano."

"To think that Italian fifi in a housecoat would dare to—"

"Yet he's failing, poor darling. Begging his doctors to keep him alive long enough to launch the Catholic revolt against you."

A farting spasm the size of the Sistine Chapel tore through Hitler's bowels.

"Eek," said the Devil. "You may have to stand in for the tubas at Bayreuth next summer."

Scowling at the slight, Hitler said "But Pius the Eleventh dies? You promise?"

"Yes—and I'm closing him down at the last possible moment, the better to shatter his everlasting hope for good in the world. That's the best way with Popes."

"And the next Pope? He'll be one of your people?"

"No, that much even I can't do. Pius picked him. A cowardly little dog, though. Nothing like his master."

"Still, still—who could ever trust a Pope? How do we know for certain that he won't try to protect the Jews?"

This next one won't even protect Catholics."

"You were given the choice between war and dishonor," Winston Churchill told Chamberlain in Parliament. "You chose dishonor, and you shall have war."

First, Hitler had to neutralize his double, Stalin, with a peace treaty that Stalin actually believed in. Then Hitler and Stalin ripped Poland apart, to exterminate her Jewish population and all elements of national leadership—politicians, army officers, educators, artists, intellectuals, priests and nuns, and other potential organizers of resistance down to police commanders. Poland is to be erased as a nation, a culture, a people.

The world's two great cannibal kings are piling holocausts like cord wood. But Hitler is using up his magic bullets: one, reclaiming the Rhineland. Two, stealing Austria. Three, mashing Czechoslovakia. Four is Poland. Then come five, Denmark and Norway, and six, France and the Low Countries.

It is now the turn of Russia. But sechse treffen, sieben äffen. The first six make you: the seventh destroys you.

Part III

THE SEVENTH BULLET

The life of Heinrich Himmler, Chief of Police of all the Reich and its conquered territory, is files and reveries. He loves to turn to his bank of applications to join the S.S., with all due genetic information and photograph, ja. Skin of the blood, eyes of the blood, life of the blood. The Erscheinungsbild!: picture of the race! Herein lies the winner's power, the evolutionary regenerating himself—but he must mate wisely. Ja. The files know of many requests to marry, denied because of dubious genetics. Leave her to some farmer's boy! The S.S. man realizes destiny by protecting the Erscheinungsbild. Next to that, all intellect, art, and science, is nothing. Sighs. Ja.

Himmler's best reveries shudder through him in Wewelsburg, his Westphalian castle retreat, done up in chivalric motif. It is a place of mystical communion with antiquity, especially at full moons and times of solstice. And there is Operation Froh. Ja. This may actually lead us into contact with fallen heroes of the Order of Teutonic Knights. Imagine a Germany before feminizing legal codes, before immigration! A land of oneness, ja, as we dispose of our traditional enemies. What of those others, of Different races? Latins, Celts, those persistent Basques, who came to Europe from alien worlds. This is a subject, we say, for future necessary discussion. Ja.

Hitler is crabbing at the Devil, who impatiently finger-ticks the times he protected the Führer from assassination.

"Who whispers, 'Run out the side door, that Wehrmacht officer has a bomb under his coat,' hey? Who sped you out of the Bürgerbräukeller before that carpenter's explosive took the roof off? Over and over, I do and I do. Your sheer survival has become implausible. People are starting to talk."

"What about Stalingrad?"

"Well, you flap your hands over the map in those wild sweeps, what do you expect? We'll attack *here*! Pincer movement *there*! Sensational Blitzkrieg formations *of course*! No one dares ask about supply lines or anti-freeze. God forbid! Because you've got that Act as infallible war lord to protect. Yet what are you really? Tantrums and vegetable pie!"

"It is the *stronger will* that conquers! *It is not a question of supply lines!*"

"Yes, and here's the shrieking again. Your adjutants joke about it—one says, 'Der Chef is trying to reach Berlin,' and the other says, 'Why doesn't he use the telephone?' And ... And! ... behind your back ...: 'Teppichfresser'!"

"*Carpet eater*! You would say *this* to me?"

"Right, let's blame the messenger!" cries the Devil, throwing his hands into the air.

Hitler's bowels erupt with a fanfaronade so savage that the paint greys on the walls.

"You know,' says the Devil, "none of my other principals got anywhere that noxious. I heard General von Manstein tell General Keitel that he has to think of the second battle of the Marne to keep from laughing at you. Manstein's Jewish, incidentally."

Hitler snorts this nuisance away.

"And what was the big idea of declaring war on the United States? We never agreed on that!"

"Symmetry?"

"Your treaty with Japan," the Devil goes on, affecting the irritated authority of a Gymnasium Latin master, "required a declaration of war only if Japan had been attacked—not if it did the *attacking!*" Bows to audience: "I thank you."

"What is America, after all? Cowboy frolics in the novels of Karl May!"

"A string of Chippewa romances is your idea of the world's greatest industrial power? Oh right, fart again"—for another seizure shakes Hitler from top to toe—"while you ruin our war! Of course," Hell adds, his head observantly atilt, "you never needed to win in the first place, did you? You just wanted to kill Jews and Slavs. And that old Nordic thing—the gods must die, the world will end. Oh! Look at you so despondent now. I prefer you screeching."

"Wars are to win," Hitler mutters.

"So depraved, yet so detached. You never get out to have a look at the death. You don't ... tingle over your kills. Stalin gloats, you know. It's a bit sexual to him. I don't trust evil without sensuality. Give me a priest who fucks the witch before he condemns her. Like Julius Streicher—though of course he's such a pig at it. No, with tact. With style! Like that officer of the inquisition who'd urge confession of the most comely of his suspects by locking them in the guillotine. A slender cord held the blade up, and this he'd place between their teeth. If they lost that grip, you see, the blade would fall. His assistants were rowdy village lads, encouraged to strip for holy work. Gracious, how hard they'd grow in their piety as they'd take up the birch rod to—"

"*Enough!*" Hitler shouts.

"You prude."

"I tell you, that *unnatural alliance of capitalists and Bolsheviks will collapse! And my people will never surrender!*"

"You despots always say My People when all you mean is Me. Why does no one ever notice that?"

Pfuikeck had his Act, too. He took it to Vienna, then to Zürich, but the police disliked Pfuikeck's spoofs of the Führer next door. Locating an irregularity in Pfuikeck's papers, the Swiss deported him to Bavaria after alerting the authorities there.

So the Gestapo was waiting. Instead of deportation to the east, however, Pfuikeck was taken all the way to Berlin under guard. At headquarters, Gestapo Müller—as they called him—offered Pfuikeck a job as Judenfänger. A Jewcatcher.

"Officially, Berlin is Judenfrei," Müller explained, as always concentrating on his dialogue, motionless at his desk. "The Jews are gone. However. It seems that many went underground. 'U-Boats' we call them. They hide and wander. They sell on the black market or perform odd tasks. They have no address, no documents, no friends. Or …"

Gestapo Müller smiled thinly.

"Or they have a route of one-night stopovers, forged or stolen papers, and help from traitors to the Reich. Their old butcher gives them chance cuttings of meat without a ration card, the beef is shared for a weekend's hostel, some further shady business is transacted. It is a culture unto itself. With perhaps ten thousand U-Boats in the city, what net can we cast to bring them to the surface?"

"Perhaps a Kalman festival," Pfuikeck suggested, spoof still his nature. "They love operettas."

After a long pause, Gestapo Müller said, "Yes, you are noted for such an original sense of humor. Here"—as he nosed into a file—"we read of a musical selection in one of your Zürich revues. 'Manheim in May' is the title. Let us quote:

> Mannheim in May!
> The world is a stage.
> Our Führer feels gay.
> Pogroms are the rage.

Looking up, Gestapo Müller said, "In some way I am missing the point of this joke."

"The Swiss missed the point, too."

"It is odd," said Gestapo Müller. "This is a perilous place, yet the arrogant come to us arrogant, unfiltered. The connivers try to connive. The jokers display their insolence. You are not in your element here, with an irresponsible public giggling at Jewish twaddle."

Thoroughly warned, and heeding the warning, Pfuikeck nodded.

"We have under our protection a most successful catcher of Jews," Gestapo Müller went on. "She is beautiful and clever, 'the Lorelei.' A suitable reference, to the famous poem by the Jew Heine. Our Lorelei parks herself at a café table with someone she suspects is a U-Boat. She feigns despair and intimacy. She is a Jew on the run, she says. Nowhere to turn. Now: emboldened by her confession, her victim admits that he, too, is a Jew. Perhaps if they teamed up ... but she has already signaled to the Gestapo men, and another U-Boat's voyage is finished."

Almost dreamily, he added, "It is not known how the Lorelei knows her prey. But she is most effective."

"I'm not Jewish," said Pfuikeck.

"I know," Gestapo Müller replied. "But you're something. You can unmask the others like you. The Different ones always show too much ... imagination. Too much art. Too much dissent. You will recognize such qualities, and betray them. If you fail to deliver a certain number of U-Boats to us each week, severe measures will be taken, of course."

Gestapo Müller smiled. And Pfuikeck likes the sound of the job. He remembers theatre managers who scorned his projects, facetious critics, handsome young men in their beautiful suits on their way to a carefree evening, thinking of how they will whore for each other and call it romance.

"Each catcher devises his unique tricks," Gestapo Müller was saying. "But we have collected some general intelligence. Bomb shelters are good picking fields—look for the Bombenscheine." The identity card of those who lost their papers in a raid. "They are very often fakes, or stolen from a corpse. The Lorelei loves café work. She is entranced by cafes. Some of the most successful catchers prefer to wait outside cinemas, where U-Boats earn money by standing in line to buy tickets for others. And now you will learn of the passwords. This is most important. Resistance groups use lines from banned writers. Quote some Jew, see what you get. Or the national traitor Thomas Mann."

Taking up a mallet made of lead, Gestapo Müller rapped on his desk, and the door flew open.

"Start him off," he ordered, and as the operative pulled Pfuikeck up by the collar, Gestapo Müller added, "It's Berlin in May."

May of 1944.

Into the narrative now enters Count Claus Schenk von Stauffenberg. Not tut ein Held. We require a hero. He even looks the role: tall and vigorous, with an artistic nature but a strength of purpose icing his eyes. He wrote poetry once; now he is Chief of Staff at the General Army Office. This is partly in recompense for his bravery in the African campaign, where he lost his left eye, his right hand, and two fingers on the left. Kurz und gut: the best man in Germany.

"No more tea parties!" von Stauffenberg cries to his Uncle Nux, also a count, von Uxküll-Gyllenband. "No more of this Goerdeler stalling while Europe falls apart!"

"Who is with you in it?"

"All and none—Die Kerle haben ja die Hosen voll oder Stroh im Kopf." That lot has its pants full or no brains. "I hear a lot of 'Yes, I won't.'"

Uncle Nux says, "Then you will do what?"

"I will kill Hitler. I've had it in mind for a long time. You know, Uncle, we haven't merely lost the war. We've lost the losing of it. We're surrounded and bombed and totalized in ruin, yet we can't surrender because of that fucking mustache and his thrill murders. Uncountable thousands slaughtered in the east! Thousands more snatched up on the streets of the occupied countries to labor like slaves! Russian women and children forced-marched into the frozen waste and left there to die. We are not fighting like Germans, Uncle. We are fighting like Hitler."

Looking away for a moment, at history's future wonder at these unpardonable years, von Stauffenberg concludes with "Von dem Gangsterhaufen kann ich mich nur durch den Tod trennen."

I will kill them all.

"Die heissherzige Jugend" is what cashiered Colonel General Franz Halder calls von Stauffenberg. The passionate youth. His energy overwhelms doubters, because he will die rather than fail, and unlike most others in the resistance he has access to Hitler. No more waiting months for the Führer to appear only to see him scuttle off to an exit just before one strikes.

"As if Hell itself had his ear," says Uncle Nux. A former military man, he has lately been in business, and has made use of his contact with Gunnlaug von Kleist, of the industrial family, a captain in the S.S., sympathetic to the resistance. The von Stauffenberg circle has been eager to attract such participation, for everyone fears a civil war at home while the Bolshevik avalanche rolls in from the East.

"What are we," Gunnlaug asked von Stauffenberg's Uncle Nux. "Traitors? Heroes? Innocent children of guilty fathers?"

"Consider the liberation of explosives at the court of the lords of misery," Uncle Nux replied. "Right at the feet of the beast. What are we, indeed? Successful. We are fine reading in history's text, and I'm so nervous I couldn't smoke if I had any tobacco in the first place." An ironic laugh. "We are awakened from our evil dream, Captain von Kleist. Ah—the sirens. National Socialism's Beethoven. Will you join me in the shelter?"

"No. I must get back to Prinz-Albrecht-Strasse." At Uncle Nux's look of alarm, Gunnlaug added, "There is time enough." At the door, he paused for a last word. "*Was nun beginnen, Tod ist überall?*" What can we possibly start now, when death is everywhere?

And Uncle Nux said simply, "*Stirb zur rechten Zeit!*"

Die at the right time.

The Allies' bombing campaign completely reinstructed life in Berlin, for there was no intermission in any real sense, and one's time was spent at work or in shelters. Time for even essential chores was scarce. People took to wearing the same clothing for days. Men went unshaven.

When a Nazi Bonze took notice of the von Kleist residence, with its all but medieval impenetrability, he told the brothers to sell it to him, and they had no choice. Gunnlaug moved in with the Baroness; Kai and Conrad took an apartment together. Kai had to leave his piano behind, and Conrad passed his puppet theatre on to Joschi and the twins. They were too awed by the gift to play with it till Old Hans roused them with a lusty reminiscence of his days as a theatre manager. A new company was formed on the spot, making debut with their version of *Hedwig the Bandit's Bride*, racy, bold, extempore.

Kai and Conrad had gone to their new flat, two rooms in Cristel Pack's building—on her landing, in fact. Behind the door of one apartment came the sound of a piano banging out miscellaneous chords.

"Perhaps they will let me visit and play a bit," said Kai, as they deposited two chairs in the front room. As they came out, Cristel Pack, in her doorway, cried, "Oh, here are handsome sirs! So, so! The fancy dress! Princes of the realm?"

Kai gave Cristel a distant bob of the head as he headed for the stairway. Conrad got out a hello while taking in the woman's unruly physique.

"One moment," she said, planting herself in Conrad's way; Kai turned back at this. "Why are two young men not in the service?"

Kai and Conrad had to carry with their papers a document explaining that their work was vital to national survival. "Longnoses"—their term for Nazi busybodies—often challenged them, to their fervent disgust, and now Kai told Cristel to mind her own business.

"Such a *fancy* boy!" Cristel observed, striding back to throw open her door. The odd piano chords from the apartment opposite made a curious accompaniment as she cried, "Those with nothing to hide from the Führer's gaze have a national duty to unmask the liars, whisperers and fainthearts betraying the Fatherland! Come view a National Socialist home!"

"We're too busy," said Kai, pulling Conrad along.

"Not a peek at least?" Cristel urged, throwing a bear arm around Conrad's shoulders and tugging him toward her door. "You will see the table where our frugal one-pot meal is consumed!"

"Who is this demented woman?" cried Kai, as Conrad failed to shake out of Cristel's grip. She actually got him inside her door—"Kai!"—as Kai came charging after. "You animal!" he said.

"And you so pretty, too! I will put you in my oven like a Jewie!"

Still struggling with her as Kai joined the fight, Conrad kicked wildly at a leg of a table decorated with Führer souvenirs. The whole thing went flying across the room, and knocked into the wall, losing Hitler porcelain plate and other pieces of totalitarian kitsch as Cristel let out a gasp.

"But he is my romance!" she said, surveying the wreckage.

The two boys had already run out, almost knocking into Gunnlaug, who had just arrived. He was in uniform, and when Cristel appeared in her door, holding bits of shattered plate, she went hard and still at the sight of Kai and Conrad feeling safe behind an S.S. captain.

"A hero of the state, mein Herr," she said, almost respectful in tone. "You will want to discipline this rowdy element at once." Then she closed her door and left the three alone.

"Chatting up the new neighbors, I see," said Gunnlaug.

"This is too late to come," answered Kai, burying his being in his brother's embrace. "I shall never forgive you."

Gunnlaug extended his right arm to Conrad, to come share in the redemption of love. Complying, Conrad thought, It's like a mountebank hawking an elixir. But it works.

"Come, I am short of time," said Gunnlaug, breaking the hold. "Which flat is yours?"

As Kai let them in, Gunnlaug looked pensively over at the door from which the piano chords were coming, then moved inside with the boys with a sense of great purpose.

"You must listen to me both," he said. Out of his attache came a large rectangular case and a small jingling box. The case gave forth a revolver. The two boys shared a look but said nothing as Gunnlaug showed them how to shoot and clean it, emphasizing safety over and over. Bullets in the box: how to load them, unload them. Precautions. The boys obediently absorbed the lecture. These days, one was alert or one got killed.

"Why this now, though?" asked Kai at last.

"It doesn't matter why, just *listen*. If they come for you, say, 'Let me get my coat' in a docile manner." Turning to Conrad, he added, "Resigned, ja? Then you come out shooting. Of course, you must keep your overcoat in—"

"What if it happens now, in the warm?" Conrad asked.

"Was it ever this frustrating to advise the reckless? Make arrangements. Devise codes. I cannot watch every second, like an angel." Resting a hand on his brother's head, he told them, "If my Freundin comes, you go with her. No stalling, ja?"

"Ja."

"Conrad?"

"Ja."

Practice cleaning the gun now, and try not to shoot yourselves too much."

As Gunnlaug left, a woman came out of the piano-chords apartment, dressed for the street. She started to greet Gunnlaug in plain language without a mention of the Führer, and he interrupted in an undertone, warning her that it was generally known that BBC listeners smoke-screened with automatic piano. Her expression did not change, but her coloring paled; attending enemy broadcasts was a capital crime.

"From now on," Gunnlaug told her, very quietly, "no piano. Just"—and here he simply lipped the words soundlessly—"play the radio very quietly. Ja?"

At such honesty in these wary times, the woman could only nod.

Back in the apartment, Kai asked Conrad, "What brings all this to us? This gun and cautions."

"I am really afraid that Gunnlaug is going into his aristeia. He must make everything final before his great battle."

Kai, suddenly realizing that this must be true, jumped through the building down to the street like a wild thing, catching Gunnlaug just as he was stepping into his car with "No! *No!*"

"Not a word," Gunnlaug whispered, most urgently. "Be von Kleist! Show them nothing!"

"... I ..."

"Speak calmly to me," Gunnlaug ordered, snapping his fingers as if in illustration of an anecdote, in case they were being watched. Two men having a merry talk.

"Yes," Kai replied, fighting tears. "But where are you going?"

"To headquarters, and then to the Baroness. What is the matter with you? Where would I be going?"

I will be brave with this ruse. My brother will be proud. "I have been wondering how you like your birthday tie."

"Yes, excellent spy talk. Remember to keep your sidearm cleaned and loaded. And 'Trust Odysseus to escape, he is fast and smart.'"

"Now you are Odysseus?"

"One of his crew," said Gunnlaug, getting into his car.

The shortages had been mounting: beer, then wine, vegetables, potatoes, and of course fuel. There were almost no taxicabs to be had, and public transportation was so vexed by the bombing that all travel was constricted and overcrowded. The KaDeWe department store was an empty barn. And soap? A unicorn myth.

That put Horst Pack in business, on the black market: medical supplies meant for the front, household goods, heirlooms of all kinds, French lingerie—imagine! at such a time—and food, of course. Horst had been through Stalingrad; now he had no fear. Berlin thinks it has a bomb problem? You try a place where every Godfucking house hides a pack of Ivans. "Fritz! Fritz!" They'd shoot from nowhere, on the next floor, on your floor, in the shithell bed with you. No one slept in Stalingrad. Every three days or so, you'd pass out, then wake up with a dead Ivan atop you. Or worse: a live one. Anytime Horst heard something, he'd whirl and shoot. Ours, theirs, *fuck*! Except that way you run out of bullets.

Horst was standing in a doorway near the Rotes Rathaus on a weekday evening—on crutches, so people didn't demand to know why he was not in uniform. He made three connections in half an hour, all cash. The principals had to meet him at a collection point later on. Or is he supposed to carry fruit and woolens around like a Galician peddler?

Cristel would turn him in if she knew of it—but would she have loved Stalingrad! Those women knew how to deal it out. Your buddy takes one of those bullets from nowhere, and suddenly three axe ladies fly out of, I don't know, the earth itself and start hacking his limbs off as he screams. "Fritz, wer essen du!" they would shout in their crazy German. You have to get to the wounded before the Ivans did, in case someone was holding on to a crust of bread. Frozen, of course. Frozen life like frozen death. Frozen shit, even—it'd hit the ground with a bump, that fast it froze. I'd like to see a frozen Führer take a shit in Stalingrad.

At least Horst got out. One and a half million didn't. It was luck; he got onto one of the last transports that left the sole airfield still operating. He had to slip past troops ordered to shoot anyone retreating, and, just before reaching the field, he perforated a soldier a few times so he'd have someone to drag in. Shot himself up, too. They had a term for that: "Stalingrad hero."

Then, all at once, there was Jimmy, right there before Horst. She was asking about the makings of a sweetbake. He was staring, not listening. She must not know him—till he turned to show the scar on his face. The one that Old Hans left there back on Führernacht in 1933.

Startled, she leaped backward, and as he grabbed at her his left crutch fell to the ground. He held her powerfully with one hand on her arm, shifting his weight to his other side with "I won't hurt you, just talk to me!"

She was instantly still, and he gently let go, drew his hand away, and made a little gesture of it: see? You have nothing to fear.

She waited, watching his eyes.

"Who was that fellow with the magic?" he went on, urgently. "What happened that night? And after … I haven't been happy even a day. Even … Where is everybody from before? Can you meet me somewhere? I would bring stockings for you."

She said, "You have a son."

After a silence, Horst said, "From that night, yes?"

A passerby bent to retrieve Horst's left crutch, saying, as he handed it to him, "Can't you help a wounded soldier, Fräulein?"

"At a time like this you're giving an etiquette course?" Jimmy shouted; and the man went his way.

"What is my son's name?" Horst asked.

"Everyone tells me I must send him to the country, but he refuses to leave me and they won't let me go because of the war work. Your son values love above all else. Can you understand this?"

"I need to see you. Please?"

"You were nice-looking once," said Jimmy. "Englishmen with heavy wallets wanted you for sea voyages, but they could not know how filled with malice you are. They saw an amiable lout with nice plumbing."

"You teased me and hurt me. You made me bad."

"Yes, that from *you*! But a friend of mine says, 'No one makes anybody anything.' He says, 'All behavior is freely chosen.'"

"What friend?" cried Horst. "The magic man? Where is he now? You will tell me?"

She took both his crutches by the edge closest to her and flung them clattering behind her on the pavement. He pitched forward with a gasp, snatching at her legs, but she had backed away.

Staring balefully, pathetically up at her. "At least, you would help me to my feet."

"His name is Josef," and she ran away.

"Noch hab'ich mich ins Freie nicht gekämpft," Gunnlaug told the Baroness. I have not yet fought my way to freedom. "But *this* man—amazing! He *is* liberation. You should meet him, with his wounds of one who has arisen, almost in a ... a mystical ..."

"Another Führer," the Baroness murmured. "And we've hardly used up the first one."

She was sitting atop him, skin to skin, straddling his loins and giving the back of his torso a "therapeutic."

"So ja," she continued, "another action for the resistance."

"It is different now. Before, it was General Beck being *not* in charge. Now it is someone in charge."

"Couldn't we just lose the war?" she asked, working on his back and deltoids. "Instead of so many fine men taking this risk, along with their families and who knows what other innocents?"

Gunnlaug moaned in pleasure.

"We *are* losing the war, ja?"

"This coup is a statement to history."

"Oh. Well, Yes, by all means ..."

"You must not mock such heroic exploits, I think."

"Yes, my friend," digging more deeply the better to delight him. "It sounds just a bit pompous to hear of history from a boy who shouts when he fucks. Bist du Erlöser?" Are you a savior now?"

She worked on his shoulders, soothing the knotted muscles and laying her head close to his. He liked her to whisper to him, and she did so now.

"When he began with the Jews and the liberals and the homosexuals like your darling brother, there was no coup. No statement to history, my dear. Then the wars. The killings, the slaves picked up on the streets of Amsterdam, Lyons, Belgrade. A coup, a statement? And through it all, my darling—the Jews, the Jews! Take away their businesses, cars, phonographs. Their pets, their books, their hairbrushes. Even their decorations from the Great War. They can't go to cinemas and parks, my pearl. They can't even walk on sections of the Wilhelmstrasse or Unter den Linden. What were they to live on? Air? Now they are not even to live, as we carefully do not mention. Then, suddenly—a coup! Now at last we are morally antagonized by Nazis, my eagle."

He rose up, throwing her off and pushing her back under him—not angrily, but in the determination to be understood.

"We thought it was so crazy it could not get crazier!" he cried to her. "And yes, now it is cataclysm. *Now*, yes … and we thought …" with his mouth on her breasts with the sly pull that she loved, toying with that place that has no name, aching down to the eternal home. He was rude there, not nibbling, to hear her call out to him at his banquet. Must he reconquer every time, make new statements to history? Prussia exacted terrible reparations of France after the war in the 1870s, so France took fair revenge at Versailles, so Hitler fucked Versailles, so half of Germany married him while the other half stood by Hindenburg, the idiot who *go! pound the bitch!* ushered the Nazis in, though even General Ludendorff, who invented the stab-in-the-back lie that damned liberals and Jews for cutting a discount deal with the enemy, predicted that Hitler would love when her head rears back in that silent scream of our juices rise between us hurl Germany into the abyss so deep in her right steep ascent breaking your nature into that sky *there* you *now* together if *I must die to save you!* on His Cross downhill now and very draining wet scared happy rest much later in somewhere.

Later on, she said, "Stop grinning."

Long pause.

"You think you're invulnerable," she said. "A fairytale hero."

"We'll meet in Switzerland."

"Wasn't Silesia dead enough?" she asked.

"After all this," touching her, making sure she was still there. "In the confusion of—"

"It won't succeed, will it?"

He thought it over as if for the first time. "Von Stauffenberg will kill Hitler. But no, it won't succeed. There are too many others to neutralize. Too many. I may not … be available …"

"Nimmst du mir alles, was einst du gabst?" So you take everything from me?

"No, my tragedy diva," he said, changing his tone to joke her along. "We'll meet in Zürich. The Grand Hotel, at afternoon English tea."

"Yes, when?"

"Whoever gets there first awaits the other. But promise me—after the action, fetch my brother and keep him safe. He knows nothing, but they'll go after him all the same. *Promise me*."

"You did not need to ask."

"He is a loving and innocent boy, not at all prepared for—"

"*You* are the one you describe! Why do you always discern your best qualities in others?"

He sighed, then said, "Where is that maid that is always hovering about?"

"Duscha is in a sulk because she wants to get away from the bombing and return to her people in the Spreewald. She thinks I could send her in a chauffered car with forged documents."

Gunnlaug didn't even have to think about it.

"You could," he said.

"Well. I could, yes."

He nodded.

"If I ..."

Leaping up and stretching himself, he said, "I don't know why I feel so good. Perhaps from looking forward to seeing you in Zürich suddenly, one afternoon when the world is free." Towelling off, he said, "Now I must go to a medical examination."

"For what?"

He shrugged. "Orders."

"Tell me—when exactly did we lose the war? At Stalingrad?"

Pulling on his shirt, he shook his head. "Stalingrad crippled us. We didn't lose till the massed tank battle at Kursk. We've been in retreat in the East ever since. Even without the Normandy invasion, we had lost."

Tie in hand, he paused, then said, "Run for the Spreewald. Stalin's coming."

Pfuikeck calls it "shoplifting." He prefers to browse in the bombing rubble, where U-Boats try to take documents from corpses. But his quarry run off at the sight of him, and those two Gestapo shadows are too lazy to chase anybody. With all Germany to pick from, they found *him* the only two Nazis who aren't fanatics. All they want to do is sit in parks, smoking.

Stalking through Berlin, Pfuikeck watches for the anxious and haunted. What's his weekly quota?—but they never tell him anything. Just do it. They're Different and you're Different. Find them—people who ask questions. Members of the Party of Doubt.

"The Lorelei brings them in like fish in a bottle," says Gestapo Müller.

Pfuikeck visited his old cabaret, intact but dark. The display cards promised some activity later in the summer, a new operetta by Eduard Künneke.

I heard he retired, Pfuikeck thinks, walking on. And isn't Künneke Jewish?

"It's gigantic," Rolf was telling Conrad. "Dr. Mabuse went wild after seeing *Gone With the Wind*—in a print dubbed into Portugese, mind you, and they couldn't find a translator because they keep getting sent to the Eastern Front ... Where was I? *Yes*. Dr. Mabuse's revenge, his ... Magische Theater. Nur für Verrückte. Eintritt kostet den Verstand." The Magic Theatre. For madmen only. Price of entry: one's mind. "Now guess the subject."

"Frederick the Great? The Führer's bar mitzvah?"

"So you *are* Hungarian!"

Conrad blandly shook his head.

"Who but a Hungarian would ... It's Kolberg."

"Who is that?"

"The city that defied Napoleon! With Heinrich George, Kristina Söderbaum, and that tantalizingly handsome Horst Caspar. Veit Harlan directs—in color! *And!* Dr. Mabuse has received Führer benediction so absolute that he has pulled well over a hundred thousand troops out of the Wehrmacht for the battle scenes! Are we making war or making a movie? Dr. Mabuse tried to make Hollywood hits and we didn't win. He tried locking cinema doors during the newsreels. We still didn't win. So he's making an epic ... and *now we'll win!*"

"Did we win at Kolberg?"

"We lost, and the city was destroyed. The point is to inspire a fight to the end, so we all die with style. What, you don't want to? You want to be held? All right, come. Yes. See, now? Conrad knows when he is safe."

It was like that now in the office—touching, flirting, taking risks. The door was always locked, and long noses who expressed suspicion were immediately listed to be drafted for the all-devouring hunger of the war that could not be won. It was Conrad's idea; he nurtured an intense hatred of what he called "privacy stealers." He told Rolf, "This is my war, and I will be as ice cold as any of them."

Twelve perfect German males, Himmler rhapsodized. The occult number twelve, at the astrological concurrence of race and destiny, must yield communication with the purest Germanic past. Through the heroes of today, National Socialism would convene with the long dead Order of the Teutonic Knights! This particular reverie so captivated Himmler that he missed lunch.

Adhering to an arcane Nordic number system, the men were selected in pairs at age twenty, twenty-three, twenty-seven, thirty-two, and thirty-eight. All were fair of complexion, with eyes gray, green, or blue and hair from haystack yellow to fawn brown. In a laboratory, the elect were stripped to be examined and summarized by doctors with pickpocket fingers. The metal spider measures the skull, something like a wrench considers the dick, and other protocols detail size of hands, shape of ears, spiking of nipples, coloring of lips. Vermillion. Rose. Scarlet. The doctors skritch for reactions, discover a pinprick navel with conspiratorial delight, shameless as S.S. guards stand immobile and unseeing.

Outside, the doctors direct the subjects to run laps around a courtyard, then examine skin, perspiration, breathing cycles. They revive the excitement on Capri during the retirement of Tiberius, details of whose escapades had to be suppressed in the chronicles. But then, it is worth remarking that National Socialism harnesses modern technology to the most primitive beliefs, and Operation Froh will isolate twelve perfect males of German blood to chop off their heads and converse through their bared souls to the heroic past by light of moon god.

The previous night's bombing has destroyed parts of the lab housing, and the subjects' dressing room is no more than a bit of hall with an S.S. guard and a curtain hung on a cord. Awaiting his own examination, Gunnlaug was listening to the doctors at their exercise.

"An angel!" one cried. "It cannot be disputed," another agreed.

Peering over the curtain, Gunnlaug watched the doctors performing a quadrille around a naked youth.

"Sit down, Captain," the S.S. guard told Gunnlaug.

Turning, Gunnlaug said, "It must be frustrating, maintaining your command while hermaphrodites sneak blowjobs off decent German lads."

The guard took out his revolver and aimed it at Gunnlaug. "Sit down, Captain," he repeated.

Gunnlaug sat.

After a bit, he said, "Do you feel good pimping for those—"

"Be silent, Captain."

When Gunnlaug's name was called, he joined the doctors, carefully looking over the lab for something he might use in an emergency. He had to remind himself that his part in the uprising was more crucial than whatever occurred in here.

"Thirty-eight years old and unmarried?" said one doctor. "Most irregular."

Before Gunnlaug answered, the air-raid siren went off, and everyone took shelter. By the all-clear, it was agreed to postpone till tomorrow. Gunnlaug was dismissed, the doctors thrilling at the prospect of unwrapping that splendid package.

Pfuikeck went shoplifting in a café on the Ku'damm, under the merry blanket of camouflage netting, to confuse the bombers. He sat with strangers to pour out a sad tale: a U-Boat without papers or hope. He couldn't even wash.

People just got up and left him. One woman screamed for the police to come arrest the Jew, and it seemed as if the entire place would attack Pfuikeck physically till his Gestapo team broke in and took him away. As they left, many threw their right arm up shouting, "Heil Hitler!" to the photograph on the wall. "Juden raus!" cried some. Jews out! Then: "Führer, befehl, wir folgen!"

Führer, command: we follow!

Nazi Europe contracted as Nazi murder intensified: manpower essential to defense was diverted to the extermination of designated enemies of the state, and Hitler dreamed of a miracle weapon with which to destroy London while sending physicists to the front lines. More were killed in the final year of the war than its its first five together; and when Stalin's army reached the German marches it was told, "Only the unborn are innocent." Yet Stalin's double gave it no thought. Swallowing a third cherry tart as another of hellish gas attack shook the dinner table, Hitler reminded himself that he was the man of surprise, an established historical fact.

Everyone knew that the generals were planning an uprising, and there was no attempt to prevent the coup. Himmler and Göring needed Hitler dead so they could make a deal with the democracies and halt the Russians at the Vistula.

"Emil made us in his image," Halder marveled. "We *are* Hitler ... and we *kill* Hitler.'

"I was never Hitler," von Stauffenberg replied.

His wife asked him, "But what is he like? Those famous Führer eyes—they fix you? Inflame you?"

"They bobble like those of a cocaine addict," von Stauffenberg told her. "He rages for hours, then goes to dreamland. They're savage eyes and sleeping eyes at once. They're eyes of nothing, of a fake. And who didn't think so, all along the way? We knew what he was, all of us. But no one wants to stand up to the aggressor. It's so exhausting. So, in the end, the bombing and death and the national dishonor that we will never outlast—all this was for a crackpot vagabond desperate for flattery."

Von Stauffenberg had only five minutes with Gunnlaug on a bench in the Tiergarten, hiding in plain sight.

"Put your men on alert," said von Stauffenberg, the man who defies. "The performance is set for July 20."

"Will we be cheering for the trinity as well?" Goebbels, Göring, Himmler.

"No. It is the comedian only."

"Too bad," said Gunnlaug.

Von Stauffenberg let out a grunt of a laugh. "No," he said, "we have plans for Goblin, Fat, and Loon."

Lichtspiel.

The drama of light and darkness, of earth and fire: Berlin in bombs. Norns play roulette and Europe loses. Der Alte Herr, beyond physical harm, strolls out during a raid, watching luminous droplets of conflagration rain down. Buildings faint with a scream or flow into the street like lava; others reject surrender, true National Socialist edifices.

Yes, civilization, the moral world: and I was once the busiest man in it. Now I am magic on the scene. I save U-Boats from the Gestapo with comic distractions. It has a spiritual aspect. And now that the Screamer isn't giving his speeches on the air, the loudspeakers are silent and one can cross the Platz in peace—perhaps to have a second look at a captivating Mamzelle. All the poets do so. Petrarch. Dante. Fritz Schiller dogged the tracks of anything in skirts. And Herder? Don't ask. At least I put mine to work. Does anyone know that Marianne Jung wrote some of my *West-östliche Divan*? The cutest rhymes, too.

Through the fantastical rumble, the searchlights rear up at the sky like maddened workers protecting the hive. *Zuuusch!* And there goes that façade. My family home's in Frankfort went down—on my death day, too: March 22. Tant pis. But fitting, no?

Yes, Marianne. I've had luck with the ladies. What security that gives a man!—freeing him from the morbid fear of imaginary enemies, when the Hated Son becomes his own Hating Father. It is the theme of the double.

Rolf and Conrad were waiting it out in a shelter when Conrad noticed someone staring at them, an old blame of a thing in shaggy dress.

"Don't look," Conrad told Rolf, "but a man over by the corner is watching us."

Rolf looked.

"He has a theatrical air," said Rolf. "Let's ignore him and maybe he'll ..." Smiling: "I'd give anything to touch you just now."

"I wish I could fold myself up inside someone like you," Conrad whispered. "You'd make all my decisions for me."

Rolf made a Blick. Then: "Hitler got started that way. The whole country moved in."

"The man who was staring has gone."

"In the middle of a raid?"

In fact, Pfuikeck hid and then tailed the two in the Gestapo men's car, and when Rolf dropped Conrad at his apartment building, Pfuikeck noted the address. The Gestapo wanted U-Boat Jews, but it wouldn't be disappointed with a homosexual.

Another sort of Jewcatcher was at work in Hungary: a Swede named Raoul Wallenberg had been authorized by his government to travel into the heart of Nazi Europe to assign Swedish visas to Jews to save them from extermination. Even the relentless Adolf Eichmann allowed himself to be confounded by the diplomatic turnaround, perhaps because Nazi war power depended on the steady supply of Swedish iron ore.

Wallenberg far exceeded his official quota for these safe-conducts, and he was able to cancel the machine-gunning of seventy thousand Budapest Jews by promising the S.S. general in charge that he, Wallenberg, would be the star witness against him in tribunal at the war's end if he went ahead with the action.

Cristel Pack's Sundays were devoted to the Request Concert radio show. All the Reich listened: to popular music, messages from soldiers at the front, replies from home, and request numbers. Private Rudolf Boelke asks for the Heinz Rühmann tune "I Break the Heart of the Coldest of Fraus," the first song that Rudolf and his sweetheart Ulla heard after she accepted his marriage proposal. "And Ulla never misses a broadcast, so here is our comedian himself, Heinz Rühmann ..."

"It is so sweet," Cristel would murmur at these announcements. "Of course we will win. After all the perverted history created by Jews and Popes, at last everyone is fighting the right war."

Casualty lists are sometimes read, and Cristel's son is cited as missing in action. She goes out into the hallway to see what's doing, and her neighbor Frau Seeringer rushes out to sympathize.

"My dear Frau Pack! I just heard!"

"It is an honor to give to the Fatherland. I am blessed."

"Oh. Yes. Yes, of course." Frau Seeringer is taken aback—but what did she expect from this mountainous fury?

Kai comes up the stairs, and unlike Frau Seeringer he has adapted to the perils of life in Hitler's Germany. He speaks only to those he trusts, and he is alert for warning signs. At the sight of Cristel, he reaches for the revolver, looking right at her. Take one step toward me, I dare you, evil dogcunt.

Cristel stays put, humming and swaying a bit. It is Frau Seeringer who presses forward with "Oh, Herr von Kleist! See how our dear neighbor has suffered the most grievous—"

Kai has slammed his door closed, leaving the confused Frau Seeringer to converse with Cristel, still trying to sympathize with a woman who doesn't know what sympathy is.

Finally, "Oh look, here's another one!" says Cristel, as Gunnlaug, in black S.S. uniform, comes pounding up the stairs. "Our soldier of the Reich, honor-bound to Führerblood. Ja, my boy?" Gunnlaug, keyed his way in and slammed the door behind him.

Inside, he said, "I am in a race now more than ever, so do not reply. Just *listen to my words*. If you fall under suspicion and undergo interrogation, you are to look right into their eyes and say 'Code Answer.' Those two words and no others. You will tell this to Conrad and—no, you *will not argue*! As always with me! What is this need to open your stupid mouth and haggle with my advice? *Now* do you hear? You will listen now?"

Kai was angry but silent.

"Code Answer. *Say it.*"

Kai said it. Angrily.

"There is more. A man is lurking around this building. Something looks wrong about him, I am sure of it. So I slide into a recess in the building opposite, and what do I see? Two Gestapo!"

"How do you know they are—"

"My own brother, *do you not know me yet?* The clothes, the hat, the way they stand, even how they smoke."

Kai threw his arms around Gunnlaug, saying, "I hate you, you should know this."

"Oh, I know this," holding him so tightly Kai feared it was conclusive.

"Where do you go next?" Kai asked. "Who are you this time?"

"Mein Name ist Meister des vollkommenen Wortes." I am the Master of the Final Truth.

Kai snuffled.

"Yes, yes, no wonder you hate me," Gunnlaug told him, stroking his hair.

When they broke apart, Gunnlaug rehearsed Kai in Code Answer, made him promise to remember to tell Conrad of it, and left. Outside, he approached the menace he had spotted earlier: Pfuikeck, lying in wait for Conrad. Gunnlaug lured Pfuikeck inside on a pretext, grbbed him by the hair, and forced the snout of his revolver into Pfuikeck's mouth.

"One noise, please, and you are dead," said Gunnlaug.

He waited, watching Pfuikeck for obedience.

"Yes. Now. I want you away from this building forever. If I see you here again, I will kill you."

Taking the pistol out of Pfuikeck's mouth, Gunnlaug bombed it into his front teeth and stifled the ensuing scream of pain by shoving the firearm back inside and upward, forcing Pfuikeck onto his toes, wheezing out tiny eeks.

"Do I have your attention?" Gunnlaug asked. "Nod."

Awash in sweat and agony, Pfuikeck nodded.

"Tell your comrades you had a fall. It is a good laugh for them, I guess. Your last warning, now: Do not return to this neighborhood unless you want to die."

Pfuikeck hurt so badly that he helplessly let out shrill moans as Gunnlaug stormed off like War Father, all powerful but very irritated.

"Let's run away, Conrad," said Rolf. "I have a sister in Stuttgart, she'd take us in." Rolf twirled a pencil. "Have you heard the Herbert Selpin story? It was another of Dr. Mabuse's pet projects, *Titanic*. Imagine: *Grand Hotel* on a boat, with calamity finale. The British are scoundrels, the Germans quietly stalwart. Herr Doktor Selpin is our director, a hero. He isn't afraid of the shrieking Brown idiot running the second unit but whose true job is driving everyone insane with fanaticism and incompetence. Selpin finally rips into him, Dr. Mabuse orders Selpin to recant. Selpin: 'Never!' Dr. Mabuse: 'Then it's Nazi justice for you!' So they throw Selpin into prison and two Browns come in and string him up. Headline: 'HERBERT SELPIN COMMITS SUICIDE IN PRISON.'"

Conrad knew the tale already, as Rolf well knew. It wasn't information, but a statement of the first theme. Now Rolf put down the pencil, reached into his jacket, and pulled out a long, thinnish black object, and tossed it onto his desktop. Instantly, a knife blade flashed out of one end.

"Yes, it seems these two noble S.S. men set Selpin on a stool and tied his suspenders around his neck and then to bars across a window high up in his cell. Selpin grabbed hold of the bars, so when they kicked the stool away, he didn't drop. They said, 'Fine—see how long you can roost up there, like a chicken in the coop.' Of course, Selpin must give up eventually. And now everyone on the set cuts the Nazi who started it all. They cut him dead. Dr. Mabuse: 'You talk to him or you'll talk to Selpin in hell!' And now he bans the film, after all! Because the panic during the sinking will remind the audience of bombing raids!"

Rolf put his finger on the knife at the handle and spun the thing around.

"American," he said. This was the second theme. "Black market special, and it's called a jazzknife. Will you come away with me, Conrad?"

"Have you been drinking?" Conrad asked.

Rolf sighed like Zarah Leander in the last reel, when they must part, my darling. "Why is it that, whenever one is simply being very direct, everyone thinks he is drunk?"

"I can't run away. I have to be loyal to my friend."

Rolf nodded. "All the best people have that line, where they make a stand. Loyalty ... honor ... I have no such line, and yes, I have been drinking." A surprising new theme in the development section: "I could cut your throat with my jazzknife, and who would care? Just one more German murder out of how many millions? Would Herbert Selpin care? I could love you, or I could kill you and say your aunt Anneliese did it. I could say you did it, as the Führer does. The English made the war. Liechtenstein made the war." His voice soured in a groan of exhaustion: "The Jews made the war!"

Rolf jumped up.

"Let's kill someone, young Conrad. Whom shall we ... Dr. Mabuse? Come, try the knife. First, let me close it up. Careful with this monster, now."

Conrad picked it up.

"Hold it away from you. Your hand well back on the ... Right. Now hold tight, don't change your grip, and press the little button."

The blade leaped free so suddenly that Conrad dropped the knife.

"A fine assassin you'd make," said Rolf, retrieving the knife. "Better leave it to me." He smiled tensely for the recapitulation. "Yes, loyalty. What to do when the new god dies? We're all mad with war exhaustion. Loyalty is all that's left us."

The two stood looking at each other till Conrad came up to Rolf and rested his head against him. They moved slightly now and again, eventually holding each other, shifting their grip, wordlessly saying goodbye.

The Devil had little to do in shielding Hitler from the assassination, on July 20, 1944. First, the strategy conference at which von Stauffenberg was to plant his two bombs was moved from a cement bunker to a wooden structure. Concrete would have congested the blast to a dense frenzy; wood simply blew apart to let much of the blast force escape.

Then restless Sergeant-Major Werner Vogel got curious while von Stauffenberg and his aide, Lieutenant Werner von Haeften, were promoting the fuses of the bombs. So they were able to ready only one of the two for detonation.

Even so, Hitler would have been dead but for Colonel Heinz Brandt. Von Stauffenberg's loaded briefcase blocked Brandt's access to the map, so he shoved the case deeper under the table, inadvertently protecting Hitler from the primary impact.

Heading to their car for their airlift to Berlin and the anti-Nazi revolution, von Stauffenberg and von Haeften heard the explosion and thought they had pulled it off. "So nimm mein Segen, Nibelungen-Sohn," von Stauffenberg muttered. Take thus my blessing, spawn of hell. And some in the hut did die: but not Hitler.

There was confusion from Vienna to Paris that day, as some of the uprising sprang into action, others issued discreetly ambiguous orders, and still others did nothing. By midnight, the coup was aborted. Von Stauffenberg was shot in the courtyard of army headquarters on the Bendlerstrasse. Von Haeften threw himself in front of his Siegfried to die first, as von Stauffenberg cried, "Long live holy Germany!"

Gunnlaug leaped into the Baroness' bedroom through her great window, long emptied of its glass in an air raid. He said, "I come by rooftop to tell you that we have failed, and you and I will have to reunite in Zürich after all."

He was moving to her, but he did not break his knees and weep for shattered ideals. They did not even touch.

"My maid," she said, "has decided to return to her people in the Spreewald. It is something of a magical place, it seems, where the Browns never go. It might be interesting for us as well."

"That would put too many in danger. I shall leave a twisted track for them and find my own secret exit. Once the torture sessions begin they'll get so many names that I might easily swim around the net. I am Odysseus this week, a man of wiles."

He smiled.

"I ask you to protect my brother, so innocent of involvement. And his friend. You could pack a car and charm your way through the stop points. Then you disappear into the water forest."

"Not possibly, my sweet. This isn't a movie—the Browns will shoot at sight."

"You can do anything, and we both know it. Or why did we ... how did it happen? If you love me, save my brother."

He took her into his power then, out of time and reason, as if he knew he could never get enough of her in a thousand years. Her love of flight urged him to soar ever higher to defeat the controllers of totem and jujufear. He has been creative with her in the past, but this is classic union, elemental to leave her reinvented with his slick magic. Then soft opera, ending serenely on the tonic chord.

"Ah yes," she said, after. "He towels himself, dresses, goes."

At the window, watching the street, he told her, "Du weisst—wo du mich wiederfinden kannst!" You know where we are to meet again!

"What a fadeout," she answered: he had gone.

So distended and immiscible were the parts of Hitler's government that Operation Froh went on as scheduled that same night, astrally favorable to the resuscitation of departed spirits. Drugged comatose, the twelve young heroes, including a susbstitution for Gunnlaug, were beheaded in the main hall of Wewelsburg Castle, their skulls then set up in swastika formation as Himmler's minions fussed about.

Quicksilver night looked in through open windows as ancient instruments were sounded. The stronghold on the hill, hidden in the pure Nordic night, the blood flags waving, and now: the transcendance of death across the centuries. Speak, Ottokar! Magnus! Germold the Bear!

And speak they did. One started quoting Heine, another told an interminable joke in Yiddish ("The Pope, the Dalai Lama, and the Rabbi of Kamyenets-Podolsk visited a nudist colony ..."), and other heads let off Bolshevik slogans of the Weimar years. The living fell back in fear, but one S.S. officer drew his sidearm and started shooting, whereupon all twelve heads broke into the hit tune from *The Threepenny Opera*:

And the shark, he shows his choppers ...

It was pandemonium in Wewelsburg; the Devil danced all night.

Cristel Pack was also up late; hearing the Führer speak always stimulated her beyond sleep. She kept her front door open, to rush into the hall and share her elation with neighbors. Did you hear? Our Führer has been saved from a clique of defeatist traitors! This proves that his work is divinely protected!

Frau Seeringer found Cristel thus, to share important news: Cristel's son, announced as missing in action, was in fact a prisoner of war in Canada!

Yes. Frau Seeringer just heard his name in a list read out on the radio!

"But that would have been the BBC," Cristel told her. "Listening to foreign networks is a capital crime. Don't you see that it cannot be done?"

Had Cristel not heard? Her son is alive!

"This is a violation of your membership in the national community," said the exasperated Cristel Pack. "I will turn you in and they will take off your head. Oh—wait as I check the oven. My sugarless cookies, such sweetness in this time of severe rationing."

Bewildered by this inexplicable reply, Frau Seeringer started to follow Cristel, but turned to Kai and Conrad as they came up the stairs.

"Oh, sirs! I just now ... I tried to ..."

"What is wrong?" said Kai.

She told them. They could smell the baking through Cristel's open door as they heard.

"Or is it a curious joke?" Frau Seeringer wondered.

"That is no joke from this woman," said Kai.

Cristel returned with "Who wants to come with me to the Gestapo, ja?"

"Why are you so evil?" Conrad asked.

Cristel loves that question. "It is how I can tell I am alive."

She started to move; Conrad cried, "Kai!," but he was too late. Cristel whacked Kai in the face with a frying pan and he staggered backward.

"Handsome sir," Cristel giggled out.

"She is mad!" Frau Seeringer cried.

"Go inside!" Conrad shouted at her, rushing up to disarm Cristel as Frau Seeringer, far from leaving, went up to Kai to help him. Struggling to recover his wits, Kai touched his face and his fingers came back bloody; he held them out to show Frau Seeringer in disbelief. Wrestling for the pan with Cristel, Conrad was amazed at her power. Yes, she was huge—but wasn't she a woman? She kept trying to kick at his genitals, but Conrad finally got hold of the pan firmly enough to smack her with it just above the eyes. Now she, too, stumbled backward; Conrad pursued her into her apartment, banging the metal on her till she toppled over in her kitchen of sugarless cookies.

Kai came in then, everyone panting and Cristel lying on the floor, looking up at them with surprise and delight. There would be more from her.

"I am not hurt, Conrad," said Kai. "That lady wanted to call a doctor, but I made her leave. She has a ... She has people to stay with."

The two comrades regarded Cristel and her hating grin. Kai pushed her cookie sheets off the table, scattering Backwaren all over the floor. "Hoppla!" he added, wiping his face with one of Cristel's cloth napkins.

"You both tuned into the BBC with Frau Seeringer," Cristel got out. "It will all be in my report. This attack on me is like the attack on the Führer. We are Germania and we never surrender."

Kai kicked at her head not hard half enough. She just laughed.

"*Shut your snout!*" Kai shouted.

"When I get up," Cristel told them, shaking her head at their foolishness, "I will kill you. First the wondrous blond boy. Then his friend." Her great arm reached up, slammed the utensil drawer open, jacked it up off its hinges, and pulled it down at her side in a rain of metal. Her eyes on Kai and Conrad, she found her way to a breadknife and, warding them off with it, got to her feet. "I want to murder those lovely eyes," she told Kai.

"Shit, Kai, what do we—"

"We are two, *we* must win! Arm yourself!"

They already had her cornered, Conrad holding the frying pan and Kai now wielding two knives that he held clutched together for extra tearing power. They stood frozen, all three, as if at the climax of an avant-garde ballet. Then Conrad, shielded by Kai, turned on the oven without lighting it.

"Can you hear it?" he asked Cristel.

"You would gas me like a Jewie?" She swung suddenly with her knife, but the two whacked back at her, Kai slashing her arm and face and Conrad crying, "*Monkey! Wizard! Helen! Witch!*" as if the words were a spell to break up time and sweep the innocent away. Cristel chuckled. Now Conrad protected Kai as he pulled open a cupboard door and threw at Cristel everything he could grab up. She turned away defensively, giving Conrad an opening: he hit her knife hand with the pan so forcefully that the knife flew across the room, and Kai lunged at her with a potato peeler. He ran it deeply into her face, getting a scream out of her, and now he and Conrad hit her with everything they had till she failed and sagged to the floor. Taking her under the arms, they dragged her along the floor to the gas.

Yet she was not unconscious; she found something on the floor as they pulled her along and stabbed at them with it. It was a fruit knife, a small one, and they dropped her and whacked away at her until she lost hold of the knife. Kicking away every other potential weapon, they pulled her the last few inches to the open oven and stuffed the top half of her into it, exhausted but invigorated by their hatred of this latest of Europe's periodic Inquisitions.

"*Explode now!*" Kai shouted. "*Explode, you witch!*"

This is when Conrad noticed the deep red stain on Kai's shirt.

"*Kai!*"

Then Kai saw it. "She must have got me at the end of it. It is only …"

"*No!*" Conrad shouted, as Kai started to keel over. He fainted even as Conrad caught him. But now the Baroness was with them, opening Kai's shirt to examine the wound, signalling to servants hovering in the doorway, arranging the flight to safety.

"There is no time for anything," she told Conrad, cleaning her hands at the sink. "We are leaving directly." Duscha brought a travel bag to the Baroness, stepping over Cristel's legs with scarcely a look at her.

Fishing a medical kit from the bag, the Baroness bade Conrad turn off the gas.

"I know the von Kleists dislike outsiders," she said, dryly. "But there are limits."

"Is he ..."

"Hush," she said, unwinding a spool of gauze.

Pfuikeck was ready to pack it in. He had been thinking for a while that he might give National Socialism the slip and turn U-Boat himself. The area around the Alexanderplatz was ideal for a breakaway; Pfuikeck knew every alley and courtyard thereabouts.

One night, he told his keepers that he had a mark, and, with their eyes off him, he fled into the heavy weather of a raid, running up Keibelstrasse to the next shelter with his papers ready to show, thence to the next shelter, on and on till the all clear. He was on Linienstrasse, not far from his old cabaret, and as he walked past it he made out the unmistakable sounds of a performance. Reading the hoardings, he figured out that it was the dress rehearsal of the new Künneke piece, *Petra Plays the Bagpipes*. So it was going on, after all—the last Nazi musical!

How long has it been since I've been in a theatre, Pfuikeck wondered as he crept inside. The first act was barely underway, it seemed, judging by trifles of plot being tossed about, as the heroine gradually undertook to travel the world in search of a set of bagpipes without which she cannot be married. Künneke gave her an amusing ensemble number with corrupt Hollywood folk who try to wed her to a cinema princeling, but her faithful boy friend, still at home, sang a tender waiting song as the seasons passed. Petra's father had a major role as well, her severest critic in private but loyal in finalettos.

Pfuikeck marveled at the colorful staging, but the action had no character. Where were the zany jests, the love of life? At least there was a production number built around the bagpipes, a vivacious galop:

> Who is the bagpiper?
> Who? Who? Who?
> Heinz and Hans and Gans and Gert
> And also WonderBert!

Pfuikeck had to admit, it was enchanting, inviting. One could hardly resist joining in—and what would be the harm, I ask you, at the last musical? It's the last everything by now. Why not seize the radio stations, conduct our own Strauss, rush every stage? It's my theatre—I ruled here once! Do they see me coming and make way for my mincing and gaping *if that's all that's left me* and which one's WonderBert *bombs away outside* while I'm dancing around up here in *Hitler's new best friend* the only part they left me with my finger held to the nose and cancan around the rapidly emptying stage till *defile the glorious myths of Europe* they call the *hate what you love if it doesn't love you* magic theatre police and cheer my turn:

> Who is the Jewcatcher?
> Who? Who? Who?
> Hitler's asshole's Judenfrei.
> Dui-dui-du!

The music had stopped; what cheek! Or is it just a rush for the shelter? The orchestra conductor was the last of the company in Pfuikeck's line of vision, staring up at him with a look of almost comprehending sympathy. But he, too, departed, and by then the bomb blasts were so loud Pfuikeck couldn't hear the uniforms crashing into the theatre. But he saw them, took off with a mischievous *Tsching-bum!*, and dove into the basement. A passageway connected with the theatre lobby, but there was bound to be a guard. It was the prop room that Pfuikeck was headed for; he recalled a mummy case standing in a dark corner—yes, there, as if waiting for him. The door was stuck and wanted forcing, and, from inside, Pfuikeck could hear the soldiers thumping through the place, the furious joy of their calls to him to give up and face the penalty.

Die Frist ist um, Pfuikeck thought. My term of employment is over. Odd what a relief it is, like getting fired from a troupe that gives nothing but Hauptmann and Tieck. But *here's* luck: a direct hit on the building next door set the theatre on fire. Waiting as long as he dared, Pfuikeck ventured out of his mummy box, sneaked upstairs, and had a look through the glass in the stage door. Flames behind him, nothing in front. He edged out onto the street and ran off.

The Baroness' sedan, using up the very last of her fuel allotment, was proceeding southeasterly toward the Spreewald, with Duscha, Kai and Conrad, the Baroness, and her driver, Hugo. Everyone's papers were in order for the checkpoints, even Hugo's. He was so plagued with war wounds that the Army didn't want him any more and he wasn't even good for factory work.

Hugo drove them along the main roads; on the back ways one already looked guilty. Conrad had concocted a story for them, and all went well under the antagonistic scrutiny known by now to all Germans.

"Do you know where my brother is?" Kai kept asking; and "How will he know what happened to us?" and "What was the last thing he said?" Then, finally: "Did you leave word for him about where we are?"

"It is dangerous to leave word in Germany today," the Baroness told him. "The war will soon be over, and we'll all have tea in Switzerland." Riding along in the darkness, as Duscha and Hugo, up front, traded the odd glance. He, too, was from the Spreewald. Duscha had got him the job.

"Switzerland?" said Kai.

"Zürich. The Grand Hotel." Sensing Kai's mounting despair while fighting her own, she added, "Vergiss nicht, dass Überall eine Vorsehung herrscht." Don't forget, Providence is still in charge.

"Truly?" Kai cried out. "You think there is God somewhere?"

"We are all going to God, sir," said Duscha.

"What God is this, I wonder?"

The Baroness said, "An incompetent one, it would appear."

"Kai!" cried Conrad. "You're bleeding again! You mustn't move about so!"

Kai let out an "Ei!" of complaint, but at least he was still.

It was quite some time—and one hair-raising check stop that provoked a phone call to Berlin from the commanding officer—before the Baroness' car reached the edge of the Spreewald. Conferring with Duscha, Hugo drove them through a maze of deserted rustic lanes. To the Baroness' anxious questions, Duscha replied, "The way in is not simple, gnä' Frau. This place is sanctuary, and must be protected."

"No doubt, but from what?"

"Doubt," Kai put in. "Contradictions. Ambivalent feelings."

"Hugo," said the Baroness, "how on earth do you know where you're going? Where are the signs?"

Duscha answered. "Signs are provocations," she said, getting out of the car.

In what was now the hazy darkness of early morning, Duscha went up to a harmless-looking brook and began to whistle. Was she raising a question, asking after the state of the place? All that the party could see, out of the car windows, was a solid treeline across the water. This is what the world looked like before the arrival of men, cabarets, institutes. No information: affection. No arguments: tolerance. No progress: innocence.

"What *is* the girl doing?" the Baroness asked.

"Whistling, my lady."

Then it seemed as if a way had appeared, or perhaps the growing light of dawn now enabled everyone to see a path curving through the woods. A small boat—a kayak, perhaps, but quite high in the stern—glided toward them out of the foggy nowhere, and the brook was now clearly established as a reasonably dense canal.

"I suppose we shall have to leave the car here," the Baroness grumbled, climbing out as Hugo held the door for her, visored cap in hand. "Who would run a car in *Grimm's Fairy Tales*?"

At a meeting of officials, Himmler said, "Die Familie Graf von Stauffenberg wird ausgelöscht bis ins letze Glied." Von Stauffenberg's family will be exterminated to the fetus in the womb.

Sippenhaft. Hitler's real goal was to use reprisals as a cover under which to kill off potential laders of the postwar Germany that would survive him. Some five thousand former members of the Weimar government were arrested, though in the end the uprising of July 20 resulted in no more than a few hundred executions, some as late as in the last weeks of the war. The subjects were among Germany's best men, and not one of them broke under torture. Some of them were hanged before whirring UFA cameras, their trousers pulled down to expose the erections typically engendered when the spinal cord is broken.

At the same time, the Americans and English were well on their way to Paris and the Russians had reached the east bank of the Vistula River, little more than ten kilometres from Warsaw. Poland now sought to shake off the Nazis with a revolt in the capital. The German response was savage, incinerating the wounded, commandeering children as human shields, and ending with a Warsaw that was all but Polenfrei. The city was bombed to the ground and, for a time, ceased to exist. Through all this, the Red Army held ground and watched. Stalin liked Poles even less than Hitler did.

The Spreewald is a labyrinth; Conrad got lost whenever he left the island that he and Kai had been settled on. When he complained to Duscha, she said there was no reason to get lost—as if one got lost for reasons. "The paths are straight, Herr Thomamüller," she said.

Not that there was any purpose in touring. There were fiddles, Bibles, and rumors, but otherwise no music, no reading, no news of where. Conrad thought the people looked like Marika Rökk's last operetta. But Duscha blended back in as if she had never left, looking up a boy she had once walked out with. His family were healers, deft with herbs; an aunt went to work on Kai's wound and he did seem to feel better, though the break in the skin refused to close.

It seemed to Conrad that they were all miles from each other on these crazy islands—yet children could collect them and, shortcutting through forest and skipping over footbridges, reunite them in minutes.

"I hope you realize we're all murder suspects," Conrad told the rest of the party on their first informal meeting together.

"If this has to do with that beast with her head in the oven," said the Baroness, "the authorities are completely distracted with the attempted regicide."

"They cannot come here in any case, sir," said Duscha. "They used to try to, but they have given up."

"They have boats, don't they?" Conrad answered.

"They do not know the signals," Duscha quietly insisted. "The barriers will not part for them"

"Duscha was raised here," the Baroness told Conrad. "She must know." Through her worry over the fate of Gunnlaug, she felt a twinge of pleasure in admiring Duscha: the prim little pretty so starched up about her wonderland.

"Who is in charge here, more God?" Kai cried out. His wound was flaring up. "I suppose He controls what happens!"

"God does not control, Herr von Kleist," said Duscha, as Conrad tried to soothe the bristling Kai. "God only redeems."

"The breakfasts are good," Hugo pointed out. "Our fine sweet juices, real eggs, and potato kartoshka."

"A local specialty, you see," said Duscha. "The recipe is older than any museum or theatre in Berlin."

"Duscha," said the Baroness, "you are quite a surprise."

Conrad felt guilty about Rolf, and Kai felt guilty about Gunnlaug. Kai could also have felt guilty about the family business; its biggest factory took a direct hit in a raid, and decisions had to be made about reconstituting production. But Kai did not care about the business any more.

"The enemy will take it soon enough," he said. "I never cared for it in any case. It was simply a chance for me to dress up and be respected like my brother."

"Don't get sulky," Conrad warned him. "It makes your wound bleed."

"Ei, stop fussing with me, I am fine enough!" Nevertheless, Kai let Conrad bed him down in the autumn air of a needling north wind.

"I should not have given up my piano," said Kai, closing his eyes to rest.

Both he and Conrad were restless in this place. They wanted art, not the spirit: what one creates, not what one is; and they would not stretch forth their hand.

January 30, 1945 was Goebbels' big day. After nineteen months in production and an expenditure of over eight million Reichsmarks, *Kolberg* was enjoying its premiere. Nothing less than the UFA-Palast am Zoo was suitable, but that theatre was now rubble in a crater. The Tauentzien-Palast stood in.

More important, Goebbels had persuaded the Führer to make a rare radio address that same evening, the perfect response to gloomy war news. The Russians had reached the Oder, only eighty kilometres east of Berlin; the Ardennes offensive, Hitler's last hope on the Western front, to discourage the democracies and shatter their bond with the Bolsheviks, had failed. But a rousing war cry from the national deity would underscore *Kolberg*'s theme: a fight to the death. Führer, befehl, wir folgen!

And how avid he is, Rolf Kümplers thought, watching Goebbels greeting the notables he had managed to lure out between the air raids. The little goblin grins and waves as if we were back at the Olympics and nothing has happened yet. He holds himself straight as a bayonet, out of fear that if he relaxed his guard for even a moment or two, he might freak and caper about like Füsli the Puppet.

Rolf sits just behind Goebbels' place, in the front of the balcony. First row was once the haunt of the Bonzen, but after July 20 there are security problems. Goebbels scoffs at these as a matter of policy; everyone else is hiding.

As Goebbels takes his place, Rolf leans forward and says, "Kolberg! What an inspiration! Even if I'd prefer Tanzgirls in a Naktballet."

Startled, Goebbels swivels around. "Oh, Kümplers. Always a prank."

The lights were going down. Rolf carefully took out his jazzknife, but just then the dimming paused and began to stutter—an electrical jumble, common in Berlin these days. That was when Rolf became aware of an S.S. officer a few seats down and across the aisle. He was very young, probably one of the volunteers from the Netherlands or France who enlisted to avoid being picked up for slavery in war production.

Something odd about this officer: he was looking at Rolf and smiling, nodding, almost ... as if he had figured out what Rolf was going to do and wanted him to do it so the S.S. could move in with its tense justice. Give violence to my cause! this Brown lout begged. He was tribe this-side-of-river discovering that there was a tribe that-side-of-river, a cleric confronted by a painting, a reeve hearing rumors of poisoned wells. He'll swing the ax for you with *chop!* and *chop!* and scream as I *chop!* with feast of *chop!* you like it *chop!* you yes? Yes?

Is he disappointed when I settle back in the sudden darkness? But it would be useless now. A stunt. If it were as simple as cutting a throat with a jazzknife, there never would have been a tyrant, anywhere, ever.

Hitler's medical men were quacks, and their injections kept his failing body alive as a spicy marinade exhilarates rotten beef. For entertainment, the dozy Führer doted upon his scale model of the great city of the future: Linz!

The Austrian town, near enough to Hitler's birthplace to be hailed as Führer-sacred, was to be a Mecca of the thousand-year Reich: a place of the prophet. Even when the European war reached its final month or so and Hitler and his suite lived in a bunker far below the Chancellery complex, Hitler would slip upstairs to gaze upon his Linz.

"See," he tells himself. "The Opera, to rival Bayreuth in Wagner productions. But no *Parsifal*—it stinks of church incense."

"I knew I'd find you here," says the Devil.

Now Hitler has someone to announce at. "You admire this town, this Linz. A German town. Skyscrapers, archives of the Reich, parks on the grandest scale imaginable are to be the wonder of Linz. What, *Vienna*? Is that what I hear?"

A rhetorical pause.

"A polyglot chowder of a city, Vienna! A genetic cesspool! Where gabbling Hungars and Turks book invasions of nigger shimmy dancers and jazz pugilists! And always, always at the heart of it all ..."

He has been doing well, but without injections and victories the energy runs down.

"I am the enemy of the conniving Jew," he croaks out.

"You're the enemy of the human race, actually. It's all I can say in your favor."

Martin Bormann, Hitler's secretary, appears in the doorway.

"Mein Führer," he says, "you must come down now." He speaks without inflection, just above boredom. "They are serving dinner."

Without waiting for Hitler to move, Bormann takes hold and force-marches him into the bunker.

"And it's enough of your ridiculous Linz for today, I think," Bormann adds, as they tramp down to the dirty basement of Berlin.

One morning, Conrad returned to the cottage he shared with Kai to find Duscha and the Baroness watching a beldam making mysterious passes over Kai, asleep in bed. The Baroness put a warning finger to her lips, but Conrad didn't like this picture. The old woman was rubbing leaves on Kai's wound, exposing him to the winter cold. Worse, Kai should surely have awakened, yet he was unconscious.

"What's going on here?" Conrad loudly asked.

"Hush," said the Baroness, and Duscha shook her head at him.

"Kai!" he cried.

"He will rise," said the old Wendish woman, in reasonably good German, tracing circles in the air. "He will rise when the trouble outside is broken."

"Oh, get out of here, you silly old thing!" Conrad bellowed, going to the bed to shake Kai awake.

They left, and Kai's eyes fluttered. He nodded, made room for Conrad to sit with him, and petted Conrad's arm, saying they must always be the best of friends. "But now I must take leave of you and find my brother Gunnlaug."

"Except you are too weak. And either Gunnlaug has been caught or is well hidden. And if the Browns can't find him, how could you?"

"Yes, I feared that you would deny him."

"No, Kai, it is that we are on our own now. Are you afraid? Because I am."

Kai put his arm around Conrad's shoulder. "We are still secret friends, and we have come out well," Kai said. "I am not afraid for myself. I am afraid for my brother."

"He's probably in Switzerland already. It is quite absurdly romantic, like everything your brother does."

Kai was weeping.

"I want to leave this place," he said. "It is so still and empty. As if a god had been here long ago, and his followers are afraid to move in case he should return." He wiped his cheeks. "I am so angry at the stupidity of Europe to have this war. And all because of the anti-Semites! Jews, Jews, they think of nothing else! I ask you, where in our civilization did this come from? You tell me, Conrad, here in this silent forest of furtive movements and unspoken wisdoms. The Greeks could be very cruel to a foe, but they didn't single out a blood group to—"

"Kai, you mustn't move around so!"

"No, I *must* be out of this *bed*! I must walk through the idiotic paradise where it is a big event if someone sneezes."

Kai was struggling into his Wendish overcoat, a woolen cloak with button-and-loop fastenings.

"I'm coming, too, then," said Conrad, with time only to grab a scarf and run after Kai. He was stamping along like someone with everywhere to go and no place to start. Conrad followed him over bridges and along several boat rides till they were absolutely lost.

"Ausgezeichnet!" said Kai, looking about in triumphant defeat. Excellent!

Conrad would have been freezing if the last boatman had not forced his own coat on Conrad. Sharing was Wendish law.

"You'll return it to me in some way," the boatman told him.

"And the Jews," Kai went on, prowling about the terrain, "are as much at fault, because they could have become Christian long ago! Ja, we will trade one stupid religion for another, and this is extinction insurance!"

Kai paced some more, then stopped, looking at Conrad.

"Well?" Kai said. "Is it not so?"

Conrad replied, "I think that if all the Jews had converted and interbred with Christians and vanished into gene pools, we would still be plagued by anti-Semitism. Europe needs it too badly to give it up. It is a periodic purging of progress. Of too much creativity and liberalism.Or, even, yes, of homosexuality. They call it 'Jews' but they really mean 'People are changing my life.'"

About to reply, Kai grew suddenly pale and fell senseless to the ground—a perfect fall, the body limp and the head protected from injury. Even before Conrad called for help, the Wends had come running. When they brought Kai back into the hut, the Baroness was waiting for them, and took charge with cautious optimism. The Wends put Kai into bed and left without a word while the Baroness spread an extra blanket over him.

"He is worried about Gunnlaug," said Conrad.

"Who of us is not? I have given everything I have for him." A rueful smile. "Of course, with the ones who turn life into opera, everything isn't nearly enough."

Amused despite his worry, Conrad said, "'Ill-starred are you, Io, in your lover.'"

"And who says that?"

"Prometheus. Another hero who turns life into opera."

We descend to the underground of Bedlam, smelling of stale rainwater and Hitler's gas attacks: the bunker. Martin Bormann, we know, is there, along with Hitler's Freundin Eva Braun and the Goebbelses and their six children. There are S.S. bodyguards, secretaries, and various messengers and drop-ins. Overhead, the Russian katyushas are breaking the rubble of Berlin into yet more minute rubble. Everyone in a basement is starving; everyone not in a basement is dead.

Order is breaking down even in Hitler's bunker. The S.S. guards laugh at Goebbels, and laugh harder when he bridles. They appear out of uniform, tieless, their braces down. They paint the walls with frescoes of defiance. There is nothing else to do.

One afternoon, Hitler found himself unexpectedly alone in the bunker. But for the humming of the generator, it was silent; the Goebbelses' children must have been napping. Suddenly, a ruckus broke out in the room where the senior Goebbelses put up, a muffled something wedded to passionate kicking on the doors. Opening them, Hitler found Goebbels gagged and bound to a chair, dressed in women's clothing that might have been called "finery" in a gypsy camp. There was even a ratty fox stole on his shoulders.

Goebbels mmphed frantically through his gag till Hitler pulled it off, saying, in mock-wonder, "Goebbels, what does this mean? You look like something out of a Tingel-Tangel revue."

"Get me out of this degenerate get-up! *Oh!* I would gladly murder *many millions* at this moment!"

Behind Hitler, the Devil plays castanets and sambas around with "Ay ay, ay ay, do he nevair be to de tropics!"

"Was it those fun-loving S.S. chaps from the switchboard room?" asks Hitler, holding back a smile as he unfastens the ropes. "They can play the knave at times."

"I don't know *who* it was!" Goebbels frees his legs himelf as the Devil wags his behind, then hits high D behind a black lace fan. "It is an offense to the Reich itself!"

"You know, Goebbels, you might consider a career in the cinema," says Hitler. "Now that Zarah Leander has gone back to Sweden …"

Goebbels lets out a *sss* of rage, throwing off the last of his bonds to jump up and tear the offending costume off, then stomp off.

But now it is time for Hitler's Wedding of the Painted Doll, Eva Braun. The S.S. guards get up a little band, with accordion and violins: *Lohengrin* and "Isle of Capri." The bride is vapidly pretty, the groom in green and yellow, the face a death mask. His doctor's intoxicating philtres can no longer still a helpless shaking of the left arm.

It was all over in a moment, for Martin Bormann was intent on getting the Führer out of Berlin to the south, where a devious construction of caves promised eternal defiance by a small band of the faithful. "Operation Seraglio" they called it.

Goebbels wanted Hitler to stay in Berlin, Goebbels' city, and as the wedding guests trailed out he brought the matter up again to a weary and enervated Hitler. He did not seem like someone who could undertake a trip of any kind—and then one of the S.S. guards came in: the youngest of them, all peach fuzz with an Alsatian lilt in his speech.

"Mein Führer?" he began. "Dr. Haase says you will not fly to the south, and I beg to take this librety ... Mein Führer, you must *please* go to the Alpine redoubt. I request this on behalf of the German people."

With Bormann's beady eye on him, Hitler just looked at the guard.

"Mein Führer, you are ailing, it is clear. From cares of state, and the disloyalty of an ungrateful clique. This, when you yourself have never faltered."

The young man tried to take Hitler's hand; hating touch of any kind, Hitler pulled away. The guard then knelt and extended his own hand. This time, Hitler accepted it.

"It is simple, yes?" said the guard. "One hand on another. But how often the simple act eludes us. We believe that complex problems must have complex solutions.

"It was you who showed how false that is. How many others said, 'We must rid ourselves of the Jews!' and it was no more than a wish. Only you, at last, showed how easy it is to exterminate the Jew for all time. Mein Führer, you have changed the history of the world forever, and that is why the people love you so. Now that it has been started, it will never be stopped. And one day it will be completed. Have you not thus redefined the very meaning of *civilization*?"

Hitler extends his other hand to brush the guard's cheek, but it is his left hand, and it shakes so. Anyway, Bormann breaks in with "Lieutenant, to your post at once!"

Jumping up, the guard insists, "The Führer must go to the Alpine redoubt, sir! He must be taken against his will to—"

"Out of here, damn you! In the Führer's presence without a tie, giving orders ... Go back to your cave paintings with the other snuffling puppies!"

The Devil says, "A paradox I simply *worship* is that this is supposed to be the war between democracy and fascism. Yet who's taking Germany? The other fascists, la! There really is only one difference between you and Stalin. You want everyone to die in despair. He wants everyone living in despair."

Hitler quaked uncontrollably and his breath stank and his clothes were spotted with his foodie menu of flora and sweets. "Stalin is Bolshevik filth," he said.

"He beat you, didn't he?"

"Not yet!" Hitler rallied, answering history's summons to go here go there in his famous pacing step. "It is the *will* to *win*, it is all there! Yes, at any moment—"

"The Russians are coming," the Devil smiled out. He held a hand to his ear, as if attending to the roar of the katyushas overhead.

"*Slavs!*" Hitler screamed out. "*Cannot! Conquer! Germans!*"

"I hear that Stalin wants your skull for a drinking cup. They're going to take you alive."

"*There speaks the Jew!*" Hitler shrieked. It's a great moment, undermined by a gaseous eructation so potent that Hitler flies around the room on its backdraft like a balloon losing air, to land skittering along the floor on his bottom.

It was time for the suicides, under Martin Bormann's direction, as the doubles were put into play. The most persuasive one, formerly a hotel porter in Klagenfurt, was to be murdered and left floating in a water tank for the Russians to find. The second-best double was brought quite suddenly into the room where Hitler and Eva were to kill themselves, and it happened so fast that Eva wasn't sure exactly what was happening. There was a commotion—distractions and bustling about. Then they were gone, and her Adolf was by her side, but he looked a little odd. No, even odder than that. And very soon after, the pair were dead. So it was the second fake Hitler whose corpse was burned and buried outside the bunker's emergency exit, where the Russians would eventually find it. They would assume that the first double was a decoy and that the second double, burned to a crisp, was the real Hitler: which is indeed what came to pass.

The real Hitler was being stupified in the Little Conference Room when Bormann's Seraglio team bundled him off to medical revitalization and freezing therapy in a secret location.

The real Goebbels knew nothing of this, or he might not have been so willing to "die with his Führer." Of course, the six Goebbels children must be put down, too. "They were born to live in a Führer Germany," Magda Goebbels announced, with the smile of a wrecker who can at least take something beautiful with her when she loses. "Come, Helga, Hilde, Helmut! Come, Holde, Hilde, Heide! Here is mama with chocolates!" She and S.S. doctor Ludwig Stumpfegger forced cyanide capsules into their mouths, one after the other. The oldest, Helga, tried to escape as her mother shouted, "Catch the little bitch and slay her! Does she think she's Shirley Temple?"

Fourteen-year-old Helga fought ferociously, but they got the poison capsule into her mouth and Magda broke it open on the girl's teeth, screaming, "Kill the children all over the land! Destroy it all for the enemy vermin!"

Goebbels had met his kind when he met Magda. "You fucking bitch," he said. "You have no feeling in you." That was why she was such good sex; he got hard now thinking about it.

"Germany has no right to feeling when it loses this war," Magda replies. Nodding at their own cyanide capsules, she says, "After you, Alphonse."

German males too young or old for the armed services had been mustered into a street-clothes militia. Any who dared retreat were shot or hanged on the spot as the Communazi urge reaches its true goal of the murder of all life.

Gustav was a proud member of the Volksturm, and when the eleven-year-old Joschi showed up with him, no one said anything. But then, no one was in charge. The nation was no longer fighting; the fighting itself was fighting.

So Gewinner and Rohling joined a group of boys who had dragged an antique Howitzer cannon out of the Zeughaus—the armaments museum—and set it up to use against the Russians. They had but three payloads, and the children who emplaced at the junction of the Dorotheenstrasse and the Wilhelmstrasse were determined to use them well. Insanely, they ignored the whizzing katyushas. Even when a Soviet tank cranked its way around a corner at them, they fearlessly set off their first salvo: a dud.

"Du blöder Grossvater!" cried one boy, kicking at the Howitzer. Stupid old thing!

"Scatter, fellows!" cried Gustav.

They ran to a secure position behind a chance embankment of debris, but Gustav took a bit of damage from the tank fire and was hobbled. There was no medical support, not even a bandage, and Gustav was losing blood. Joschi volunteered to run for help.

It took him a worrisome amount of time to pass even two streets, but at the first break in rocketfire Joschi dashed toward two men in Wehrmacht uniform.

"We need some first aid!" he called to them, running up. "We've suffered a—"

"Why so fast away, young soldier of the Reich?" said one of the men, grabbing hold of Joschi by one arm. "The Führer commands you to defy Stalin, not run from him."

"My friend Gustl has been hurt in the shelling!" Joschi shouted in frustration. "He needs help quickly!"

"Is that why you run away like a Jew?" said the second man, as he reached for another coiled noose from the pile lying next to him.

This was Horst Pack.

"No, I am *trying* to get help for a wounded comrade!" cried Joschi, as the first man held him under the arms with a casual "Yes, they always struggle." Suddenly, he screamed into Joschi's ear: "*You should struggle with the enemy, spawn of a pig!*"

"Trying to *help* by running away," Horst mused, throwing the rope over the horizontal of street map. Though he limps, Horst has recovered from his handicap. He's quite vigorous; this is his eighteenth hanging today.

"If you do harm to me now," Joschi pleaded, "then I cannot rescue my friend Gustav from the Russians!"

"This is not Italy," said Horst Pack, looping the noose over Joschi's head. "This is not Sweden or mysterious Asian China with clacking jade tiles and ten thousand dialects."

"*Mutti!*" Joschi shouted, as he fought to free himself. "*Alte Hans! Herta! Frau Kraus!*"

"Here it is Germany, "Horst Pack implacably went on, "and here we do not like when you are *running like a coward in the wrong direction!*"

The other man yanked Joschi high over the street, fixed the end of the rope at the base of the lamp, pulled in the slack till the strangling boy was caught at the zenith of the geometry, then let him drop and bounce. With the grim delight that had ruled Europa for twelve years, the two Nazis heard Joschi's neck snap like an autumn twig.

Something was happening, Conrad thought. Duscha's people, habitually taciturn and strolly, were rushing and chattering. Then Kai came out of the hut, shirtless in the morning cool, and Conrad saw that the wound had begun to heal.

"Kai!"

"Yes, you see? Now I journey to find my brother and become whole again! It is *The Saga of Kai.*"

"*Finally!*" said the Baroness, coming over the footbridge with Duscha and Hugo beind her. "Berlin has fallen and Hitler is dead."

"We heard it on the radio," said Hugo, all smiles.

"I wonder if the car is where we left it," said the Baroness.

Germany, under the Führer-designated Chancellor Dönitz, was stalling its surrender to allow servicemen to head west and give up to the democracies. The Russians were as murderous with German prisoners of war as Germans had been with the Russians they captured.

In Berlin, the war was over. The katyusha rockets were still, the Nazi hangmen were gone, and the Russians had begun imposing order, locking up Party Bonzen and raping every woman they saw. "Frau, komm!" Next time, don't start World War II.

Jimmy might easily have been taken many times over, for she was out all night looking for Joschi. Frau Kraus had ventured out, too, to find Gustav. But they had no idea where the two boys had gone.

It was a long night for der Alte Herr. His time was up; he fretted over having wasted it. But he was all but powerless anyway, and one longs to discover the private life—a flaneur's spin through town, a conversation *not* taken down by the relentless Eckermann. One would enjoy getting off a bon mot and then forgetting it without having to believe that one is betraying one's legend.

Herta was asleep in Joschi's bed, the faithful Quizli at her cheek. Old Hans jumped when he heard the knock. Was it Joschi and Gustl, then?

It was Gustl, swathed in bandages, but alive. He fell into the Old Man's arms, telling how terrible the fighting was, how he had been hurt, how Joschi ran for help.

"Where is Joschi? Quickly, Gustl."

"But I was hoping he was here. Where is Mutti?"

Herta had awakened. "Mutti is looking for you, Gustl," she said.

Warning Herta not to go out for any reason, the Old Man took took Gustav off into the first light of postwar Berlin, a city of stories waiting to end badly. Gustav would guide the Old Man to Joschi's likely whereabouts.

The city was up: Russian soldiers everywhere, natives coming out of cellars to find food and water, and, already, Trümmerfrauen organized to clear away the debris. Rubble women. The experts thought they'd be at it for thirty years.

At Unter den Linden, in front of the wreck of the Hotel Adlon, Russian soldiers were protecting the Trümmerfrauen from rape by other Russian soldiers. A dump truck with Nazi insignia stood by, and an officer was coming away from a conversation with the driver. The Old Man and Gustav stood right before him, and he addressed them as amiably as if they were all old friends.

"Do you believe it has full tank of gas?" the Russian said in fluent German, albeit with comical vowels. "Fresh from garage!"

The Old Man nodded.

"Because I speak language, they give me this detail. So I am seeing a lot of Berlin, like a tourist!"

The officer offered the Old Man a smoke.

"No, thank you."

"For trading, at least!" he urged.

The Old Man bowed and pocketed the cigarette just as a commotion drew everyone's attention to the middle of the avenue, where a Russian soldier was trying to take a man's bicycle. The man fought to keep it, to the sour interest of his countrymen and lively commentary from soldiers with five or six wristwatches displayed on their forearms. The officer called out something in Russian and the cyclist was able to go on his way.

"What does a Soviet fighter want with a bicycle, anyway?" the officer wondered aloud.

Gustav had been scouting around during all this for a sign of Joschi: nothing. The Old Man thanked the officer once more, and he and Gustav started off again.

Suddenly, Gustav shouted, "*No!*" He had stopped, staring down the Wilhelmstrasse. Shouting his "*No!*" over and over, he raced around a hill of junk, his voice breaking into sobs as he reached Joschi's body. Someone had cut the boy down; the noose still held fast around his neck. The Old Man—the officer, too—came running after; scavengers in the buildings on the streets, their sides ripped off to create comic-strip living from floor to floor, turned to watch.

Gustav had thrown himself over Joschi, his noisy mourning aggravating the tragedy. Opening the noose, the Russian officer took it off the corpse and, for some reason, showed it to the Old Man. "Who kills a little boy?" the Russian asked.

"Are you sure he is dead?"

The officer stared at the Old Man. Then he answered: "One thing I have recently learned is what death looks like."

Yes, of course. But until the great humanist of the moral world vanish from the transformations of time on more glorious wings, he, too, must be good for something. It is all in the tour de main, you know.

So Goethe knelt, gently pushing Gustav to the side. He took Joschi's body into his arms and warmed the child in his wisdom and art. Stirb und werde!, which means

Die to become!

And with a terrible writhing and one storm of a sneeze, Joschi was looking up at a friendly face. "Mutti?" he croaked out. The Old Man altered his grip to let Joschi's feet touch the earth. Standing in the steadying grasp, Joschi felt at his neck, but his guardian quickly took that hand away from there. "It will be tender for a while," he warned.

"Joschi?" said Gustav, peering up close in disbelief. He tried to dry his eyes with a few furtive movements. "Your voice sounds funny."

"Gustav," Joschi managed to get out, with difficulty, as he reached for his friend. "Are you all right?"

"What a question for *you* to ask!"

Looking quizzically at Old Hans, the Russian officer said, "So now the boy lives twice!" He laughed, shaking his head at humankind's ability to survive anything.

The Old Man nodded at the officer, saying, "I can use that insight." To Joschi, he added, "'One death is sufficient for most beings, but you will have two in the end.'" For he, too, knew his Homer.

"Joschi's back!" cried Gustav. "Rohling, we have to go home and impress Herta!"

Still wobbly, Joschi held on to Gustav, asking, "Was I knocked out by a rocket concussion?"

Gustav thought it over, then nodded yes. It's not a lie if you don't use words.

"You boys go on," Goethe urged them.

Joschi tried a few steps on his own, and decided he was capable after all. As they started off, Gustav observed, "We should form a club now. To watch out for each other. Herta and Quizli could be in it, too."

"Very well," as they headed back across the road. "But that Quizli better not make one of his fiendish remarks."

A now a crane shot: a junked Berlin of movie-set facades and rock heaps, with a brutalized citizenry trying to restart a culture perverted by the Nazi stone age. The two children move on homeward, the Russian officer watching till he is called over to some minor mishap in his detail. As the camera's eye rises, the bashed in skyline astonishes: only the wounded Reichstag still stands. Covering music plants the hope that Providence somehow had some lesson to teach, however savage the text.

But then I appear in closeup. The democracies fought me down in the end, but you cannot last because you will not fight. Your refusal to identify the aggressor emasculates and cripples you, Munichs you. I am the eternal no and I will never give up. I hate your liberty. I hate your books and music and sense of humor and happiness: and that is The Act. I hate all in Creation except murder and terror and I am coming for you.

EPILOGUE

Not all that long ago, a tour group sponsored by the American Green Life organization visited the jungles of Brazil, and one of the party, straying from the path, found himself lost. Then he blundered into a small settlement of curious looking buildings of a kitschy middle-European feeling. No one was abroad in the afternoon heat, yet he heard accordion music from somewhere. Stepping into the nearest building, the man found himself in a tavern, empty but for Carlos the bartender and a lone man watching an American football game on the cable television screen over the bar.

Carlos, who spoke excellent English, hosted the visitor to a call for emergency assistance for his Green Life group, and, expressing surprise at finding this bit of civilization in so remote a spot, the American took a second look at the man watching television.

"Holy cow!" he murmured. "Are they making a movie around here? That guy's a dead ringer for …"

"Hitler?" asked Carlos, setting a beer down and waving away the man's money. "He comes in here all the time."

"Yeah, right."

"Go over and ask him yourself."

Curious, the man moved to the end of the bar, taking in the hair, the eyes, the moustache, the dandruff flakes.

"You *are* Hitler!" he cried.

"Yes," said the other heavily, turning from the television screen. "And I shall rise again and kill the Jews and three N. F. L. linebackers."

Bewildered, the American stuttered out, "Which three?"

"See, Carlos, what did I tell you?" said Hitler as the barman joined them. "Nobody cares about the Jews!"

978-0-595-51664-3
0-595-51664-5

Printed in the United States
116673LV00002B/77/P